To my family and friends

Thank you for always being there for me

Chapter 1: Overture

"Greetings everyone, and welcome to this special lecture on the most interesting of subjects, the topic of Nothing." The rail-thin man paused for effect.

"I am Professor Gerald Nullo, Doctor of Nothing. I hope you are very excited to learn more about this amazing domain of study!" The lights in the room dimmed and all focused on him. The lights followed him as he walked around the room as if laying out his path on the ceiling.

"I have spent a long time studying nothing. I have written countless papers, chaired various seminars, and authored several books on the topic."

The man came to a stop and a large holographic screen manifested behind him.

"Among my many works are some you may have heard of. These include *The Art of Nothing, How to Talk with Your Partner About Nothing, Throw That Donut into the Nothing-Zone, Nothingnomics, 92 Tips about Nothing for the Stock Market, How Nothing Led to the Fall of Rome* and others." While he spoke, holographic projections of each of his books appeared on the screen behind him. Tomasz was able to count over a dozen.

"I have been featured on many news shows, been a guest on many late-night shows, and toured around the world. I have made it my life's mission to bring my message of nothing to people across all walks of life. To people who span the breadth of the human experience." Videos of Professor Gerald Nullo, Doctor of Nothing, popped in and out of existence next to him.

The first couple of videos showed him speaking on various news channels like INN and America! News. The next showed him appearing on *The Show at Night with Jonesy Gerry.* It then switched to him speaking to people in various remote locales around the world. The last video showed him in deep conversation with Pope Pius…whatever number they were at now.

"This is a topic that is very near and dear to me. I hope that by the end of this lecture, you will come to appreciate a bit more about nothing." He made sure to place special emphasis every time he said the word *nothing.*

It was clear that this man was very passionate about nothing. Of the dozen or so students in the dim room, only about half seemed interested in what he was saying. That did not seem to faze him at all.

"You may ask what the study of nothing focused on. What exactly do we mean by studying nothing? What does nothing encompass? You may say 'You mean to tell me you study nothing and think it is worthwhile? That there is anything valuable to learn from nothing?' Well, to that I say, yes! I say that the study of nothing is without comparison. It transcends time, it transcends space, and it transcends all fields of study. There is nothing quite like it!" He laughed at his clever remark. It is one Tomasz was sure he used every time he talked about the topic.

"One of the greatest discoveries in mathematics was the idea of the number zero. Zero? A concept first conceived in India over two thousand years ago represented by a simple dot. You are telling me that is one of the most important ideas that humanity has devised? A dot that means nothing is a great idea? Something so simple, something so ubiquitous, yet this was a great discovery?" The man looked wide-eyed around the room.

Tomasz looked over to Monique. In the dim room, her face was hard to see, but it was enough that he noticed how enthralled she was in the lecture. Although Tomasz found the lecture more interesting than he cared to admit, he was more interested in looking at Monique.

Her hazel eyes were fixed intently on the presenter. Whenever she showed interest and focused on a topic, she would purse her lips and play with her long dark curly hair. Tomasz never got tired of seeing it. As Tomasz kept staring at her, she turned her head in his direction and smiled at him.

Being in a stupor, Tomasz smiled back at her. It was then that he realized how long he had been distracted. He snapped out of his trance to focus back on the lecture.

"…happened before the big bang, they will say that it is not worth studying. That there was nothing of interest there so do not even bother with it. Nothing, you say?" The professor looked beyond incredulous at what he had said.

He peered around the room and pushed his glasses further into his face. With a smile, he added, "But to that, I say no that nothing IS interesting!"

"But it does not stop there, because the study of nothing impacts many aspects of our daily life as well." He interjected as if interrupting himself.

"Let us consider several questions. What were we before we were born? What do we become after we die? Is there a purpose to this daily struggle we go through that we call life? What is that agonizing feeling we sometimes feel deep in our souls that wrenches at us?" He looked around the room with a self-satisfied smirk. Tomasz was unsure if he was waiting for an answer or if this was a part of his speech.

Tomasz could not help but roll his eyes at the professor. People who claim they have simple solutions to complex problems always irritated him. Despite this, Tomasz did find the man entertaining.

"Is the answer nothing?" a weak disinterested voice in the back of the room replied.

"That is correct! The answer to all those questions is nothing. And when you realize just how ubiquitous nothing is you realize that you have to study it. Because the study of nothing is quite unlike any other."

Even though the lecture went on for around another hour, the professor's enthusiasm for the subject never wavered.

At the end of the lecture, some students stayed behind to talk to the professor. Tomasz was only interested in talking to Monique.

"Tomasz, wasn't that amazing?" she said as they walked out of the dim room into the well-lit hallway. The sparkle in her hazel eyes shone brightly. While looking deep into her eyes Tomasz forgot what exactly was going on.

"Oh yes, wow!" Tomasz replied, coming to his senses. "Um, I uh, I never thought about nothing that much before to be honest."

"I have read a lot of his books, but to hear him talk in person, it was nothing short of amazing! I was happy to see you come to his talk. I did not know if you would find it interesting or not." Monique smiled as she spoke to Tomasz.

It was that smile that Tomasz could not help but think about on a near-constant basis. Well to be fair, it was not just the smile, but that was a big part of it. There was also her dark skin, her hazel eyes, and her long dark brown hair that tumbled into curls.

"Well, when you first mentioned it to me, I thought it sounded kind of well, crazy? But I would be lying if I said that by the end, he did not have me convinced. As of now, I proclaim myself a true believer of nothing!" Tomasz declared which Monique laughed at with glee. He always loved any opportunity to make her laugh.

"You are always so silly," she said.

"Oh well, it's easy when you have nothing to work with," Tomasz responded, which again caused Monique to laugh.

"By the way, I hope your plans for later tonight do not involve nothing," Monique said with a reserved look.

Tomasz knew exactly what she was referring to, but he did not want to make it seem as if he had been preparing for this very night for over a month now.

"Tonight, umm, what's going on?" he said as he gazed into the air as if in deep thought.

"My show starts! You'll be there right?" Monique beamed with joy as she spoke.

"Oh yes, of course! Your show starts. The show! What was it called, hmm was it *The Nothing Burger*?"

"Hah hah, very funny," Monique replied.

"Oh, I remember—*The Thieving Raven*," Tomasz said.

"Sometimes you think you are cleverer than you are," Monique added.

"Oh don't worry I know the limits of my cleverness," Tomasz replied.

"Hmm, I don't know about that. But yes, it is at the Starlight Theater," she said.

"Oh yes of course. Good because I was getting ready to head to the Starship Dealer. Completely different location." Tomasz had looked at the map many times and knew that it should take him approximately forty-five to forty-seven minutes to get there from his apartment. That was of course accounting for the average traffic expected at 7 PM on a Tuesday. "Yeah, I'll be there."

"Great! Did you see if there was anyone else that wanted to come watch it?" Monique asked Tomasz with a curious look.

"Oh yeah, well I, um, oh that's right I forgot to ask anyone, sorry," Tomasz replied in a soft tone.

The truth was that he could not think of anyone to ask. He considered asking two of his classmates. But he did not know them well enough to think that it would have been anything but awkward. The only other person he considered was his neighbor, Francisco. But it had been a while since he last saw him. This brought the total to zero people who could accompany him to this musical.

"Oh well, at least you are coming." Monique smiled.

They continued down the hallway and out into the open air of Cahuilla Tech. It was a warm, clear sky, sunny Fall day. The kind of day where nothing of note should happen.

"Oh, I have something to show you Tomasz! It's something that my cousin sent me from one of his recent trips. Do you mind if I share it with you?" she asked Tomasz so that he would give her permission to share direct to his interface. The truth was that Tomasz had added her as a trusted user a long time ago.

"Oh yeah sure, I need a quick minute." Tomasz acted as if he was going to update some settings on his interface. While looking at his display he saw a request for a delivery. Not something he expected, but that could wait until later.

"Um, ok, access granted." Tomasz tried his best to be as convincing as possible.

"Ok, there you go! What do you think?" Monique asked as an image was being processed by Tomasz's occipital lobe.

Tomasz studied it for a second and his only reaction was confusion. The image he was looking at seemed like any starry sky he had seen before. What the picture showed were different arms of the Milky Way high up above the sky. This was visible every night in Cahuilla City, provided by the city's artificial nature initiative in an attempt to make citizens feel closer to nature. Tomasz looked at it for a while trying to determine what about it was so impressive that Monique felt the need to share it.

"Well, this seems like the Milky Way..." Tomasz began.

"And?" Monique replied.

"Well is this a display from another city? New York?"

Monique shook her head.

"Los Angeles Display?"

Monique shook her head again. Tomasz studied the photo a bit closer and tried to see if there were any discerning features. At the bottom of the image, he could see large craggy mountains. They reminded him of those in the VR worlds he frequented.

"I see mountains, so was this taken near Denver? Do they have constellation lighting over there as well?"

"No silly! This is not from artificial constellation lighting, what you are seeing is the real deal! This is the actual Milky Way!"

Tomasz spent a second or more trying to understand what Monique was saying.

"Wait, I'm confused. So they are not using artificial lights?" Tomasz asked.

"That's right!"

"So are these like some sort of modified lantern flies in the atmosphere?" Tomasz asked as he studied the image more.

"No!" Monique laughed at Tomasz's confusion.

"What you are seeing are the stars from the Milky Way. There is no human intervention here. No modified lantern flies. No drones. No fireworks. No satellites. This is what you see on a clear night sky. It's impossible to see it anywhere in the US anymore. My cousin ended up going to the Andes in South America to get a glimpse of this."

Tomasz was completely astounded at the revelation.

"So was this taken with a filter? Is this in infrared? Did they do some post-processing to get this?"

"No. You can see this exact image with your plain old eyes, no enhancements are necessary. No need for filters, interfaces, or any of that. As long as there are no clouds and there isn't any light pollution nearby this is what you would see above you in the night sky."

Tomasz couldn't believe it. It seemed so much brighter than the lights he saw over Cahuilla City on a nightly basis.

"So?" Monique asked.

"Huh? Oh right, I mean I have a hard time wrapping my head around it. I always thought you needed some sort of visual aid to see this. This is amazing. I bet your cousin must have been awestruck." Tomasz himself was in awe. Even the artificial replicas did not seem as impressive as the image he was currently seeing.

"Ugh, I am so jealous. I hope one day I'm able to see it myself."

"Yeah, no doubt. Now I want to see them too," Tomasz added, still engrossed in the image.

"Well, maybe one day you and I could see what we need to do and then plan for it. It seems like it would be great." Monique said.

"Well I guess, but traveling that far seems kind of hard right?" Tomasz did not even think while he spoke as he kept staring at the image.

"Oh, yeah that's true I guess," Monique said, a bit less enthusiastic than she had been a second ago.

"It's a shame," Tomasz replied, still unaware of what Monique had been suggesting.

"Hey, Monique! You coming with us?" Someone from afar called Monique. There was a group of about ten people huddled together trying to get her attention.

"Oh, that's some of the other cast members from tonight's show. I almost forgot we were meeting here at ten past the hour. I can't wait for you to see us all. I'll see you then!" Monique waved and she walked away to join the rest of the group.

Tomasz replied in an almost inaudible voice, "See you then."

He looked at the time on his display, 1:12 PM.

Tomasz thought for a second. It seemed as if there was something important that he was about to miss. The concert!

"Oh crap!" He said as he started a mad dash.

Tomasz dashed past the stone buildings that composed the Cahuilla Tech campus, going straight to the music hall. Although the campus itself was only around thirty years old, the façade of the various campus buildings was designed to resemble stone buildings that had been standing for centuries. As he ran, he kept an eye on the time: 1:12:45, 1:12:46.

Tomasz had a show that was about to start broadcasting to a global virtual audience in less than three minutes.

He finally saw the main auditorium and went straight through the doors. The inside of the hall had more people in it than usual. Musicians on different instruments blared dissonant symphonies. A cello occupied in the front row by Rebecca played a slow melody, while Ren played a fast-paced melody on a keyboard. Around the corner, a fiddle player wailed away, while someone else banged on a xylophone. Without taking much of an interest in the cacophony occurring Tomasz spotted his favorite drum set. It was empty so he ran to it and as soon as he sat down his vision completely changed.

Instead of being in a crowded music hall, he found himself on a floating platform in what seemed to be outer space. Around him, he saw a singer with a keyboard, a guitarist, and a bass player who were glaring at him. He struggled to adjust his seat while ignoring the glares from the people he was playing with for the first time.

"Great timing there." The singer's comment dripped with sarcasm.

"We start now, so hurry up!" the guitarist shouted at him.

"What are we starting with?" Tomasz shouted back.

"This guy! You're killing us!" The singer shouted at no one in particular.

"It's Denial by Fantasy of Rhodes, you know them?"

"Ah got it," Tomasz replied.

With that Tomasz started the count off.

Tomasz led into the performance with a wild drum solo that is unique to Denial. The others would then come into the song at different times. They would all start unsynchronized on purpose. It sounded as if multiple groups were playing at the same time. Over several minutes, the intricate song would meld together the melodies. At that point, the second part of the song would begin.

It was one of Tomasz's favorite songs, a very challenging and complex piece. Despite its complexities, Tomasz could play it without much effort. There were a handful of things that Tomasz was good at, and this was one of them. When he sat there and his kit surrounded him, he felt as if he was away in a different world. And to anyone looking at him in the auditorium that is what they would have seen: a guy banging away at the drums, feeding off of some unknown energy and reacting to invisible cues. But what Tomasz saw was different. In his field of view, he was at the back of a stage, surrounded by bandmates on either side, all playing to the same tune now.

The band found themselves in the center of an arena composed of a cosmic palette of colors that floated in outer space. The crowd, made up of thousands of virtual avatars floated and flew around the band, enjoying the show. Some of the crowd would push against each other, moshing around in space. Others held hands and made big circles that would rotate at a slow pace, flying in front of the band. There would be amazing creatures flying through the crowd. Tomasz saw whales, elephants, and even a fire-breathing dragon appear in front of him. He also saw other fantastical creatures that he could not even identify. The stars in the background would pulse in and out of existence. As they did so they would radiate different colors while they orbited around the band. It was an amazing experience. But it was an experience that Tomasz wanted to be done with.

Tomasz kept pounding away at the drums, knowing that each beat got him closer to the end of the show. Anytime there was a break he would sit in silence. He did not have much interest in interacting with the other band members, he wanted to leave.

There used to be a time when he enjoyed this when the thought of playing to live audiences around the world thrilled him to no end, but that time had passed. Tomasz did not know when or what happened, but at some point, he stopped caring for it. It had become another thing he had to slog through. Another meaningless chore. He hoped one day he would feel excited about it again. But he was not sure if that was ever going to happen.

The thrashing continued for close to an hour. Mechanical motions one after the other as Tomasz banged away, waiting for the whole affair to end. Once his set ended, he looked towards the crowd. Floating and mindless, with no awareness of anything but this little virtual world they now occupied. This virtual world would continue even after Tomasz left. As soon as he did another group would come on and the show would go on.

Right on cue, Tomasz disconnected and he found himself back in the real world. He sat covered in sweat and the former occupants of the music hall had all changed. Now the piano was playing a soothing slow melody. Instead of a cello, there was a group of trumpets, all blaring. And now there was a choir singing in the middle. The discordant rhapsody continued, with everyone connected around the world and disconnected in the room.

Tomasz had enough of Cahuilla Tech and decided to make his way back to his apartment. As he walked past the front gardens of the music hall a familiar voice greeted Tomasz.

"Well, do my eyes betray me, or is that Tomasz I'm seeing?"

"Hey Zeno, what is the weather looking like today?" Tomasz asked the school AI mascot. Even though Tomasz did not feel like talking, he did not mind Zeno's company.

"Well it's looking like it's going to be rather warm today, no clouds and very sunny. If you like the heat, then today is your day. But I know that is not your thing, so no luck for you!" Zeno said in an almost apologetic way.

"But hey I understand your predicament, I'm sweating a storm up over here myself," Zeno added as he walked next to Tomasz.

As always, he was smiling. His appearance was of an old barefoot balding man with long hair and a colorful toga that matched his personality. The AI mascot would manifest in people's interface. This meant that at times it could seem as if the entire campus was talking to themselves. Zeno always ranked as one of the best things about Cahuilla Tech.

"So you got any plans for later on today, Tomasz? Perhaps frolicking through the Fox Botanical Gardens? An intense FoxFit session later? Or maybe even a nice evening stroll down the river walk?" As Zeno spoke to Tomasz about the different activities his outfit changed to reflect each occasion.

"Oh well, I do have some plans. But I had to push my frolicking back to tomorrow because I'm going to go see a musical later today." Zeno faked laughter at the reply.

"I even got myself a nice outfit for it and everything. It seems like it is going to be a good time," Tomasz mentioned to Zeno who now hovered next to him.

Zeno sat next to him on an old worn-out chair and read a book titled *Zeno's Paradoxes* by Zeno. Zeno was one of the few people that Tomasz spoke to regularly. Well, that was not true, but because Zeno was not a person.

"Oh, might this be Monique's musical you are going to see?" Zeno asked with a knowing smirk. His gaze did not move away from the book he pretended to be reading.

"How did you know about that?" Tomasz asked.

"Oh me? Well what can I say, you're not the only one who loves talking to your friendly holographic school mascot! I don't know if it's my elegance or my carefree attitude but I can't help but have everyone's ears! It's always Zeno this, Zeno that, Zeno I may have invited a certain someone to a musical I'm starring in on this particular warm fall day. You know, those are the kinds of things a dear devoted mascot such as yours truly gets to around these halls." Zeno added with an exasperated tone.

"Or I don't know, it could be that my language processing model misheard what words were uttered. Maybe someone was handing out invitations to a nice relaxing reading session in the Crow District Fish Factory." Zeno now looked pensive as he stared beyond his book which now bore the title *Zeno's Book of Happenings*.

"Did she say anything else? Did she mention me?" Tomasz came to a sudden halt which made Zeno's chair screech to a halt. The hologram appeared to be struggling to hold on to his holographic chair as it stopped. Zeno took a couple of seconds to collect himself.

"Oh dear me, Tomasz, you know I could not tell you anything about that. Just think about it. If I did how could others bring themselves to trust their friendly school mascot Zeno with their thoughts?" Zeno smiled as he looked at Tomasz. His book now bore the title *Zeno's Secrets*.

Tomasz eyed the holograph.

"Well one last question, what do you think of my outfit for later tonight?" Tomasz asked as he transmitted to Zeno a photograph of himself wearing the outfit.

Zeno studied the image for a second.

"I must say Tomasz, I would not have expected you to be so bold and wear something like this!" Zeno remarked as he got up from his chair.

"Is that good or bad?" Tomasz asked.

"Well, my opinion of it is that it is fierce and dangerous," Zeno replied.

Tomasz looked at him confused.

"Yes, I do like it, Tomasz. If I may say, Monique will like it as well. But I'm sure I'll hear about it later anyway."

Tomasz was happy to hear Zeno's approval for his outfit. The outfit was not anything Tomasz had planned for but it was what he ended up with.

"Thanks, Zeno," Tomasz said as he continued toward the train station.

Along the way to the train station, Tomasz encountered a smattering of people here and there. Whenever he did come across someone they did not even bother to look in his direction.

Everyone acted as if they were the only person out in the open. He did not see a single person acknowledge or greet anyone else. Tomasz reciprocated and did not acknowledge any of the people that were around him.

Looking above, Tomasz could see the clear sky dotted with various screens. These would flash advertisements to those passing underneath.

"FEELING HOT? PICK UP A HEALTHY TURBO-HYDRATING LORENA TEA!" One of the ads read as it flashed an image of a woman enjoying an ice-cold drink.

The floating screens would hover near the train station and move to where the majority of the people were gathered. The tall glass-paned train station mirrored and distorted the hovering images, producing a rainbow-like effect from the reflected advertisements.

As he approached the doors of the train station the advertisement changed once again.

"Do you have a date in mind? How about—"

Tomasz walked into the train station only to have the advertisement follow him in without any pause.

"—a night at Drusilla's Ristorante?" the ad continued. Now it showed Tomasz dressed in a fancy suit in front of a candlelit dinner sitting next to a beautiful woman. She looked so much like Monique that it made him uncomfortable.

"Having trouble with love? Met the woman of your dreams but she isn't paying attention to you? Well, I have what you need! If you want to learn what women want to hear and how you can get the girl you deserve, subscribe to my world-famous winner's club!" The man pointed straight at Tomasz, doing everything he could to grab his attention. He followed him as he walked down the train station continuing to blab on about his secrets to romance. Tomasz thought he recognized him from somewhere. He was sure he saw him in the news recently getting arrested for something.

Tomasz saw the train approaching the terminal. The train made no sound as it neared the stop. He got in and his interface alerted him that his preferred seat was open. Once he sat down a virtual store appeared in front of him.

Tomasz went for his go-to drink, RED MOON, a tea brewed with leaves harvested from soil mixed with lunar minerals. A virtual acknowledgment from Tomasz and soon an ice-cold can of his favorite drink fell into his hands.

As Tomasz sipped the drink his entire view changed in an instant. One second, he had been seeing the inside of the train and now he was in a room with two women sitting across from him behind a desk. They engaged in a conversation as the letters INN floated above and behind them, the Cahuilla River flowed in the background.

"Teresa with the weather. That's right citizens of Cahuilla City, this week we expect it to be warm. So don't get rid of your summer clothing just yet." The woman speaking was Lucilla "Lucy" Kassa. She was a local celebrity, one of the city's most well-known anchors. Tomasz met her once and always remembered her charming personality.

"Sophia, what else are we expecting tonight for Cahuillans?" Lucy turned to the woman next to her.

"Well Lucy, authorities say that those in Crow District should be on the lookout tonight. There has been an increase in reports of violent gangs around certain neighborhoods. Some businesses have had their windows smashed and their patrons harassed. Authorities have warned people in Crow District to be careful if they go out later in the night."

"That sounds very serious Sophia, I hope authorities can catch those culpable for this soon. Do we know if the city is looking to do something about them?" Lucy asked.

"Lucy, as of now City Hall has not given a definitive answer on what their plans on this matter are. But I have heard reports that Madam Sonali herself has begun to take a personal interest in the matter. We are still unsure of what sort of statement we can expect from her, but if she is to be involved with this we can expect that City Hall will make some sort of formal statement soon."

"Well if Madam Sonali is already on alert with these groups then I already feel more at ease. But I understand there are some other serious news that we are hearing, is that correct?" Lucy uttered every word with the utmost gravity. Tomasz sat dazed and enthralled.

"Lucy, that is correct, we have breaking news. We have received confirmation that Kayden Clemens, the star linebacker for the Cahuilla City Ranchers has been spotted in Monaco with Jennifer Von Hofen, the heiress to the Von Hofen Jewelry Empire." Sohpia stared straight at Tomasz as she said this.

"What?" Tomasz replied in disbelief.

"Wow Sophia, in all my years I would not have expected this. To think that the one ranch hand who is notorious for his constant breakups and juicy late-night escapades is now official with a member of the Von Hofen family? I don't think I could have ever imagined this."

"Well, it's not just you Lucy. Most Cahuillans say they are flummoxed by the news. We expect that Jennifer Von Hofen will be at the next game that the Ranchers—"

"Reminder! Unread Message!" A notice read on Tomasz's interface, interrupting his broadcast.

"What?" Tomasz looked through his interface. He remembered the delivery request he had received earlier.

Oh, that's right! I got a job! he thought to himself as his view returned to his actual surroundings. It had been quite a while since he had gone on a job. He was glad to have something else to do instead of just waiting until Monique's show.

The alert read: "Delivery requested by: Caring Angels Organization. Pickup destination: Strawberry Plains Apartment Complex at 21 Charleston Court, Apartment 37B, Fox District. Pickup time, 4:00 PM. Package Description: Seventeen by two by one inch. Twenty pounds. Delivery Destination: 101 Lowray Street, Crow District. Delivery time requested: 7:00 PM."

"The Caring Angels?" Tomasz read to himself in confusion. On his interface, he looked up 101 Lowray Street. The image he saw must have been wrong. All Tomasz could see was a rundown bar with a sign that was half-lit between other derelict businesses.

This does not seem like a good idea, Tomasz thought to himself. He was about to deny the request when another message came in.

"Alert Updated. Pay for delivery: $10,000. Requestor note: 'We looked up other services but we think you are THE MAN for us! The Caring Angels! Hope to hear from you soon!'"

Tomasz read the update several times. He wanted to be sure there were no details he was overlooking. He checked the distance from the bar to the theater.

Well, I guess it's not too much more that they are asking for, he thought to himself.

He accepted the request and smiled.

***

It was only several more minutes before his train arrived near his home. The apartment complex Tomasz lived in was like a city in itself. The complex included four gargantuan parallel buildings, each of which was two miles long and thirty stories tall and housed around twenty thousand residents.

Each had a grocery store, a shopping mall, a suite of restaurants, and any other type of amenity the residents could want. It had taken him a long time before he was able to tell without any help which entrance was the one nearest to his room. To Tomasz, it seemed as if someone had designed a single segment of the building, built thousands of those, and placed them all next to each other as far as the eye could see. One of the enduring legacies of the post-Conflict building boom. The only discernible features around the various entrances were the different trees. Outside of the entrance near his apartment, there was a row of fiery red royal poinciana trees in full bloom.

Inside the building, just as it was on the outside, Tomasz saw no activity. He made the five-minute trek to his hallway without even once seeing another person. As he neared his apartment door, he saw his neighbor walk up to their door at the same time. For no particular reason at all Tomasz acted as if he had not seen him. Tomasz had lived in the same complex for the past three years. Despite that, he only knew around five people by name. Two of them he mixed up regularly.

"Oh hey, Tomasz! It has been a while since I last saw you." The man smiled wide at Tomasz.

Tomasz turned towards his neighbor with a feigned look of surprise.

"Francisco? Wow, it's been so long since I saw you that I thought you had moved out!"

"Oh yeah, something came up and I had to go stay with my parents for a while. Thankfully everything is fine now so I was able to get back here yesterday." Francisco's reply made it seem as if some heavy burden, he had been carrying had been lifted.

"Oh, I see," Tomasz replied with no idea of what else to say.

"What have you been up to?" Francisco asked.

"Oh me? You know, um…" Tomasz had to think for a while for anything of note that he might have done since the last time he had seen Francisco.

"The usual?" Francisco smiled as Tomasz was still caught up in his world.

"The usual," Tomasz replied in a defeated tone.

"So you got any plans for later today?" Francisco still smiled at Tomasz in his usual friendly manner.

"Em, nope didn't get the best sleep yesterday. I finished a gig about thirty minutes ago so I was hoping to start resting early today," Tomasz replied without even thinking. Francisco looked disappointed.

"Oh ok, well one of these days we ought to meet up!" Francisco mentioned, still clinging on to whatever shred of friendliness he could muster. It was more than Tomasz could muster even when he tried his best.

"Great idea," Tomasz said and went straight into his apartment. He had lost track of how many times he had promised to meet up with someone and didn't follow through.

Once inside his room, Tomasz went to the beanbag splayed across the floor and plopped face down on it. With his head still buried in the bean bag, he scanned his interface to check the time: 2:48 PM. He rolled over staring at the plain white ceiling.

On any other day, Tomasz would scan his interface for a live event and spend hours without even moving one inch. But he had actual things he needed to do today, and he needed to prepare for those. And one of the things he needed for tonight kept eating at him.

The outfit for tonight's event. He had tried to convince himself that it was not that bad. That it was a unique outfit and would make him stand out but in a good way. He even received Zeno's approval, which he thought would have quelled his doubts. Instead, he found himself feeling nervous about the whole thing. There was only one solution to his current conundrum.

He scanned the inventory of nearby garment stores, trying to see what was available in his size. The first option was from a store in his building. It was a black and white pinstripe suit with a red pocket square and red tie. Tomasz saw a virtual display of how he would look with it. The virtual Tomasz walked around in his room showing the real Tomasz all the angles of him in the outfit. Tomasz was sure his virtual counterpart was more handsome than he was. His face was more chiseled, his cheekbones more pronounced, he stood a tiny bit taller, and seemed to have more muscle mass than his real self. Tomasz did like this outfit and he could have it in his room in the next two and a half minutes if he wanted, then he saw the price—$3000. He looked at his bank account. It was not even half that.

"Ok, let's see." He muttered to himself as he ignored that option.

The next store he looked at was out of stock on the outfit he liked, the next could not deliver in time, and the last one was even more expensive than the first.

Tomasz looked toward his closet with dread. A quick scan showed him that aside from what was in the garment bag, the fanciest clothing he had in there were khaki pants and a tropical-themed shirt.

Maybe I'll just stay in today, he thought.

But then he quickly remembered Monique's smile, remembered what Zeno had told him and decided he would go through with his original outfit. With a defeated gesture Tomasz waved at the closet. A robotic arm came down from the ceiling, brought out a single garment bag and placed it on his bed. The bag was emblazoned with *Angelica's Fine Wear and Tailor Shop*.

Tomasz rolled off the bean bag and made his way to the bed. He stared at the garment bag.

"You are my last hope," he sighed as he reached for it.

He zipped it open and pulled out the clothing within. A tailor-made, sleek, silky smooth, custom fit, dazzling Pink Tuxedo.

"How the fuck did I end up with this?"

Chapter 2: Mementos

"A life of luxury is closer than you think, Tomasz. With a home in Io Enclave, you'll be within reach of all you could want."

The screen inside the cab showed Tomasz pictures of him sitting next to Felix, Rui, Andres, and Jakey. In one, they all sat around a cozy-looking fireplace, laughing without interacting with each other. The images that kept appearing emphasized Tomasz and his friends at various locales within the state-of-the-art neighborhood. Tomasz could not begin to imagine what it was that made the five of them look in such high spirits.

It had been years since he had seen any of them. The only thing Tomasz was grateful for was that this ad did not include Joshua, as other advertisements have sometimes done. Remembering the last time they all had met in person brought back unpleasant memories. Of course, the ads are not that well-educated on people's personal history.

"Here in Io Enclave, you'll never be too far from anything you would like to do. Feel like hosting a tabletop session with your friends? Then you should grab a table and a pint at the Feisty Orc, one of the most popular gaming bars in the area."

Now the images showed Tomasz playing a board game with his brother Aleksander. Seeing his brother enjoying a board game gave Tomasz a laughing fit that took him quite a while to calm down. One of the things Alex had stated many times was how much he hated board games.

"Or come down to the VirtuaStadia, the most advanced immersion theater in all Cahuilla. Featuring over a hundred isolation pods that can sit up to four people, feel free to come by yourself, with a companion, or even with a group. Each one of our pods promises to give you the most realistic immersive experience. They will transport you to the edge of space, bring you to the depths of the ocean, or transport you anywhere you and your companions can dream of. All this is possible right in the heart of the Io enclave."

This time the ad showed Tomasz sitting next to Monique in one of the isolated pods. It showed both of them engrossed in whatever they were watching and then it transitioned to the virtual world. One second, they were sunbathing on a warm tropical beach, the next they were skiing downhill a snowy Olympus Mons. The last image showed them stargazing while they stood atop a mountaintop in the middle of the night.

Even though Tomasz had seen ads like these before, compiled from various memories, they still made him feel odd. Especially the last one. The thought of him being with Monique in any one of those locations made him feel a certain type of way. Did it make him happy, sad, anxious, excited? Whatever that jolt that he felt was, it did not last for too long.

"Strawberry Plains Apartment: Arrived," the voice in the cab announced.

"We hope that when you consider your next move you think about Fox District's hidden gem, the Io Enclave." The door opened and Tomasz stepped out. As soon as he set his feet down the motorized pod moved on.

"Well, this is an interesting building," he said to himself as he stared at the apartment complex in front of him.

The building was about twenty stories tall of brutalist concrete. On its walls was a shiny gleam of iridescent colors that seemed to meld into each other and change hues at a slow pace.

Even though he had been a lifelong resident of Cahuilla City, it had been many years since he had been to this neighborhood, now known as the Io Enclave. His recollection of this place seemed alien compared to what he was seeing now. None of the buildings seemed to follow any specific pattern. That was clear when looking at the buildings on either side of the Strawberry Plains apartment building.

The two tall glass-covered buildings were around twice as tall as the center building. They were connected by a glass bridge that loomed over the Strawberry Plains building. On the bridge, some more of the same ads that Tomasz had seen in the cab were being presented. Looking in the direction of the ads made the sound transmitted by them register straight to Tomasz's auditory processor.

"A life of luxury—"

Curious about his surroundings Tomasz looked away toward the opposite direction. Across the street, more buildings dotted the landscape. Tomasz noticed several more apartment buildings and the massive VirtuaStadia. The outside of the cylindrical building was a massive display depicting all manner of things being experienced by its current guests. These views included mundane hospital visits, flying atop a dragon while soaring through the sky, and even a journey into the sun.

But the VirtuaStadia was not the only building decorated in displays. Many of the apartment buildings near it also featured their massive displays. These seemed to be showing live feeds of its residences and the on-goings of its inhabitants.

In one Tomasz could see someone cooking in a state-of-the-art kitchen. On the next a person lay asleep with a dog next to them. One of them showed a room so dense with plants that Tomasz was not sure if a person could live there. The last one Tomasz saw showed a couple arguing and now and then pointing to the screen. It seemed as if they were blaming the viewer for their issues. This made Tomasz not want to look anymore.

Tomasz walked up to the Strawberry Plains building. As he approached the door a friendly voice greeted him.

"Hey, hey, Tomasz! It seems like you are here to meet with Mickey! Well, let me be the first to tell you that is one particularly swell muchacho! He is just about ready for you and I will let him know you are on your way! Follow that blue line and you'll be there in no time! Well, it will take you three minutes and forty-three seconds but close enough!" the building's AI concierge announced.

The blue line appeared inside Tomasz's field of view and led the way down the hallway. The light along the hallway slowly pulsated as he continued and Tomasz noticed a nice faint smell of strawberries. A low-playing tune jingled in the background; it sounded like someone was playing the piano far behind Tomasz. The sound seemed as if it came from the lobby, but even as Tomasz got away from the lobby the sound stayed at the same volume.

Tomasz found the door. As soon as he looked at the placard on the door that read 37B, it swung open.

On the other side of the door stood a man who was only wearing a bathrobe. He was shorter than Tomasz, with long black hair, a sizable unkempt beard, and deep blue eyes. He looked to be in his late thirties. It seemed as if he spent a lot of time in the sun as he had a very distinct tan line around his neck. With only a bathrobe on Tomasz could tell that the man was as stout as a log, with biceps as wide as Tomasz's legs. The man stood, staring at Tomasz, not saying a word.

"I have concluded my visual inspection," the man spoke in a low voice and then paused.

All of a sudden Tomasz grew concerned about what this inspection entailed. What database had the man scanned to investigate him? What exactly did he find?

"I have determined that you are a person of high mint." He smiled as he spoke in a higher voice than Tomasz expected. The words were uttered at such a slow pace that they seemed to be in no hurry to escape his mouth.

"Oh, you have retinal scanning gear?" Tomasz responded, unsure of what the man meant by high mint. The man did not look like law enforcement to Tomasz, but there must be other ways of getting the gear.

"Hahaha, no kindred soul, I am free from any cybernetic implants, that is way behind me. What I have is communication with the cosmos. And they let me know that you are high mint. Also, only high-mint people could embrace threads as smooth as that."

Mickey pointed to the Pink Tuxedo.

"Oh yeah, this." Tomasz was still embarrassed about his loud clothing choice.

"Oh, I'm one hundred percent being low mint right now!" Mickey gasped as if he had come to a terrible realization. "Where are my manners? Come in, kindred spirit, and make yourself comfortable. Enjoy the energy that permeates my abode, I got the package almost ready for you."

"That's not necessary—" Tomasz started to say but by then Mickey had already put one of his arms around Tomasz and dragged him into the apartment.

"This here is my little corner of the world. Feel free to grab yourself a drink or food, I'll be back in a sec."

"No it's ok—"

"Hey Jeremy, get this profile in good taste here a nice warm herbal tea, Mickey style," Mickey said as he walked into one of his rooms.

An arm swung from the ceiling, bringing down a drink for Tomasz. He grabbed it and felt obliged to drink. First, he sniffed it. The smell was pleasant enough that he followed up with a quick sip.

Not what Tomasz expected but he enjoyed it. He felt unsure of what he should do as he found himself alone in the large foyer of the apartment. As he sipped on his drink, he looked at all the decorations in the dwelling, familiarizing himself with the interior of the apartment. All over the apartment, he could see the mark of its owner.

The walls were covered with paintings, decorations, pictures, and various other art pieces. In addition, Tomasz saw some sculptures that seemed to resemble… Well, to be honest, he had no idea what they resembled.

Tomasz noticed that some paintings had an MT printed at the bottom. Those with the MT insignia had a similar style. As Tomasz was no art connoisseur, he was not sure if they were well made or not, but he thought they looked nice. That made them no less interesting to look at. He noticed that a majority of them featured the ocean as a background.

Tomasz saw a frame displaying pictures that would alternate after some time. The first picture showed a group of eight all dressed in camouflage. They all had rifles and stood in front of a building that was smoking from the inside.

The next showed a vast expanse of sea, nothing distinguishable in it. The same eight faces came into the next frame. This time they all seemed intoxicated, smiling at the camera, Tomasz recognized the one on the right. He was clean-shaven and had much shorter hair, but it looked like his host, Mickey. Another image flickered by, another image of the sea, this time Mickey smiled as he waded in the water.

The next photo showed seven people, covered head to toe in armor, sitting inside some type of armored vehicle, all looking towards the front. Out of the window, a long line of vehicles was visible stretching up a long road. On either side of the road foliage of varying density was visible. In some spots, the trees were so thick that it was impossible to distinguish them. In others, the only thing left were stumps between still-smoldering craters. Another image of the sea. This time two people were looking at the sea, with their backs to the camera. In the distance, a large fire raged in the sea. The last image showed five people sitting at a bar, he recognized one of them as Mickey, and this time he had his long hair and beard. None smiled. Each of them held a glass high. Between them, three full glasses stood filled. Above the frame hung a small patch with the word 'SAPPER'.

"Meow."

Tomasz's heart nearly jumped out of his chest. He looked down to search for the source of the sound and saw an orange cat staring straight up at him. After recognizing the source of his fright Tomasz laughed as he bent down to pet the small creature. The cat was happy to accept attention from the unfamiliar visitor. The cat closed his eyes in appreciation as Tomasz scratched the middle of the feline's soft head.

"It is complete," Mickey said as he walked back into the room carrying two bags, one large and one small.

"Ah, I see you have met my friend Pedro." Mickey smiled as he looked at the cat.

"Oh, Pedro is it? Pedro gave me a scare," Tomasz chuckled still petting the cat.

He saw Mickey looking beyond him, at the pictures behind him.

"Oh I'm sorry I didn't mean to intrude, I saw the pictures and—"

"No worries my friend, I invited you into my home. I cannot be angry if you happen to look at the pictures I have set out in places where eyes could meet them." Mickey seemed genuine in his statement.

There was a moment of silence between the two.

"So you were in the Conflict?" Thomas asked. "My uncle was there, he was a ranger I'm pretty sure."

"Oh is that right? Well, those guys are missing something in their heads, but they would say the same about us," Mickey laughed in response.

"Jeremy, can I get a tea myself and a refill for my guest."

The robotic arm swung down and grabbed Tomasz's drink while two other arms came down with hot teas for both of them. Mickey sat down at a small table and Tomasz sat across from him. Pedro followed them and sat on Mickey's lap.

"You are correct. I was present for what is now known as the Conflict. Well, when I first got there, it was still an 'operation'." Mickey said as he got comfortable with Pedro.

"You see, nobody likes the word 'war'. So, there was an unspoken agreement on all sides to never use that word. At first, it was a theater-restricted operation, with minimal support. That's why when I got there, we thought it was going to be a quick job. One of our ships was attacked in a freedom of navigation exercise and of course, we were told it was an accident. But we needed the world to know that it was unacceptable. Nobody went into that thinking they were going to start a war. But sometimes you go into a situation trying to make the best of it and completely fuck everything up." Mickey finished.

Tomasz nodded in agreement, unsure of how to follow up.

"Do you remember when that happened?" Mickey said.

"The attack on the Roosevelt ship?" Tomasz replied.

"Yes," Mickey replied.

"No, I was too young," Tomasz replied.

He knew the incident Mickey was referring to, but he was only several weeks old when the Reef incident occurred.

"Yeah sorry. I'm used to talking to those higher on the age spectrum." Mickey laughed at his remark.

"A quick operation turned into an eight-year Conflict with a death toll of three hundred and sixty-five million. Close to one hundred and twenty million were wounded. Those numbers are so large that sometimes I think they're made up. I mean they're crazy right? " Mickey asked out loud.

Tomasz nodded. He had heard the numbers so many times he didn't even give them much thought. He never thought about the staggering amount of carnage that must have entailed.

"Day after day with more news of how the situation was worsening, nobody could believe it. It did not matter that they had live feeds showing them the carnage as it unfolded. It did not matter that they could see satellite imagery of the different smoldering craters of what used to be entire cities. It didn't matter what you showed them, people could not believe that such atrocities were possible in the civilized world we had all grown up with. A world in which humans erased each other from existence en masse on a regular basis was the world of a different time, not our time. I mean, I was living it and sometimes couldn't believe it," Mickey said while still focusing on his tea.

Tomasz took a sip of his tea emulating his host. Although he had not come here to discuss history, he could not help but be engrossed by the conversation. The Conflict was a unique topic that Tomasz was fascinated with, although one he wasn't very knowledgeable about. The Conflict was still not very openly talked about in society.

"I'm sorry you probably don't want to hear this," Mickey said with a sense of abashment.

"I don't mind. Honestly." Tomasz replied all too quickly. He was curious to hear what the man had to say.

Mickey gave Tomasz a surprised look and continued.

"I'll be honest. After going through that, the best way I would describe it, and I am trying not to exaggerate here, but I would say it was not fun. I was hungry all the time. I slept like three hours undisturbed at most on a good night. Hated a lot of the people I came across, both our guys and theirs. I got diarrhea and constipation more times than I can count. And to top it all there was stuff blowing up around me all the time. It really sucked." Mickey said. He took another sip of his tea. Tomasz once again emulated his host.

"Wow, I mean that sounds horrible. I'm sure you must be glad to be back from that Conflict." Tomasz replied.

"Oh of course I am. Who wants to be in a warzone? But you know there was something about it. Something I miss. I don't know, sometimes I feel as if you were to ask me to go back and do it again, I wouldn't even think about it. I'd do it in a heartbeat." Mickey laughed.

Tomasz stared at Mickey wide-eyed.

"It's terrible I know. I sound like a fucking monster, right? Well, it makes me feel like one. Anyone listening would think that I was some sort of psycho who loves killing and murdering. But I swear I'm not!" Mickey added as he laughed.

"I didn't even care about whatever it was that we were doing out there. I didn't think that we would end up in such a massive conflict when I enlisted. But when I was there, it was, it was just so simple. They told me where I had to go and what to do, and that was it. No worrying about any other dumb bullshit. No worrying about taxes, about making rent this month, about having to go visit my friend because it has been a while since I have seen them, none of that. All I had to do was focus on what the mission was, nothing more to it," Mickey continued as he scratched Pedro's head.

He paused to look at Tomasz, who spun his wheels thinking of something to say but nothing came to mind.

"I'm sorry my man, I'm being so low mint right now," Mickey said. "I became the thing I swore I would never be, an old man telling the new ones how it used to be back in my day."

"No worries, I don't mind one bit. I never get the chance to talk with veterans of the conflict and I never felt comfortable talking about it with my uncle, so I don't mind at all." Tomasz was deeply fascinated by the topic.

"It's like, I hate conflict you know, I can't even argue with my mom if she asks me to do something I don't want to. It's not some jingoistic idea that I got that we're the best and only we know what's right, I can't even figure out my stuff. But I miss being there. I miss my guys," Mickey said as he looked beyond Tomasz to the pictures on the wall.

"I miss the people from my platoon. Dolan, Velez, Barrios, Bezukhov, Goldberg, Moore, Taylor, and so many others. We had so many moments we were so sure we were going to die and yet somehow we, well, well not all didn't." Mickey sighed.

"But no matter what they were there for you. The only thing they needed to know was where the fire was coming from so they could shoot back. They would be there for you regardless of what is going on out there. It's so damn hard to find that out here. I mean, aside from Pedro, of course. Feel like there must be something wrong with me feeling so lonely in this city of millions." Mickey laughed as he snuggled up to his cat.

Tomasz could only look at his host. What even could he say?

"Oh, I understand," Tomasz said finally.

But Tomasz did not understand. He did not and was not sure he could understand what the man cuddled up to his cat was talking about. He used to be close with his friends, but those were childhood friendships. He had no clue what it would feel like to trust others with your life in the middle of the deadliest war in world history. But there might have been something Tomasz understood. That feeling of isolation, of wanting a connection. He had never thought about it in that way.

"But enough about me, if I keep telling you more of my stories you'll be here for a full week! What you came here for is this."

With that, Mickey slid the large package across the table. Tomasz looked at the paper bag and grabbed it.

Now that he held it in his hands, he was surprised at how heavy it was.

"Pretty heavy right? That's how you know it's good!" Mickey chuckled as he saw Tomasz struggling when he picked it up.

Tomasz was curious about what exactly he had in his hands. But as a courier, he felt as if whatever was being delivered was between the deliverer and the recipient. He felt that having some separation between himself and the package was an important professional quality.

"Well, are you going to open the bag?" Mickey asked confused as he looked at Tomasz who still held the closed package.

"Are you sure? I never open stuff that I deliver," Tomasz replied.

Mickey became wide-eyed upon hearing this reply.

"Are you serious? That sounds crazy. You're going to deliver a package across the city without knowing what it is?" Mickey said in disbelief. Even Pedro shot Tomasz a dubious look.

Tomasz felt very unsure about how to proceed. He had been delivering packages as a side job by himself for close to two years and not once had he even bothered to see what he was carrying. Most times the people receiving the packages would pick it up and thank him. That was the end of it. Sometimes if the recipient was old, they would invite him in for coffee and cookies and tell him what the package was, why they needed it, and on many occasions a full life story. But most of the time he delivered the packages without knowing anything about it. But this was also the most he had been ever paid to deliver one item.

In the entire time he had been working as a courier, he had not even made half of what this job paid. The thought that he could be transporting anything dangerous had never crossed his mind, but now that little thought did pop into his head. For the first time, he felt scared of what he could be carrying. A surge of anxiety started to swell inside him from the deepest pit of his stomach. He stared at Mickey. He would not stop looking at Tomasz until he pulled out the contents of the package.

What even was he supposed to do if it turned out to be something crazy, something illegal? What if he had a huge brick of Hydro? Tomasz had seen someone in the news get arrested for making some in his basement in Crow District and the penalty had been harsh. Or it could be some sort of weapon?

He had seen something about gangs earlier in the day and that was something he felt he ought to steer clear of. Or it could have been…well, something else that criminals want! Tomasz was so removed from any type of criminal activity that he could not even think what they would be transporting. He could not understand why it had to be him that they picked for this crime! Maybe it was a recommendation? Since it was illegal how would he get out of it?

Would Mickey let him say "No thank you!" and then let him go? He doubted that was the case and started regretting his choice to accept the job, but there was little he could do now.

With every measure of caution, Thomas opened the bag and put his hand in it. Without breaking eye contact with Mickey, he pulled out the contents of the bag. He glanced at the object in his hand expecting the worst. Then his heart sank deep in confusion.

Grasping the object, he turned it around, looking at it from different angles. As he studied it, he concluded: He had no clue on earth what he was looking at. All he could tell was that it was a rectangular shape that seemed to have some metal pins at one end.

Mickey had a big smile with his mouth open in anticipation. He wanted to see if Tomasz would be able to deduce what exactly he had in his hand.

Tomasz kept studying the dense block in his hand. The majority of the object was plastic aside from the metal pins. In a sudden flash it hit him, he recognized where he had seen it before.

"Is this like some sort of ancient battery for one of those mobile computing devices?" Tomasz asked with a mix of bewilderment and confusion. Out of all the things he was expecting this was not even close to anything he had in mind.

Mickey roared with laughter.

"Yes! He is correct. Not only is he high mint but he is also high speed."

Tomasz kept looking at the battery while Mickey laughed on. Pedro seemed to not even notice, or care, about his companion's laughter.

The device in Tomasz's hands was so old that he had only seen it in pictures on the Internet, on sites dedicated to outdated technology. The thing that surprised him the most about the device was how heavy it was. It was not even that big, but it must have weighed about twenty pounds. The more he thought about it the less sense it made. He could not even fathom why someone would pay so much to have it delivered. Something like this could be found by the thousands at any old dumpsite or an antique tech shop.

"Not what you were expecting, right?" Mickey asked after he regained his composure.

"Well, I hadn't thought much about what I would be carrying, but if you asked me to guess this would not have been it."

"Well, some things are better small, maybe heavy but still small. Like me." Mickey said with a slight grin.

"Is this thing charged or something? Does this work? I never expected something like this to be so heavy. Did those people walk around with hundreds of pounds on them?"

"Boom boom boom! Rapid fire question session, begin!" Mickey said as he mimicked finger guns towards Tomasz.

"First question. Is it charged? Hmm." Mickey thought for a second.

"Well depending on your definition of what constitutes a charged object, then I would say yes. Yes, it is charged, in a way." Again Mickey started laughing at his joke. He was the biggest fan of his comedy.

Mickey had to control himself before continuing.

"Does it work? Well depends on how you define that something works. Well ok, I am being a bit silly, but if I had to say I would say, yes. Yes, it does, but like all things, you won't know until you try it. Once you do try it though, you will know. You will know in an instant if it works. A lot of people will, I suppose. And last question, did people walk around with hundreds of pounds on them? Well, I mean I am old, but not that old!"

Tomasz ignored Mickey's comedy routine and looked at the device. He felt silly for having been so worried about the potential of carrying something dangerous. But now he felt relieved that it had all worked out. Having made peace with the relic he had been tasked to deliver, Tomasz put it back in its bag and set it down. He kept sipping his tea while Mickey composed himself.

"I'm sorry, I don't get many visitors so I come across as someone who might not be all balanced. But I do have something else." At this, Mickey seemed more serious. He brought out the smaller bag that Tomasz had seen before.

This time he pulled out the contents of the bag and Tomasz recognized what he was looking at.

"Is that an early twenty-first-century mobile telephone?" Tomasz asked. It looked like something that was state of the art close to a century ago, near the beginning of the millennium.

"That's right." Mickey smiled as he looked at Tomasz. "It's hard to get anything past you huh?"

Mickey slid the device over to Tomasz, who grabbed it. This outdated device, unlike the battery, did not weigh a lot. It was as small as Tomasz's palm and it had actual physical buttons on it. Tomasz looked at it, wondering what else Mickey had in store for him.

"So I'm confused. Do you want me to call you or something?" Tomasz asked.

"That's right," Mickey replied.

"Why can't I call you the usual way? What's wrong with that?"

"Well there is nothing wrong with that, but it would be better if we used this phone instead," Mickey said, but he could tell that Tomasz was not pleased with his answer.

"You see the regular methods that we could use to communicate are, well, let's say less than secure. You see, the frequencies this phone operates on are by all standards outdated and no longer in use. Nowadays the frequencies the phone transmits over are saturated with machine-to-machine communication. That means that there are not a lot of ears listening to those conversations," Mickey explained with a small smirk.

Tomasz understood what Mickey was saying, but he had no idea why they would have to resort to something like this.

"Ok, so you want me to call you using this so that no one else listens to what we talk about?"

"Bing-bing-bing! That is exactly why I want to use the cell phone." Mickey replied.

Tomasz and Mickey stared at each other for a second.

"I'll be honest, you do not have to take the phone, Tomasz. If you want to, you can grab the battery, walk out of here, drop it off, and it'll be fine. The sun will still rise tomorrow, the tide will still go in and out, and dear old Mickey will be a-ok. Of course, he will be deprived of the privilege of talking to his new friend Tomasz again."

"And if I take the phone?" Tomasz replied.

"If you take it, all that I ask is that after you've spent some time with the patrons of my fine goods that you call me. You see, I would like to know what exactly they have in mind to do with it. Make sense? Simple as that! Whenever you can you get the little phone out, call me, and say, 'Mickey you got no worries, those were some upstanding people I met and your battery is in good hands, so sleep tight and give Pedro a kiss, ok?'" Mickey ended and patted Pedro on the head.

Tomasz looked at Mickey. All he would have to do was take the phone and call him. Of course, he did not have to do so, but it did not seem like anything problematic. A silence crept into the room between the two of them. Mickey was the first to speak.

"Let me ask you something first, have you ever hurt anyone in such a way that no matter what you do you cannot fix it?" Mickey looked dead serious as he stared at Tomasz. His heart started racing and he felt if he lied Mickey would know.

"I, um, I don't know. I mean I've said some hurtful stuff to my brother, but we always find a way to make amends."

Mickey nodded. "I have been there before. But see sometimes you can't do that. Sometimes you can't go over and say sorry and things go back to how they used to. What you end up doing is spending hours, or in my case days of my life thinking about what I could have done differently. But you know what?"

Tomasz shrugged his shoulders.

"It doesn't matter," Mickey emphasized with his hands. "It doesn't matter. Look."

Mickey picked up his cup and threw it on the floor. Shards of glass flew in all directions around the apartment.

Tomasz jumped from the scare. Pedro leaped from Mickey's lap.

"Sorry," Mickey said as he looked at the broken cup.

Tomasz thought there might be something more to come. But Mickey kept staring at the shattered cup.

Mickey turned his head towards Tomasz.

"See, it's still broken. The only thing that could have stopped that was if it didn't happen in the first place. Does this make sense? I know I am rambling here," Mickey added.

A robotic vacuum came from one of the corners and cleaned up the mess. Both Tomasz and Mickey stared at it.

"With the robot cleaning up the mess I don't know if my point has the same effect. So please feel free to ignore him," Mickey added.

"I follow you…well, I think," Tomasz replied, his heart still racing.

"OK, because this here is the important part. This battery that you have is something that I was asked to provide to some friends I have not seen in a long time. These are people that I used to respect a lot and still do, but well it has been a long time and people do change. So if you are ok with it, all I want is for you to give me a quick call after you've met them," Mickey said as he held up an identical device to the one he gave Tomasz.

"And again what you do here is up to you. You can walk out of here, no battery no phone and I will not say anything. You can leave here with the battery and that is fine with me as well. That is what you agreed to deliver and I cannot hold it against you to do exactly what was asked of you. Or you can grab both the battery and the phone and when you deliver the package, get to know the people buying it. See what exactly they plan on doing with it, and give me a call later. If you think they might end up hurting anyone with it, let me know. I don't want anyone to get hurt by anything I make. You don't have to do anything, just call me, let me know and I'll take care of it. You'll get your payment and be set." Mickey emphasized those last words.

Someone could get hurt from this? How the hell would that even happen? Tomasz felt the same nervousness he had staved off several minutes ago start to creep in. He knew he could not go through with this. He got ready to let Mickey down.

"I'll do it," Tomasz blurted out. "I'll make sure I call you and tell you what I learn about what they are planning to do."

Somehow in the split second between making up his mind and speaking Tomasz changed his mind.

Mickey looked both relieved and concerned. "Thank you, Tomasz, you are a high-mint person." He smiled and Tomasz was not sure why but he smiled along.

***

Tomasz found himself going down Seventh Avenue. It was only a short walk away from the Io Enclave and it provided him easy access to the train to Crow District. Seventh Avenue was also the busiest street in all of Fox District and at this time of day, it was more crowded than the norm. Beyond the fact that Seventh Avenue was the best-known street in the entirety of Cahuilla, there was something that made it unique.

In other streets, ads bombarding passersby regularly and intruding on their personal space is normal. Walking down Seventh Avenue made one feel as if they were intruding upon the advertisements' personal spaces. Passing in front of a sunglass shop, Tomasz's entire surroundings shifted.

Instead of being on a busy city road, he was now on a beautiful beach inhabited by nothing short of what seemed to be Greek Gods and

Goddesses. Their every physical feature was sculpted to perfection and all were wearing name-brand sunglasses. Once Tomasz left the perimeter of the store he found himself once again on Seventh Avenue, but not for long.

The next step had him in a large candlelit room, with various tables displaying all sorts of fine foods. This was the famous Ithaca Steak House and as Tomasz walked by it, virtual waiters would walk in front of him carrying plates with succulent meals. If it wasn't for his current predicament he might have felt hungry. Tomasz moved away from the storefronts and into the middle of the street to avoid the constant interruptions. He was wary of his surroundings and hyper-vigilant of the crowds around him.

On any other day, Tomasz would not have cared about the masses around him. The citizens of Fox were infamous for ignoring those around them. The interfaces implanted in the majority of the population would provide subtle stimuli to the wearer if they were about to collide with someone. It was so ingrained into people that it was possible to walk with eyes shut down the busiest walkways in Fox District and not run into anyone for miles.

Tomasz had tried this out many times. He was aware that nobody should be looking at him for more than half a second. But this time it was different. Tomasz was dressed in such bright colors that he felt eyes on him all the time. And not only that but there was also the package. That bag that Tomasz had in his hand was deceptively heavy. He still was unsure what the hell happened at Mickey's apartment and why he agreed to deliver it. The instant he set foot outside Mickey's apartment he regretted it. He held his head down as he walked.

Well, what if I go back and give it back to him? Tomasz thought to himself. *Maybe he'll think I tampered with it or something. Shit.*

Deep in thought Tomasz raised his head and saw someone about to collide with him.

"Ah!" That was all Tomasz could say.

The man avoided Tomasz without so much as a visible reaction. Tomasz kept staring as the man blended into the crowd behind him.

Tomasz stood in place trying to calm himself down. The waves of people walked around him as if he were some sort of lamppost. Some immovable, inorganic structure that was part of the city's layout.

"Ok stop freaking out. Look!" Tomasz ordered himself.

Tomasz opened the bag and peered inside it. Inside he found the same battery he had seen earlier inside Mickey's apartment. The same old harmless battery that he had made such a fuss about.

"Ok, this is what is going to happen. Step one I will deliver the battery. Step two I will call Mickey and that will be it!" Tomasz reassured himself louder than he wanted to. He looked around the throngs of people around him. Once again multitudes were walking past him without even noticing him. This man was arguing with himself in a bright Pink Tuxedo and nobody even batted an eye.

"Well if they don't give a shit, then I shouldn't either!" Tomasz muttered as he steeled himself and continued on his way to the delivery's destination.

Chapter 3: Across the River

"Oh, but is the package delivering you or are you delivering the package, hm?" A middle-aged bald man sat next to Tomasz. His eyes were wide open as they stared into Tomasz's eyes. He had a wry smirk on the corner of his mouth.

"Um, I don't know, what do you think?" Tomasz replied as he looked around him trying to find some way to get out of this conversation. The train car was full to the brim but nobody even dared look in their direction.

"Well, but it would be wrong of me to come out and divulge the answer! First off it was I who began this line of inquiry with you. And if I were to go and speak the truth, I would have stolen the opportunity for you to expand your horizons. Depriving you of this journey you are undertaking would not be in line with my principles as a student of Socrates. So, you tell me, which one is it, eh?" The man continued in his probing. He seemed to not notice how uninterested and uncomfortable Tomasz was to be partaking in this awful ad hoc philosophical debate.

"I mean, I um, what was it again?" Tomasz asked. He did not care, but he wanted to see if the man would get a hint.

"Well young man, you see, you tell me the bag you have there is an item you are delivering. But I ask you, are you delivering the item or is the item delivering you?" The middle-aged man could not help but smirk every time he presented Tomasz with a new question.

The man had seemed friendly enough when he sat down and greeted Tomasz. Tomasz did not feel like talking but he did not want to seem suspicious and figured he would reciprocate and move on with it. That was not the case.

He complimented Tomasz on his choice of clothing. Tomasz thanked him and let him know he had picked this outfit for a musical later that night. Tomasz was sure that after that the man would be content with his brief interaction and leave it at that. The man's next statement was to the effect that true philosophy is only expressed through music. After that interesting remark, ten more minutes had slogged by and somewhere they had moved on from that to talking about deliveries.

"So, tell me young man, which one are you?"

"Umm, well I don't think I am a delivery. I mean for something to be delivered it has to move from one location to another. And the package would not move if I wasn't transporting it, so ... I am not a delivery, but the package is the delivery. Right?" Tomasz answered but all the man did was to keep looking at him.

"Oh, so you are not the delivery, is that so? But what if I were to say—"

Tomasz realized his torment at the hands of his seat neighbor was not done yet. He fought the urge to roll his eyes with every fiber of his being.

"—aren't you moving because of the package? You find yourself currently here because the package requires it of you. Without the package, you would not be here. So are you moving the package or is the package moving you?" The man pushed in his glasses, which Tomasz could tell were purely cosmetic, before continuing his diatribe.

"If your whole childlike premise rests upon the very banal fact that the package is moving because of you, then I think we ought to reconsider the very conditions of how you came to find yourself here today! If I were to cling to the same ignorant mindset that seems to pervade the streets of Cahuilla, then I too might say that you are delivering the package. But after many years of seeking true knowledge and having arrived at a higher thought plane far removed from such simple thoughts, I know better. So I must say that not only are you incorrect, but also blind to the fact that you can't be delivering the package. In fact, it is the package that is delivering you. For you would not be here right in front of me if the package did not dictate that you be here!" The man finished his inane speech and fell silent.

The silence between them indicated to Tomasz that he was now expected to say something.

"Wow, I would have never considered that, to be honest," Tomasz replied. He was honest. But he did not mean it at all in a positive way.

"I admit when I first came upon true knowledge it also surprised me. What you have heard will no doubt shift your entire perspective. Hm." The man seemed very pleased with himself.

Tomasz stared off into the space hoping that this would be the last thing he heard from him.

"Now arriving at – Crow District. The next stop is – Sonali Station. Next stop is in – 87 seconds," the loud voice announced over the speakers.

"Oh ho, I have three more stops to go," the man announced aloud as he continued smiling.

He turned to Tomasz.

"How about you young man? Do you think you have it in you to continue challenging your worldview?"

Tomasz looked at his interface. He had two more stops to go after this one. But he could not even tolerate even one more minute of speaking with this man. He found an alternate route as fast as possible.

"Oh umm, what a breeze this ride has been, I did not even realize that my stop was coming up so soon. Umm, thanks, eh, I guess for instructing me, you know packages, deliveries, a lot of stuff I learned." Tomasz could see the disappointment in his seat neighbor since his unwilling conversation partner was leaving.

"Young man, let me tell you something else before you leave. I'm sure this will surprise you, but I am Dr. Ray C. Schwartz. I know you are probably surprised to have found me out in the city. But now you probably understand how I challenged your entire worldview with so little effort, because you recognize me from my online catalog, correct?"

Tomasz's blank stare let Ray know that he did not recognize him. Tomasz could tell that it miffed Ray a bit.

"Well, then you are even luckier than I thought." Ray seemed to flip a switch and seem upbeat once again. "I host a series of very popular online video teachings called *The Conquerors and the Vanquished*. If you want to learn more from me you should go to Paryte dot, s, c, m. In there, you can find hours of content from me and other high-caliber individuals. And because I can tell that you do not support mediocrity, I'll even give you a small bonus. I don't do this very often, but if you use the code 'Omega Level', and please don't share this with anyone else, you'll get fifty percent off our exclusive 'Conqueror's Club'. At 'Conqueror's Club' you will be able to talk with other like-minded high-intelligence individuals, other conquerors. Just like you, they are eager to learn how to become conquerors and not the vanquished. Remember, the code is 'Omega Level' in Paryte dot s, c, m. I guarantee that your life will change."

"Sonali Station – arrived," the voice announced.

"Remember young man—" the man started.

"Yup got it, "Conquering empowerment" I got it!

"Young man—"

"Don't worry I know! Gotta deliver the package—"

"It's actually—"

"Oh that's right, I'm being delivered! I'll remember next time, packages and the packers, delivery, deliverer, yeah a lot. Ok wow, it's been great bye!" Ray once again started to chime in with something but Tomasz had hurried off the train.

As he walked away he kept glancing over his shoulder trying to make sure Ray was not right behind him. Once he was far enough from the train he stopped. He turned around to look at the spot on board the train where he had been 'educated'.

He saw Ray place his chin on his hand with a big smile, ecstatic that he had found a new convert to his ideals. Tomasz was sure that Ray felt as if he had completely turned Tomasz into a new person after their conversation. In the meantime, a teenager walked up and sat down next to Ray. As the train departed, Tomasz saw Ray strike up a conversation with him.

"Poor kid, he is in for a class in stupid," Tomasz laughed to himself as he gripped the package and walked away.

As he walked he took in his surroundings. He was in a massive open-air train station, the Sonali Station, that had hundreds of platforms at different levels off and on the ground.

Sonali Station itself was so massive that it was hard to believe that it was all enclosed. At the top Tomasz could see giant extractor fans. These existed to regulate the various weather patterns that would form inside the building. The organization of the various rail lines that crisscrossed the station was so amazing that to behold them was inspiring. The only place where there were no lines was in the exact center of the structure. Instead, a giant stream of water poured down in a cylindrical shape. In the exact geometric center of the water, a massive holographic sign floated. From Tomasz's perspective, he read:

nali Station

row District

It felt odd being here. Despite Crow District being part of Cahuilla City and only being separated from Fox District by the Cahuilla River, it was a part that he rarely visited. He was a lifelong Fox District resident, yet had only visited Crow District around ten times or less. The last time he had been in Crow was over a decade ago. He had come with his dad to visit his uncle. He never much heard from him these days.

As he looked around he could not believe the sheer amount of people coming and going from this single train station. Tomasz thought that Seventh Avenue was a busy street. He was sure he could count many times more people here than he had ever seen on the busiest day on Seventh Avenue on each one of the floors of this station.

He currently found himself on the eighth floor. Despite the massive structure he found himself in and the commotion of the busy station he felt an almost inexplicable calm.

The faint blue hue that radiated all over the station seemed reminiscent of a nice dream. A smell of lavender permeated the air. Tomasz could see an artificial overlay faintly pulsing in his internal display guiding him to the exit. It was hard to perceive and it was only when he was halfway to the exit that he noticed he had been following it.

This helped keep the massive crowds of people moving as if it were a steady stream. Tomasz also noticed how quiet the entire station was. Despite the vast number of trains that were moving without pause, all he could hear was the faint murmur of conversation and the splashing of the water. Tomasz felt somewhat stupefied and entranced. This first experience he had contrasted with the mental image Tomasz had of Crow District before his arrival.

As he walked out of the station and into the district proper the entrancing feeling he had started to dissipate. Now in the center of Crow District Tomasz could finally see it all.

All that he could see were large buildings that shot up from the ground straight into the sky, blocking out a majority of the sunlight. Even though it was only early in the evening, one would assume it was almost nighttime. But despite that, it was nowhere near dark. Signs and screens all over the buildings were broadcasting a cacophony of content. In one display Tomasz saw INN. Now it was Lauren River who was anchoring. On a different screen, he saw a live basketball game. The screens were so massive that they covered the majority of the buildings. As he scanned from one screen to the next the audio feed from that specific screen would broadcast into his head. At two different locations, Tomasz saw gaps between buildings, where various rail lines protruded that fed into the massive building Tomasz had left. He was so enthralled by the view that it came as a major surprise to him when the next thing he was admiring was the pavement.

"Hey! Pink boy, get out of the way!" Tomasz heard someone shout.

He reacted as fast as possible before his face slammed into the ground. By the time he looked around he couldn't even see who had pushed him.

"Well, I guess people moving out of the way not to bump into you is not a thing in Crow," Tomasz muttered to himself.

He adjusted himself and prepared to go on with what he came here to do. He checked the time: 5:12 PM. He had a package to deliver. Or maybe the package was delivering him?

Regardless, he needed to get the battery to Lowray Street. His interface lit up and he saw the directions to his destination. It was twelve miles away and he had less than two hours to get there. There was no way he was going to get there in time walking.

The interface brought to his attention a tram that was a minute away. While waiting for the tram he looked across the street. A sea of different modes of transportation bustled and swerved, missing each other by mere inches.

People and robots unloading cargo would move in and out of the traffic without pause and at no point would they collide with the traffic. As the tram approached, he noticed something peculiar, something completely unexpected.

For a split-second, Tomasz could swear he saw two people dressed in very similar Pink Tuxedos to the one he wore. They were across the street and before Tomasz could get a good look at them the tram stopped in front of him, blocking his view.

Tomasz got in and looked across to see if he could see the Pink Tuxedo duo, but he had lost them. As he scanned the street, a sudden surge in motion sent him staggering and almost falling to the ground.

As he fell forward he felt a tug on his collar. The force pulled him to his feet and set him upright. Tomasz looked back as a mechanical arm settled into the roof of the tram.

"Caution: tram is underway now." The warning shone in his face.

"Yeah, no shit," Tomasz whispered.

As he got over the fright of almost smashing his face into the ground yet again, he found a pole on which to hold on. Tomasz studied his fellow passengers as the car moved along. The majority of them resided only in their thoughts as they stared ahead. Tomasz could see the flashing lights in their pupils indicating that they were watching something via their retinal display. Those who went without either slept or sat in silence. Amongst all the passengers, no one seemed to pay Tomasz any sort of attention aside from two at the very end.

As soon as Tomasz had entered the tram the two cops had noticed him. At first, he thought they were staring at him due to his unique clothing. But enough time had passed that now he started to feel uncomfortable.

The two individuals sported all-black ballistics-grade gear over the entirety of their bodies. The only difference between that kind of gear and the type issued to the military was cosmetic. That was thanks to the Safe Home Act, enacted a year into the Conflict when there were fears of a continental land invasion. That act ensured that all law enforcement on US soil had the same equipment and training as those overseas in the Conflict.

The face shields they wore made it impossible to see their faces. If one was not used to their uniforms, it would be easy to mistake them for robots. The one thing that identified them was the white letters CCPD emblazoned across their chest. Tomasz's retinal display identified them: Lucas A. Happe and Jenn Brown. Tomasz held the package close to him.

"It's ok. Be calm, just be calm," he whispered to himself as he looked away from them.

Still, he could feel his breathing intensify. He had no real reason to feel concerned. But the more he thought about calming down so that those two would stop looking at him the more nervous he got. For what seemed like a lifetime Tomasz waited for his stop and it finally came. As the tram came to a halt Tomasz readied himself to leave. As soon as Tomasz let go of the pole he saw the two cops get up as well. His heart started racing.

"You, we need to talk to you." The man in all black pointed in Tomasz's direction as the doors swung wide open.

Tomasz pointed to himself and prepared to respond. Instead, for the third time in a very short interval, he once again found himself falling forward. Falling out of the car Tomasz was able to stop his face from hitting the ground again. He heard horns blaring all around and saw a silhouette run past him.

While he struggled to regain his balance, he heard the word "Stop" shouted many times. As Tomasz tried to turn to the cops he felt a push from behind away from the tram. As Tomasz lost all balance he could hear the same "Stop" being yelled. Only this time it was not in a commanding voice but in a frightened tone.

Before he saw it Tomasz felt it. The impact of the fast-moving vehicle sent him flying. Even though he wasn't in the air for very long it felt like a lifetime. Shortly before hitting the pavement, Tomasz could see the bright yellow car that hit him screech to a halt. The next thing he remembered was lying down on the pavement.

Tomasz was now staring into the sky. He saw the same tall buildings that had mesmerized him earlier. Even now when he was lying in agony, he could not help but admire the spectacle before him. His retinal display interrupted his view with a flashing message: "WARNING! Traumatic injury detected. Emergency services, Allwyn Medical Experts, dispatched. Arrival expected in 37 seconds."

His retinal display cleared and a small timer appeared in the corner of his vision. Amid his misery, Tomasz received another message across his field of vision.

"This emergency service is brought to you by Lokos Tacos Restaurant and Drone Service. Skip Ad in: 5, 4, 3,-"

Tomasz did not want to watch whatever it was they were about to show him but he was unable to move any part of his body to stop it.

"Hey, there amigo! I hope you didn't forget what day it is. It's TACO TUESDAY! You're missing out if you don't come over to your nearest Lokos Tacos for some crazy amazing flavor!" A bleached blond-haired young man spoke in a carefree manner.

"Lokos Tacos guarantees that no animals are harmed in the making of our ingredients and we still bring you the best flavors!"

The shot now included images of the various food items served by Lokos Tacos.

"Whether you're just looking for something to eat in the city, something to bring home, or something for where the adventure takes you, Lokos Tacos is for you!"

Now the scenery changed and the bleached blond man was at a beach. He was enjoying the food with a group of people. They all laughed as they ate tacos they had picked up from the sand.

"Don't forget to enjoy tasty tacos on this beautiful TACO TUESDAY! Enjoy vida with some pique!"

"Those tacos do look good," Tomasz muttered as his whole world faded to black.

Chapter 4: Underground

"Look kid, we know that you guys are planning something. We have been patient enough with you. Now you have to come clean and tell us what it is, ok?" Lucas leaned into the bed and stared straight into Tomasz's eyes. Tomasz preferred him with the helmet on than without it.

"How many times do I have to tell you? I have no idea what you are talking about!" Tomasz was beyond frustrated at this point.

"Tomasz, I understand that you think these people are your friends, but they are not. I know you guys think that you are some sort of heroic resistance group, but you are not. Your group is dangerous. If you keep insisting on protecting them, I can't guarantee things will work out for you. We've seen what some of your colleagues are capable of and to me, you don't seem like you fit in with their way of life," Jenn said to Tomasz. She followed the "good cop, bad cop" pattern that the two cops had established around half an hour ago.

The hospital room in which Tomasz found himself felt suffocating. The bed was tiny and the room itself seemed only big enough for two people at a time. The two cops with what seemed to be an entire arsenal of equipment made Tomasz feel like he was inside a prison cell.

The lighting was dim, which made the two officers seem like two floating heads with all their black gear. The medical equipment which beeped and hummed along to Tomasz's vital signs provided the majority of the light in the room.

His heart had not stopped racing during the incessant questioning from the two officers. He had even forgotten what had brought him there. The intense pain from his collision with the car had faded. He lost track of all the concoctions that had been administered to him after about the tenth. He could see himself in a mirror across the room. Aside from a gauze that covered his right eyebrow, he looked as if nothing had happened. It was hard to believe that a half hour ago he was hemorrhaging and was minutes away from death.

"I know, I know, you already told me. And like I said, I don't even know what group you are talking about." As Tomasz spoke these words Lucas scoffed loud enough that the entire floor was sure to hear him.

"I keep telling you the same thing because it is the truth! This group, the Thread Barons, or whatever it is. I have never even heard of them! You guys tell me that they have been planning on doing something big for a while. You tell me they have stolen corporate data, destroyed personal property, committed arson, and are suspected of various cyber crimes, petty theft, and other things. And you think that because I am wearing this Pink Tuxedo I am involved with this?" Tomasz paused and then continued.

"I mean I know that the first thing you did when you saw me on the tram was scour the web for my records. You know that there is nothing on there about me being part of some gang or anything even close to that. The last time I was in Crow District I was only a kid. You know that is true because you haven't disputed that. So how is it that you think that I am part of this Thread whatever group? Is it a crime to be fashionable?"

Jenn laughed at Tomasz's remark. Lucas did not.

"OK kid, let me tell you something, there are currently close to ten million people in Crow District. Guess how many are wearing threads like yours?" Lucas retorted.

"I don't know but I saw two people wearing similar clothes so I'm not the only one!" Tomasz exclaimed.

"Oh, you did? You had not mentioned this before. See your story keeps changing! How do I know you are not hiding anything else?" Lucas sounded angsty as if he was nearing something important.

"Come on Tomasz, work with us here, all we want is to make sure that no one gets hurt." Jenn tried to appeal to Tomasz's better nature to see if he would come clean.

"Aaaghh! On my name! How many times have I told you? I swear I already told you everything I knew! Let me repeat this to you for like the millionth time! About a month ago a friend invited me to their musical. I wanted to look nice so I asked around where I could find a nice outfit for cheap. By word of mouth, I found a very low-key tailor near my school, Cahuilla Tech. Her store is old-timey, with most equipment being over half a century old. The woman's name was Angelica and I went to her and I said that there was a play I was going to or something like that. She replied that she knew exactly what I was looking for, so she took my measurements. Two weeks later, when I went to pick it up, she had made this custom Pink Tuxedo for me." Tomasz said exasperated as he pulled at the vest.

"Did you think I would have picked this to wear? THIS?!" He was gasping for breath and in the now silent room, the only sound came from the racing heart rate monitor.

"So you are telling us that you didn't argue with this lady when she gave you those clothes that you didn't like and you accepted them as they were?" Jenn looked at Tomasz wide-eyed.

"YES!" Tomasz shouted. He felt as if he was stuck in a time loop explaining the same thing again and again.

"Who does that? Who takes something they don't like and accepts it and pays for it? You didn't even know what she was making for you?" Lucas responded.

"Well, I had never bought something like this before! I had no idea what I was doing! I thought it was normal. When I went into the store I mentioned I had liked one suit she had on display. I thought that meant I was getting one exactly like that! I only realized that wasn't the case when I picked it up. And I felt awkward since she was so nice about it. I didn't want to make her feel bad! So I thanked her and went on my way! What else was I supposed to say? Did you want me to berate her for making me this Pink Tuxedo?"

"So you expect us to believe that you would rather take clothes that are hideous rather than have an awkward conversation?" Jenn replied.

"You think this Pink Tuxedo is hideous?" Tomasz calmed down but now he felt hurt.

"Well I wouldn't say it's my taste, but if you like it that's fine," Jenn added with a hint of disapproval.

"I like it kid, don't worry," Lucas interjected. It was the only nice thing he had said so far to Tomasz.

"Well, thank you."

"But I still don't believe you," Lucas added in a quick reply.

"Look I wouldn't even be here if it wasn't for you two. Because you two decided to call me out on the tram, those two pelt heads ran out thinking it was them you wanted and knocking me into traffic, almost killing me! All I was going to do was go to this play in my Pink Tuxedo and that was it. Now I'm stuck here and my head is hurting like crazy after hitting that car."

"Ok well, first of all, we are sorry about that. But you're fine now and accidents happen all the time. But yes, we understand that and we're sorry," Lucas said with only the barest hint of remorse.

"Yeah, we are," Jenn added in such a low voice that Tomasz almost didn't hear it. She didn't even try looking at Tomasz when she said it.

"But we had no idea that they had like twelve arrest warrants out for them. We saw you in your, well opinions differ on whether it is fashionable or not, in your Pink Tuxedo. Which is very similar to the outfit we have heard the Thread Barons might be wearing. So excuse us for being a bit suspicious of your story and wanting to question you."

"And then there's this," Jenn added as she held up the battery.

Tomasz had tried to avoid the subject the entire time, but this was the third time they had asked about it.

"That's right, we have already asked you about everything else many times. Nothing you have said so far we trust, but you have been open with us. Yet out of all the things you have spoken about you have not said anything about that!" Lucas said as he walked around the small room. He bumped into the bed with his right thigh, visibly recoiling. He tried to play it off as if nothing happened. At the end of his accusatory speech, he used one hand to point to Jenn and the other to rub his thigh.

"Well, guys what do you think it is?" Tomasz asked, trying to stall for time.

"Well to me it looks like a—" Lucas stopped mid-sentence and Tomasz and Jenn both stared waiting for him to finish.

"Look kid, we ask the questions, now what the hell is it?"

"Is it an old-timey battery?" Jenn asked as she handled it from various angles as if the answer were etched somewhere on the device.

"Yes! That's precisely what it is!" Tomasz replied with glee. He decided now was the time to try out the story he had come up with at the last minute.

"You see, there is an old computer that I am trying to repair. I am kind of a fan of old tech. New stuff is just so intangible. I like being able to get my hands on a piece of tech and make it work. So that's what I was doing with this computer. I'm talking something very old here, like close to a hundred years. But there I was, I'd found everything that I needed for it. Fixed the monitor, and the keyboard, found a hard drive that would fit it, and even found a disc that I could use for the operating system. You know, spent a lot of time trying to get this thing working. Then I try to start it up, and it doesn't work. I mean I had worked on getting all these parts together for so long, so what is going on here? Well, I take the battery and run it through a multi-meter. That's another piece of old technology. You know I love that old tech. Got tons and tons of it. So that's when I realized that it was… can you guess?"

Neither officer cared much for Tomasz's story.

"That's right, the battery! So since I was going to be in Crow District I was going to look for a place that might sell these. I mean, they sell everything here. And I was on my way to a place I had just found. You know, just going about my day, having a grand time before I am almost killed thanks to you two!" Tomasz felt proud of himself for the way his story turned out. He thought it was pretty believable.

He looked at the heart rate monitor. It was skipping so fast that Tomasz could not believe it. Both Lucas and Jenn stared at it too.

They then stared at each other.

"Right. So and the place that you were going to take this battery, what was it called?" Jenn asked.

"Umm, hmm. Yeah, what was it called? Oh, that's right! Mickey's! Yup, Mickey's Old Computers Shop, that's right. It took me a long time to find it let me tell you!" Tomasz grinned as he answered. He was almost one hundred percent sure that neither Lucas nor Jenn believed him. He just hoped they wouldn't try to search for it on their interfaces.

Suddenly, the door to the room swung open. A man in a crisp white uniform, a doctor, ran in struggling to catch his breath.

"Oh thank the heavens you are here! There is a lady on the thirty-fifth floor who grabbed some chemicals off our storage room and she's threatening to poison everyone, please, we need your help!" the doctor begged the police officers.

The two cops looked at each other and swung into action. In the blink of an eye, they grabbed their gear, donned it, and were making their way out of the room.

"We're still questioning him, so don't let him leave yet," Jenn said to the doctor before she left the room.

The doctor nodded. "I'll make sure this deviant lowlife doesn't leave!"

Tomasz felt offended by the doctor's tone. He had done nothing wrong aside from wearing some very fancy clothing and this doctor already decided he was a deviant and a lowlife. The cops left the room, but in less than a second they returned when they realized they did not know where to go.

The doctor followed them into the hallway and pointed them toward the elevators as he shouted.

"Yes! Please, the elevators are around that corner! They will take you to the thirty-fifth floor the quickest. Please, that floor is where we keep our sick children, you have to help them!" The doctor's voice cracked as he pleaded with the officers. Whatever was going on sounded very serious.

The doctor, now outside the room, kept staring into the distance. He kept repeating loud enough for the whole floor to hear "Please help them, please I have not seen anything like it before, it's terrible! The old people are in danger!" It was hard to understand the doctor as he had started crying. Despite not appreciating those cops' attitude Tomasz hoped they could help the children and the old people that were in danger.

After a couple of seconds, the doctor wiped his face with a handkerchief and ran into the room. He closed the door behind him. Tomasz felt a sudden pang of anxiety hit him as he saw the stranger come in.

"Well? What the hell were you thinking?! You could have messed us up with this stunt! Getting caught like that?! Don't you know to avoid public transportation?!" The man had a bewildered look as he stared at Tomasz.

Tomasz tried to make sense of what the doctor was going on about. He read his nametag: "Dr. Satya Bose".

"Never mind, never mind. Look those two cops will be back here in about two minutes at most, so you better get the hell out of here before they get back."

"What—" Tomasz tried to plead.

"You know you better have a real good explanation to Mel for what you pulled. She is not going to be happy that you decided to take the scenic route. Especially today and even super duper especially when you are wearing the Pink Tuxedo! Do you have shit brains or something? You know how hard we've been working at this and you almost ruined it!" The doctor seemed keen on continuing to berate Tomasz.

"Wait—"

"But I did see your chart. Damn, that car hit you HARD! You had massive head trauma, like oof!" The doctor laughed.

"Well, I didn't—"

"I mean, you probably have no idea what's going on after all those meds they gave you. But you seem like a trooper, not surprised, Mel knows how to pick them. Although she doesn't always go for brains, as we can see," Dr. Bose said as he motioned toward Tomasz.

"But to be honest I don't recognize you. You must be a newer guy." He now eyed Tomasz with a curious look.

"I was—"

"OK, enough talking. Look, you might not know but there's an old subway line underneath this hospital. The train there stops at Godel Station near the bar. Take the third elevator on the right out there and go to the basement. There you'll find the line, it's very old so there won't be many people there. You for sure won't see any more cops. But you better be careful cause if they already found you once then they'll find you again. So no more public transportation, got it?"

Tomasz could only stare, still unsure of what exactly was going on.

"Alright, so when you get on the subway take it to Godel Station, ok? Once you leave Godel you'll see our spot right there. It'll be the one that has the only functional sign on that street. Once they see you, they'll let you in. Got it?"

Tomasz still stared. He was not sure of what was happening. The doctor mentioned something about getting on a subway in the basement but that was as much as he understood.

"Good, now hurry up, 'cause those guys will be back any minute." The doctor started unhooking Tomasz from all the medical equipment.

Tomasz was beyond confused at what was happening. One second he was being interrogated and the next he was being set loose. He did not feel like leaving in the middle of an interrogation was the best idea. But at the same time, those cops were very sure that he was guilty of something, so sticking around wasn't the best idea either. If he did, he might miss Monique's show.

"Well, are you going to stay there all day?" Dr. Bose sounded exasperated.

Tomasz finally decided to follow the questionable doctor's advice, got up, and went towards the battery.

"Oh, and tell Mel that I'll be there in a bit. I have to come up with a story about how you escaped. See you later."

Tomasz started to leave. Now he was going to be on the run from the police. He hoped that was the worst that could happen to him today.

***

Tomasz saw the train car in front of him and entered. As the doctor had told him it was pretty desolate. There were only around six people all spread out over the train car.

"Destination?" a notification on his display read.

"Erm, Godel station?" Tomasz said, unsure whether this would work.

There was a delay as the machine processed what Tomasz had said.

"Um, how about—"

The subway started moving as Tomasz spoke causing him to lose his balance.

"I am getting sick of these things that keep trying to knock me down!" Tomasz fumed as he regained his balance. The subway's abrupt start seemed to let Tomasz know that it understood his request.

Tomasz sat down and the subway continued on its way. While it seemed insane to follow the doctor's request, he did not feel like he had too many options. Once outside the subway, he would see how close he was to his original destination. After that, he would have to figure out what to do about the Pink Tuxedo. Tomasz was kind of bummed out about the negative attention it had brought him. He liked it and did not want to part with it. But there was no way in hell that he would want to encounter the police again.

Tomasz was about to dive into his interface but decided against it. Although the doctor had told him the subway was safe from any more cops he could never be too sure. If he went into the interface he might log out to find himself surrounded by a whole squad. He thought it would be best to stay in the present.

Without much else to do he studied the old subway he found himself in. As he scanned the metal walls of the car Tomasz could not find any type of digital interface. The conductor seemed to be the only piece of technology on this subway that was in any way modern. Everything else was very old technology.

There were no holographic signs on display anywhere, only static displays with ads for movies that he had never heard about. Amongst the ads he saw were *FREAK SHOW* and *BLACK OX*. Alongside the movie posters, Tomasz saw an old map. It showed the different stations this line would go through—Peart Station, Portnoy Station, Rev Sullivan Station, and Jordison Station. He did not recognize any of those.

Tomasz tried his best to occupy his mind to calm himself. The ambiance the subway gave off was anything but calming. Its lighting was not the soothing blue hue that Tomasz associated with public transport. The lighting on this subway was a bright white, glaring down harshly. The seats were a very hard material and Tomasz could not get comfortable no matter what he tried. Then there was the noise.

All Tomasz could hear was the ceaseless whine of the subway train as it moved along the tracks. He had never been on any type of transport where he could hear any part of the ride at all. Added on top of that was how turbulent the ride was. It seemed that every second, the subway was bumping up and down, giving Tomasz a nauseating feeling. He was starting to doubt whether leaving the hospital was the best idea.

Tomasz looked at the others in the car to see if they shared in his discomfort, but he seemed to be the only one bothered by any of this. His fellow riders all seemed to be either napping, which seemed impossible to Tomasz, or reading physical print media. That was an interesting choice. As he snooped further he spotted an oddity.

One of the passengers, a young woman, had a bare metal arm starting from her shoulder down. Tomasz had seen prosthetics like that before in old films or documentaries from decades ago, but never in person. The woman who had it on did not even seem to be that much older than Tomasz. He could not help but notice how beautiful she was as well. With her simple sundress, short blonde hair, and deep blue eyes, she was beautiful without effort. Once he looked up he saw that she was staring back at him.

"You see something you like?" she asked Tomasz in a tone that hinted that she did not appreciate his ogling.

"Um, I'm sorry!"

The woman's lips curled at the corners, revealing a beautiful smile.

"Oh, I am only teasing you. I'm sure you're not too used to seeing these," she said as she pointed to the arm. Tomasz shook his head.

"You must not be from around here then?" she asked.

"Em, no, not really. I'm here from Cahuilla Tech," Tomasz answered feeling sort of awkward. He was not good at small talk, especially with strangers.

"Oh wow, from Fox District?" The woman looked wide-eyed in surprise.

"That's right."

"Ah, now I can understand how you are not used to seeing some metal on people. They probably only show those in old films over there. You are either lost or you have a very specific place you are going to."

Tomasz did not know how to answer.

"Both?" the woman asked.

"Yeah, both." Tomasz laughed.

The train bumped and squealed, startling Tomasz for a second. No one else seemed to react. Upon seeing his reaction, the woman laughed a bit.

"Don't worry about it too much. It feels like it's going to fall apart, but it won't. I've been taking this subway line my entire life. This is built to last," she assured him.

"I'm Lisa by the way."

"I'm Tomasz."

"Nice to make your acquaintance Tomasz. So are you going to a party or something?" Lisa said as she pointed to the Pink Tuxedo.

"Oh, I'm going to see a friend's play and, well, this is all I had that was fancy." Tomasz blushed as he once again remembered his unique style of clothing. The Pink Tuxedo which had somehow been the cause of him being in this subway that seemed like a death trap.

"Well I would not have thought that a Pink Tuxedo could be fashionable, but I am going to say that you pull it off well."

"Really?" Tomasz blurted out. Lisa could tell she had made him blush.

"Oh yeah, your friend will be very happy to see you supporting them with such good fashion. But try not to steal the show."

The train whined as it slowed to a stop. Lisa got up.

"Well, enjoy your play and I hope you enjoy your time in Crow. We here don't think too well of those Fox elites, but you seem all right in my book. Be seeing you around, Tomasz."

"Thanks."

Lisa got off the subway and went into the dim station. Tomasz could not help feeling giddy after she left. It was not just that he had been able to talk to her without tripping over his words, but talking to her was such a nice change of pace. She seemed like a genuine person. It also was the first interaction he had in Crow district that did not devolve into something crazy. The subway moved on.

After a while, he heard the loud voice announce "Godel Station". He got up and exited the subway. Once in the station, it was hard for Tomasz to believe what he was seeing. The subway seemed like it moved him not only across space but backward in time.

The only thing decorating the walls were spray-painted figures and words, the kind of which Tomasz had never seen in person, only in old art archives.

The lights flickered and did not adjust as people passed by. There was no sound dampening in here so as the subway train sped away he could hear everything. No holographic displays were popping up as he walked by announcing the station at which he had arrived. Instead, there was a sign hanging a short distance away with the words "Godel Station" painted on it.

As Tomasz walked through the station he saw pockets of people every so often. They weren't waiting for a train, they weren't looking for something, they were there going about their day. Some were talking with each other, others were sleeping, and a group was cooking over an open fire. As he walked by, the strangers would greet Tomasz and smile at him. When Tomasz passed the people cooking he peered into the cauldron to see what they were making.

"Would you like some?" asked the woman who was mixing the ingredients into the cauldron. Before Tomasz even replied the woman was getting a bowl ready for him.

"It's cornmeal porridge! It's delicious!" A pale man sitting next to the woman spoke as if reading the question in Tomasz's mind.

"Oh I'm, I'm sorry I would love to, but I have something I need to do. But I appreciate the offer. Thanks!" Tomasz replied feeling guilty for some unexplained reason.

"Well, you know where to find us." The woman smiled and returned to her cooking. Tomasz continued walking through the station. He entered a long hallway and found some kids playing with an old ball. As he walked by a kick flung the ball over to Tomasz.

"Hey, pinky, can you kick the ball back to us?" One of the kids called out. He had dark hair and dark features but beamed as he smiled and spoke to Tomasz.

Tomasz swung his leg and almost tripped as his foot made contact with the ball. It swerved as it went towards the kids but they were able to catch it.

"Thanks, pinky!" The kids went on with their game with loud laughter, not a care in their world. Tomasz stared at them for a while with no real understanding of what he was seeing. He realized he felt sorry for them. He did not know what their situation was, he didn't know if they lived there, but it seemed like such a desolate and sorry environment, especially for children so young.

"Hey pinky you want to play with us?" The same dark-haired kid spoke to Tomasz. He seemed excited at the thought of having someone else join them.

"Oh, I'm sorry I have something I have to do. But thanks," he said as he waved to the kids.

"Alright pinky!" The boy went back to playing with the other children. They seemed as happy as any other kids Tomasz had seen. To them nothing was amiss. This old station they were playing in had more than what they needed and it was ok for them. Tomasz heard the children laughing as he walked towards the exit and up the stairs.

The scene outside the train station was similar to the one inside. It seemed as if this one section in Crow District had never progressed from how the city looked about half a century ago or more. There were roads, but no traffic was going by. The tallest building that Tomasz saw could not have been more than five stories. There were stores everywhere, but any signage that might have indicated what they once were had long since disappeared. There was only a single building that had a sign that somehow worked.

"That must be the one the doc mentioned. On my name, I ain't going in there," Tomasz muttered to himself.

People clustered in different areas around the street. Some were on the sidewalks, on the road, kids playing games in the middle of the street, and gaggles of people sitting eating up and down the street. There were around a hundred people on this short street. No one seemed surprised to see a man in a Pink Tuxedo coming out of the train station. When people saw Tomasz they greeted him as if they knew him.

"Hey there how are you?"

"Looking good!"

As others walked by they waved or said hi and kept doing whatever it was they were doing. It seemed like such a jovial atmosphere.

"Need any help finding your way?" a passerby asked Tomasz.

Tomasz declined the offer. He needed to find 101 Lowray Street so he could be rid of this battery and move on with his day. In his display, he asked for directions. The interface answered, "Destination arrived."

Tomasz looked confused. Maybe there were some signal issues from being underground for so long, so he waited a couple of seconds and asked again. "Destination arrived."

Tomasz looked around for any indication of where he was. He asked someone who was passing by what street he was on.

"Oh, son you're lost? How come you don't know which street you're on? You must be new then!" The thought process this person used to come to this conclusion made no sense to Tomasz.

"Why you're where you're supposed to be at, this is Lowray Street!"

"Really?" Tomasz replied.

"Yup, this right here is the one and only," the man said.

Of course, there was something else Tomasz needed to know. He felt as if he already knew the answer but he wished he was wrong.

"Well ok, would you happen to know which building is 101 then?" Tomasz asked.

"Oh, you must be really really new! Why it's that building right there." The man pointed behind Tomasz.

Tomasz did not even need to turn around to know which building he was pointing to. It was the one he had sworn less than a minute ago he would never enter.

"You ok there, son? You look like you ain't heard some good news?" the man asked Tomasz with genuine concern.

"Oh hah, no worries. I ate something that is making my stomach feel weird." Tomasz gritted through his teeth.

"Well feel better there, son." The man smiled as he walked away.

Once alone, Tomasz muttered to himself.

"What exactly in all the fucks is exactly going on?"

Chapter 5: Face to Face

Tomasz walked up to the door of 101 Lowray Street. He stood in front of the door for several seconds. He expected a sensor to have alerted someone on the inside of his presence, but nothing happened. He stood there, waiting, unsure of what to do.

"Hello," he said to the door. Maybe they did not have any type of motion sensor and it would pick up on sound.

A couple more seconds and nothing. Tomasz looked around and the street was still as lively as ever. No one seemed to pay attention to the man wearing a Pink Tuxedo talking to a door. Tomasz had come so close to his objective and would not stop from delivering the package now. He had to finish what he started. He steeled himself and pushed on the door. He was surprised to find that it was not locked and it opened a bit. Tomasz could hear music playing and shouting. He was not sure if the people inside were fighting or arguing but they were making a lot of noise. Tomasz kept pushing the door open and looked inside.

The inside of the establishment was done up in a style that Tomasz recognized as an early twenty-first-century bar. The lighting was dim, there was a long bar around which a gaggle of people crowded over each other. There were tables set all over the rest of the room where people sat trying to hold conversations with their neighbors.

Despite only trying to talk to those sitting next to them they all seemed to be shouting. An unoccupied stage was set with a variety of instruments. There was no one on the stage, but loud music still blared. Inside the bar, Tomasz saw around fifty people in total. All the people in there shared one thing in common, something that they shared with

Tomasz as well. They all wore the same Pink Tuxedo. Tomasz was so confused by the sight that he was stupefied.

But while Tomasz stood there staring, something began to occur. It started in an almost imperceptible manner but it spread. Like a single blade of grass that catches fire and shortly thereafter an area the size of a city is aflame.

One person near the front of the bar noticed someone had opened the door. They turned to look at the new visitor and stopped talking. The person next to them, curious about what caught their acquaintance's attention also turned to look. Little by little the itch of curiosity jumped from one person to the next. Like a flame leaping from one blade of grass to the next. And in a very short amount of time, the entirety of the bar was staring at the door, silent and in abject confusion much like Tomasz.

There was no chatter anymore. The music had died. An entire room full of Pink Tuxedos were all staring at a stranger wearing the same clothing they were. One woman marched to the entrance. Tomasz was frozen as she approached.

"Hello?" Tomasz said to the woman as she stomped up to him.

She was tall, over six feet, even taller than Tomasz, and fast too. She was Asian and had long dark hair, tied in a ponytail. She grabbed Tomasz by the arm and dragged him into the building. He heard the door shut behind him. She pushed him to the middle of the floor and glared at him.

"Who the hell are you?" she inquired as she leered at Tomasz.

"I have something for you?" Tomasz said as he showed her the bag he had been carrying since he left Mickey's apartment.

She snatched it from his hands and peered inside. Her angry scowl morphed into a confused look.

She kept looking Tomasz over as if expecting something to happen.

"I don't know you, do I?" she asked Tomasz. The anger still simmered under the surface.

"I don't think so."

"Well, you need to tell me who the hell are you and why are you wearing this?" She prodded him while she poked her finger into his chest.

"Well, I'm Tomasz, nice to meet you, and I picked this up because I am going to a musical later and I had nothing else nice to wear to it," he said as he rubbed the area she had jabbed her finger into.

"Who made it?" The questioning reminded him of the two cops he had escaped earlier.

"Erm, Angelica? Does that ring a bell?"

"The one near Cahuilla Tech?" The woman's anger seemed to somewhat dissipate.

"Um, yeah?" Tomasz nodded.

"What did you say to her?" the woman demanded.

"What do you mean, what did I say to her?" Tomasz asked.

"I mean exactly what I asked."

"Well, I don't know. I said 'Hey how are you? Are you having a good day? Boy, this weather—'" Tomasz started but she cut him off.

"No! I don't need to know what kind of small talk you make! How is it that she made you the same outfit she made for us? That is what I need to know."

"Oh, that. Let me see. Well, I told her that I had a special event to go to in Crow district and I heard from a friend that she was the place to go for special occasions?" Tomasz seemed very confused as he kept staring at everyone around him.

"Let me get this straight. You went to Angelica and told her you were going to Crow District for a special event. You told her that a friend of yours recommended her, and said that she was the person to go to for special occasions. That is what you said word for word?" the woman asked in an icy tone.

"Well yeah, I mean what else was I supposed to say? Hey old lady, hurry up and get me a nice suit?"

"Ok and after that she gave you this Pink Tuxedo?" The woman once again poked Tomasz, though not as hard this time.

"Yeah pretty much."

"And you didn't say a word when she gave it to you? You took the Pink Tuxedo without even questioning why she decided to give you such a unique outfit?"

"Well, I had no idea what she was making for me. I thought it would be something completely normal! It was the cheapest outfit I could find anywhere! I never would have thought she was going to come out with this," Tomasz said as he pulled on his collar.

"And what was I supposed to say when she showed it to me? She was so happy about it and kept going on about how I would look so good in it! Was I supposed to tell her who the hell asked for a Pink Tuxedo? Was I supposed to tell her I didn't want it? I took it because I didn't know what else I was supposed to do! And then when today came and I had to get ready for the musical I had nothing else to wear. Is that a crime?" Tomasz could not take any more questioning at this point. He felt that if he kept getting asked about why this or why that he might snap.

For a second the entire room was silent. The woman could only stare at Tomasz. She then stared towards the crowd and put her hand on his shoulder. She looked at him once again.

"You have got to be fucking kidding me," she said to Tomasz before she burst out laughing.

As soon as she started laughing everyone else in the bar erupted with laughter also. Tomasz stood in the center with no understanding of what exactly was going on. How was it that he kept getting himself in these situations?

"Everyone, meet Tomasz!" the woman yelled and everyone started shouting in approval.

"Tomasz, I'm sorry but I realized I never introduced myself. You may call me Mel." Mel smiled at him.

A cry from the crowd went up "TOMMY BOY!".

Tomasz could not even point out who started it but like the blade of grass on fire, it spread throughout the crowd, "TOMMY BOY!" was shouted at Tomasz from all corners.

"One of us!" another shouted from the crowd.

Pretty soon everyone was coming up to Tomasz patting him on the back and laughing with him as if they had known him for ages. Tomasz was still at a loss for words. A couple of seconds earlier he was being questioned and now they were all rejoicing around him.

"Sorry about the interrogation there, Tomasz. We were not expecting anyone else to come in wearing a Pink Tuxedo so we were quite surprised when we saw you. But you seem like a very decent guy. And to think you were also our delivery guy! Talk about a crazy coincidence!" Mel laughed again.

"Here have a drink on us! Jerry!" Mel motioned toward the bartender, a middle-aged short bald black man, who whipped up a drink in a few seconds flat.

"I think you'll enjoy this." Jerry smiled at Tomasz as he handed him a drink.

Mel sat down at the bar and Tomasz followed suit and sat next to her.

"Thanks," Tomasz mumbled in reply. The previous events had all unfolded so fast that he was still unsure of what had happened. As he sat down he took a sip. He was not sure what to expect from the drink but he ended up enjoying it a lot.

"Wow," Tomasz said out loud.

"That's pretty good, right!" Mel smiled.

"Yeah, I mean I have no idea what it is but it is pretty good."

"I figured you'd like that," Jerry said.

"Jerry here is our secret weapon. He just knows what people like," Mel boasted.

"Anything else you'd like? Are you hungry? We got food if you'd like some," Mel offered as Tomasz made himself comfortable.

"The soup here is really good," Jerry added.

"No, I'm good. But thanks I, um, I appreciate it," Tomasz replied.

"Well let me know if you change your mind," Jerry said and went back to tend the bar.

The bar had returned to its earlier lively atmosphere. It was hard for Tomasz to hear anything more than a few feet from his face.

"So Tomasz, seeing as you got this suit from our mutual friend Angelica, I take it you live in Fox District?" Mel asked. She seemed like a completely different person from the one who had just dragged him into the bar a minute ago. Her terrifying demeanor was now replaced by a warm friendly attitude. To Tomasz, it seemed as if they were two different people.

"Yeah, I do. Lived there my whole life. I am currently a student at Cahuilla Tech, been there for around three years. I don't venture outside of Fox often. This is my first time in Crow in quite a while."

She nodded. "Makes sense. I grew up in Fox too, the Meadows area. I understand not leaving Fox much, it pretty much has everything you could want. Might seem crazy but I actually left Fox and moved to Crow about five years ago. It's hard to believe these places are only separated by a river, they seem like two different worlds. So were you scared when you ventured into Crow? I know it doesn't exactly have the best reputation amongst Fox denizens." Mel smirked.

"Well, I mean…" Tomasz started and then remembered what he had seen in his short time here. The overcrowded streets. The people bumping and pushing into each other. The ancient subway system. The people in Lowray Street.

"It is very different when compared to Fox, that's for sure. One of the first things that happened was almost getting shoved into the ground because I was staring at the skyscrapers. So quite different from Fox. Also a lot more people, like a lot lot more. That is for sure," Tomasz added.

Mel laughed at Tomasz's earnest response.

"It takes a while, but you get used to it. When I first started venturing to Crow I would have to prepare myself mentally. But now it's the complete opposite. If I ever have to go to Fox I dread it."

"Really? Why is that?" Tomasz asked, perplexed. The thought that someone might dread going to Fox over Crow was one that Tomasz could not even begin to understand.

"Hmm, that's a good question." Mel paused to think.

"Well, it's hard to describe. But I would say, the people there are very cold. They are so distant from each other. They seem more like robots than most robots I've met. Everyone does what they need to and then hides away in their little apartments. There is no life in that district, it's like an empty husk. I always felt like I never had any meaningful connections there. I couldn't understand how living in such a big city I could feel so..." Mel trailed off.

"Alone?" Tomasz finished for Mel.

Mel was silent for a second and nodded as she looked at Tomasz.

"Yes, alone. I couldn't deal with the isolation anymore. I knew I had to do something. Even if that was to start my life again. I had no idea what I would do, but I wanted to do something where I would feel connected to others. And I couldn't see myself doing that in Fox. I tried, I did for a long time, but I never was able to find that. That's why I decided to come to Crow. In the beginning, I thought I was crazy and that I was the problem. But it didn't take long before I found others that felt like me. Others that could not understand how it was possible to be so detached from other people in such a dense city. We formed a little group. At first we were only in it for ourselves, but then we realized this was something larger than just us. So we decided we were going to try to somehow get the word out. We knew we couldn't change society at large; I don't think that's possible for anyone. But at least we could make a space for ourselves where we felt something deeper, where we all had a genuine connection, and try to reach as many people as we could. And well little by little that has grown into this group right here!" Mel said as she motioned all around her.

A man walked up to the bar. Before he even said anything Jerry was handing him a drink.

"Tommy boy, this Jerry is the best!" The man smiled at Tomasz as he picked up his drink and walked back into the crowd.

"That was George by the way. But that's a very condensed version of my life story and how this group started. Which then led to us wearing these nice Pink Tuxedos! Which somehow spread outside the group!" Mel said with glee as she pointed at Tomasz.

Tomasz could see genuine joy in her face about the stranger that had come into their midst. Tomasz could see it in everyone in the bar. The initial impression that Tomasz received from the group, the icy reception, was more in line with what he would have expected from such a first meeting. But once they moved beyond the initial confusion Tomasz no longer felt like an outsider. These people treated him like one of their own. It was all of them, in the same Pink Tuxedos.

"Our group is not perfect and we still have our issues, but I think we do a good job of being there for each other," Mel finished.

Tomasz was quiet. It wasn't the first time this night he had heard the same sentiment, but something was different this time. Earlier he heard it from Mickey. Back then he couldn't understand what Mickey was talking about. He thought that since Mickey had experienced something as extreme as war, Tomasz could never relate. He figured that Mickey's issues stemmed from not being able to readjust to life outside of a warzone. But here Mel was expressing the same angst as Mickey. Yet her experience was one that Tomasz could understand. What led her to feel this angst was something that Tomasz was starting to see in himself.

"Well, I'm sorry I think I've been rambling!" Mel sounded embarrassed.

"No, I'm sorry. I didn't mean to seem like I was ignoring you. I was just, it reminded me of something else, that's all," Tomasz said, not wanting to seem rude.

"Well, that reminds me. Let's take a closer look at this package you brought for us."

Mel grabbed the package and pulled out its contents. As she studied it she could not hide a huge grin on her face.

"Fred and Oscar were right, that Mickey sure knows how to make these things look uninteresting." She smiled as she looked at Tomasz.

"When I told him to make it look like old tech, I didn't think he would go that old!" She laughed as she raised the hefty brick in her hand. "It's a lot heavier than I expected."

Tomasz could not understand why this old battery was so interesting. But he was happy to see that he had brought the correct package.

"Do you know what this is?" Mel asked Tomasz as she handed it back to him.

"Well of course, it's an old battery and let me tell you, it caused me a lot of trouble to bring it here. I got hit by a car getting off a tram earlier and I ended up in the hospital!" Tomasz laughed as he clutched the brick in his hand.

Mel looked at Tomasz wide-eyed and then at the battery.

"You're telling me you got hit by a car with that thing on you?" Mel looked astounded.

"Yeah, it hurt like hell, but thankfully the hospital patched me up to the point where you can't even tell I got hit!"

Still stunned, Mel could not take her eyes off the battery.

"Wow that Mickey is damn good! I would've figured if a car hit all those explosives it would have taken out a whole square. Good thing we went with him!"

Tomasz was still laughing, thinking about how silly the whole situation had been. He then replayed the sentence Mel had said in his mind and stopped laughing.

"I'm sorry. Wait a minute. We were talking about this battery, right?" Tomasz was sure he misunderstood. He pointed to the device in his hand.

"Well, it looks like a battery," Mel replied in a matter-of-fact tone.

"Because it is a battery," Tomasz laughed as he replied.

"Oh no. What you have in your hand is a very compact high-yield explosive. That thing will blow up this entire bar if it goes off." Mel sounded very serious.

"No, it can't be," Tomasz muttered. He looked to her and then to the brick in his hand. He thought about the entire situation once again. Why would someone pay him so much money to transport a battery? And why would they need to be so discreet? They could have used a thousand other delivery services.

"Oh." Tomasz now understood. This was not a battery, as Mel had told him. In his hands, he held some sort of dangerous explosive. One that had he carried through a lengthy trip from Fox to Crow District. The realization made him achieve a unique state of clear-mindedness. So clear was his mind that all thoughts escaped him, such as the one controlling his limbs. Now Tomasz, like a feather swaying in the air, fell off his chair in a very graceful manner and slumped on the ground.

***

Tomasz found himself back in his apartment. It was nice here. He was sitting down at his desk. He looked at the screen before him and realized that the big project he was working on was already complete.

"Wow, neat! Well, now that I have all this time what should I do? I know—I'll go online and play some 'CHAOS MALLET Forty Million'!"

Tomasz logged into his lobby and all his friends were there, waiting for him.

"Hey, Tomasz are you ready?" Felix, his good friend from back home asked him with a big smile.

"We've all been waiting for you! I know it's been ages since we've played together, or even talked, but we thought today we should all get together. Like the good old times!" Rui added.

"This is great!" Tomasz replied, not believing his luck.

Tomasz played with his friends for over an hour. It was the most fun he could remember having in ages. After a while, he got an alert. He had a visitor.

Well, that's odd, Tomasz thought to himself. He didn't remember anybody making any plans with him to visit.

"Visitor: Monique," his interface alerted him.

Tomasz could see her waiting at the door, dressed in the same school clothes he had seen her earlier in the day. Like always, she seemed like a dream manifest.

"Guys, do you mind? I need to take this," Tomasz said to his friends online with a hint of guilt.

"No worries Tomasz, we will be waiting right here for you," Andres replied.

Tomasz got up and opened the door. Monique waited behind the door in a dashing black cocktail dress. That was not what he remembered her wearing when he saw her only moments before. But he was so enthralled by her beauty that he did not mind.

"Hey, umm, it's so nice to see you. What brings you here?" Tomasz asked.

"I was wondering if you'd like to go out on a date with me. I've been meaning to ask you for a long time. I felt like there's no time like the present."

"You have?" Tomasz replied dumbfounded.

"Oh I have, and it seems you are all dressed up for the occasion," Monique replied.

Tomasz looked down at himself. He dazzled in a dashing dark purple three-piece suit and even had a bouquet in hand.

"Are those for me?" Monique asked as she blushed. "They are so beautiful."

His hand reached out and as he did Monique told him "Wake up!"

"What?" Tomasz did not understand her suggestion.

"Hello there! Wake up!" Monique said once again, but it did not sound like her.

Tomasz opened his eyes. He was staring at a ceiling with cool blue lighting. He looked down. He no longer had a fancy three-piece suit. Now he had on his Pink Tuxedo and he was laying on the ground. He looked around and realized he was now in the center of the bar. All the other people in Pink Tuxedos crowded around him. He felt something soft behind his head.

"He's awake!" Mel shouted.

"Tommy boy!" The whole place erupted again.

"You gave us all a scare! We thought you wanted to blow us up," Mel chuckled. "That Mickey is worth every dollar, I tell you!"

"I'm still here," Tomasz muttered under his breath to no one in particular.

He got right up. Mel helped straighten out his collar and brushed his hair on the back of his head.

"Thankfully George was coming back for another drink and caught you before you hit the ground too hard," Mel added.

Tomasz looked over to the bar and saw the brick once again. That was also still there.

"I'm sorry about not being honest with you earlier, Tomasz. We didn't mean to deceive you when asking you to transport it. We knew Mickey was an expert at crafting explosives so we felt safe with it being transported here. But I want you to know I don't have anything else to hide. So if you want to know something go ahead and ask," Mel said.

Tomasz took a second to straighten himself out. This was reality. There was no helping the fact that he had brought a bomb here.

"What are you going to use it for?" Tomasz asked. He tried to be discreet but the fact that the majority of the room had gone quiet meant that all had heard his question.

Mel looked at him and replied without hesitation. "Tomasz, I don't know if you have heard of us before, the Thread Barons. If you have, you might have heard about some of the things we have done. And yeah, it is more than a group that gets together and drinks and gets loud. There are times when we see wrongs in society and we try to send a message. But what we never do is hurt people. Never. We are also not trying to cause panic. All we want to do is send a message. And that message will be delivered at three AM when we use the bomb, you brought to take down that hideous statue of Madame Sonali that towers over Yurok Park."

Tomasz hesitated at hearing this. He had no reason to believe this person whom he had met only a couple of minutes ago. He wanted to believe that was all they planned to do with this, but this person had used him to transport an explosive across the city without his knowledge.

"I understand where you are coming from, Tomasz. I was not honest with you when I requested you deliver the package, and you probably would not have agreed to it if you knew what it was. I'll tell you what." Mel reached out to the battery, or explosive as Tomasz now knew what it was. She held it out for Tomasz.

"If you do not believe me, Tomasz, you can take this and do whatever you want with it. Give it to the police and report all of us. You can go straight to the Cahuilla River and dump it in there. You can give it to your best friend, or sell it somewhere else. I will not ask questions. I won't stop you from leaving here with it. And I will still pay for the delivery because I did lie to you, Tomasz. And I'm sorry because regardless of my reasons it is not something you do to others."

Everyone seemed to be looking at the both of them, curious to see what would happen next. They wanted to see what Tomasz would decide to do.

"So you would let me leave here, with the explosive, with no harm done and you would let me be?" Tomasz asked. He tried to distance himself from the explosive without actually moving.

Mel nodded to Tomasz as she still held out the explosive.

"But why?" Tomasz was even more confused now.

"Because I do not like the thought that our relationship began with a lie and I am trying to do right by you, Tomasz."

He looked at the battery and back to Mel.

"But why this statue of Madame Sonali? She's the Cahuilla Medical Center, the CMC CEO, right? Why are you guys so dead set on blowing up a statue of this lady? All I've heard is that she's done a lot to help the people of Crow?"

At this, Mel smiled. "Oh, that's what you have heard right? Do you see Maria over there?"

Tomasz looked over to where Mel was pointing. A short woman with a bubbly smile waved at the two of them and nodded. The Pink Tuxedo seemed to match her cheerful personality.

"Her mother's house was torn down to build the new hospital wing that Madame Sonali generously gifted to the residents of Crow District. Even though a different parcel of land had already been allotted for that specific purpose in a previous year's budget. The only difference is that the neighborhood in which her mom's house was had a better view of the Cahuilla River. Then you have Raul over there." Mel pointed behind Tomasz.

He looked back and saw a dark man with slicked-back hair and dark sunglasses. If it wasn't for the Pink Tuxedo he might have been mistaken for part of someone's security detail.

"Raul used to work in the Dent Farms CMC branch and he got fired when they started 'downsizing' because he was not the right fit. And did you ever hear about the approval of Yurok Park?" Mel asked Tomasz.

"Well, that Madame Sonali helped fund the park," Tomasz replied.

"Hah of course! That's the story that made its way into the news release once city hall finally approved the park. What they don't talk about is how much the citizens of Crow had to fight City Hall to have the park built. City Hall has always aligned with the wants and wishes of Madame Sonali. So once they finally relented to the demands of the citizens from Crow they did so with one stipulation—that they would build a statue of Madam Sonali in the middle of the park since she helped fund it. Never mind that she contributed a meager amount to the actual cost. That statue is a great hundred-foot reminder to those in Crow, that no matter how much they struggle they are still under the thumb of those with real power. The people of Crow have lived for years with no real representation from City Hall. They are always treated as a lower class than those of Fox District. So that's why we decided that the best way for those in power to listen was to topple that hideous statue that they built as a reminder for us." Mel finished her fiery speech.

Tomasz was quiet after listening to all that. He had never heard about any of this. He knew of Madame Sonali by reputation as the richest person in Cahuilla. Even though she held no elected office, it was no secret that power in the city flowed through her. It had been so for close to two decades. Everyone whom Tomasz had spoken to had always said only positive things about her.

"And that's not all!" Tomasz heard Jerry speak up.

Jerry shook before he could speak, suppressing something deep inside.

"I served her at the Cahuilla Annual Gala about five years ago. Out of everyone there, she was the only one who did not TIP!" He placed special emphasis on that last word.

"She is the richest person in Cahuilla City and she could not even be bothered to tip!" Jerry was getting riled as he spoke about this event.

"It's also like in really bad taste, it looks terrible! Who the hell wants to look at a massive statue of some lady when taking a stroll in the park!" a random woman from the crowd shouted.

"Yeah, Leslie has a point," Mel agreed. "I've been to Yurok Park many times and aside from that hideous statue the park is perfect."

"It kills the vibe," another man chimed in.

A lot of "Yeahs" followed.

"It's also too tall. Over one hundred feet! No one needs a statue of themselves to begin with, and not that big," Mel added.

Tomasz was so taken aback by everything he had heard in the last several minutes that he had lost all ability to try to think of a response. At this stage, all he was able to do was listen.

"So what do you think about all of this?" Mel asked Tomasz.

"Oh, me?" Tomasz sputtered. "Umm, I guess I have no clue what to say. To begin with, I only heard about you guys earlier today from those cops."

"What cops?" Mel asked perplexed.

Tomasz explained to Mel and the rest of the bar the story of his time in the hospital and how he had endured an interrogation from the cops for his possible connection to the Thread Barons. He also explained how another member, Satya, had helped him escape.

"Ah that Satya, he's always sticking his neck out like that for others," Mel said with certain glee.

"But those cops weren't wrong. We have stolen corporate data. That was Raul when they fired him from the Dent Farms branch. There is also an incident where we used stolen credentials to steal a lot of Delian Defenses money. Some might say that constitutes some form of cybercrime. But the arson? Yeah, that was a mistake on our part. We were finishing a group cookout and threw away ashes that were still burning. I mean we didn't realize how dry the forest was that day! We tried to put the fire out but it got out of control fast. It was an honest mistake!" Mel exclaimed with remorse.

"And that's it?" Tomasz asked.

"Well, I mean there might be other cases that you didn't hear. But we always want to make sure we target those who are in power. We will never do anything to harm the common people or those who are in need. Those funds we stole from Delian Defenses helped pay for what some of the people around here live off of. We only want to help those who have no other means of help," Mel explained.

Tomasz's mind raced. What he was hearing was admission to multiple crimes. Things he never would have considered ever in his life. And now for their latest plot, they had made him an unwilling accomplice. But he heard their reasons and he didn't even know where to begin. As he stared around the bar there was one thing that came to mind that he still did not understand.

"But what's the deal with these then?" Tomasz asked as he pulled on his collar.

"Ah yes, the Pink Tuxedo! Well, we always dress up when we go out on our misadventures. This time it was Maria's turn to choose and this is what she chose! Angelica is our go-to tailor, so we told her that anyone who goes to her saying they 'had a special event in Crow district and that she was the place to go' meant they wanted a Pink Tuxedo. Now we know for the future to be a bit more particular in our wording." Mel laughed.

"So that's it? You guys like to dress up and do these things like they're fun?" Tomasz asked, befuddled at the glaring display of carelessness of the group. They had admitted to all sorts of crimes, admitted to planning more crimes and acting on them this very night, and to them it seemed like a game. Tomasz could not understand it.

"Why? Because what is the alternative?" Mel replied.

"Is it to go back to my old job where I would pass each day trying to find a single thing that would keep me going? To ignore how some view people like replaceable cogs in a machine that would not care if anything happens to them? To live in a system that alienates us from our neighbors and gives us a digital world that tries and fails to mimic the sense of community that we have lost? Is that what life should be like? Living with so little meaning and so much apathy for others? I lived that way long enough and during that time I felt nothing. It was when I met these guys and we found a common ideal, that is when I felt something. By myself, there was nothing I could do. But together we have made a difference. We no longer live a life without meaning, now we have a purpose. So yeah, we all find silly get-ups when we go out. But that's because we are proud to belong to our group. Everyone in here knows that when one of us faces a challenge, we all face it together," Mel concluded.

The bar erupted into "Yee-yee-yee-yee" shouts.

Tomasz was silent as the bar cheered Mel on. Certain things require time to process. This was one of them. Eventually, the enthusiastic bar quieted down.

"So what will it be?" Mel asked as she once again held out the explosive.

Tomasz looked at it. He grabbed it.

"So if I walk out of here with this, you won't do anything?" Tomasz asked Mel.

"I already told you, Tomasz. What I did was wrong. If this is what you feel is right, then we are not going to stop you." She motioned towards the door. Everyone crowded to the opposite end of the bar to let Tomasz know he was free to go.

He looked at the device in his hand once again and then to the rest of the people.

Tomasz walked towards the bar and placed the brick on top of it.

"Well, I wish you luck," Tomasz said to the group.

"Oh, you're leaving?" Jerry sounded disappointed.

Tomasz stopped for a second, hesitating. Whatever had just happened was something he needed to think about for a while. He needed some time alone.

"Yeah, I got a show to catch at eight at the Starlight Theater," Tomasz said as he dusted himself off.

"That's still an hour away, you're only about a ten-minute walk from Starlight," Maria added.

"Well, I don't visit Crow all that often so there are other things I wanted to see." Tomasz smiled, but he knew that it was obvious that he was lying.

"Is it supposed to be a good show?" Jerry asked him.

"I would say so. You're welcome to go if you want to." Tomasz replied without much thought.

Jerry thought about it for a second.

Tomasz walked toward the exit. Mel stood by the door.

"I don't want to make any assumptions, but I want you to know this. We would love to have you here again." Mel smiled as she looked straight at him. Tomasz could sense no hint of deceit coming from her.

The rest of the bar erupted in shouts of "Tommy Boy!"

Tomasz looked back to the group. He felt a sudden sensation that he could not explain. He was not sure whether he wanted to stay or to go.

"Thanks. That means a lot," he finally said as he smiled and walked out the door.

As he stepped out he heard the bar go back to its lively atmosphere. Outside on Lowray Street, it was still as crowded as it had been earlier.

There were people all over. Some are sitting around a bonfire on the sidewalk. Children were playing in the middle of the street. Despite the situations they all found themselves in they all looked more than happy in their community.

Across the street, a blinking light caught his attention. It was an old neon sign that flashed on and off. It was over a building that had long ago stopped serving its original purpose, but it was still in use. The lettering above the store spelled out "Eclectic Diatribes". But the neon sign only illuminated certain letters. Now and then when the lights flashed, all that read was "tribe".

Chapter 6: Interlife

Tomasz was falling to the ground at an astonishing speed. The earth in front of him was dark as he fell in the night. With each second he picked up more speed. The dark clouds that covered the few smatterings of light on the ground were fast approaching. Large and small flickers of light indicated to him that they were storm clouds. As he grew closer he saw tendrils of lightning zigzagging and carving a path through the clouds, the path of least resistance.

Tomasz continued gaining speed as he fell through the clouds, feeling an instant chill as ice crystals battered his body through his descent. Thunder exploded around him, crashing with a fury that could awaken primal fear. As he kept falling the clouds passed him and now Tomasz could see the ground. In the far distance beneath him, he saw the largest structure humanity had ever dreamt of.

The city was so expansive that anywhere Tomasz saw ground it was covered by bright lights and large edifices. There was no portion of solid ground untouched. Even in the surrounding ocean, there were specks of light, evidence of the reach of the city.

Tomasz now approached the city at a faster pace; he was crossing one mile every thirty seconds. The lights that seemed like specks only a few seconds ago now started to take shape. The specks became solid structures thousands of feet high and miles deep and wide. Within seconds, Tomasz was no longer observing the tall structures from a distance, now he was falling next to them. He looked to the windows of the buildings as he sped by. In some windows groups gathered around a table, in another, a family gathered huddled around a television, in the next a woman lay on a couch reading a book.

Tomasz seemed to pay no mind to the approaching ground, which was now a few seconds from impact. His focus never wavered from the buildings around him. As he prepared for his inevitable meeting with the ground Tomasz turned his back to it. It was as if ignoring the ground's existence would deny the impact its chance to occur. Just as he was about to slam into the pavement he stopped.

Tomasz floated above the air for a quick second before readjusting himself and stepping onto the impeccable pavement. Crowds flowed around him, uninterested in the fact that a man had fallen from low earth orbit and had landed on the surface without so much as a light thump. As he landed an announcement in his interface greeted him "Welcome to Quixos, humanity's city."

Encompassing an area of over three hundred thousand square miles, the virtual city of Quixos was humanity's shared accomplishment. It was the largest digital structure ever built. It was so large that it was impossible to visit its more than three million stores or cross all one billion blocks that comprise the city in a single lifetime. Yet despite the overwhelming size of Quixos, Tomasz felt at ease in the vast digital utopia. It was his place to go to when he needed to decompress.

He had landed in the middle of his favorite street, Valois Lane. As always people filled the street singing to different types of live music. The sides of the buildings flashed a variety of dizzying signs. One of them showed virtual dancers that seemed to be hundreds of feet tall.

"Looking good!" a random passerby shouted in Tomasz's direction.

He instinctively looked down expecting to see the Pink Tuxedo. Instead, he found himself in the latest ancient fad outfit he had picked out. He had on a black and white shirt with the sleeves ripped off, arms covered in tattoos, black jeans, and a metal spiked belt.

Tomasz enjoyed picking outfits from different eras to wear in Quixos. The latest one he had happened upon was late twentieth-century punk rock. In this outfit, the only colors Tomasz could see on himself were black and white.

Tomasz went down the road in his usual routine. He would pick up a vodka tonic and start drinking. Thanks to the virtual interface it would be as if he was drinking it in the real world. From there he would prowl down the street, seeing which establishment had the best music.

On a usual visit, he would spend an hour or two per establishment but he did not have that luxury tonight. Despite that, he knew it would be no hassle to find a place to relax until he had to attend Monique's show.

As Tomasz strolled down Valois Lane he stopped in front of his usual haunts to see what interested him. The first stop, Lucky's Spot, was not his favorite, but Tomasz liked it enough to give it a try now and then.

He went inside and stood in the corner. The wood-adorned bar and stage were glimmering in the lights as the place teemed with people. He was surprised to see who was playing at the moment. It was one of his favorite groups, Distant Ensemble, playing one of his favorite songs. He settled in to enjoy the show.

As he did so he could not help but look around and take in the crowd. He noticed that as the crowd came together, no matter how close they were to each other they could never actually touch. A curiosity of the virtual world, but as commonplace as breathing in the real world. He also noticed an oddity between the interacting avatars.

They would talk and listen to the music, but many times there was a clear lack of expression of emotion when they communicated. The action of delivering a message was being carried out, but it felt incomplete. Tomasz grew irritated at himself for not being able to focus on the music. He figured the place was too crowded and went on to look for a different place.

He stopped at a couple more places. First was Lenny's Kitchen, but Tomasz did not care for the music. He sauntered over to Nandu's but like Lucky's, it was too crowded. Again and again, Tomasz tried location after location and could not find anything that he could enjoy. As a last-ditch resort, he decided that the next place he came across he would stop in.

That place turned out to be Keiko's Tavern. The group playing music was decent enough and the place only had a handful of patrons, so Tomasz decided to sit down. He finally started to feel more at ease. He had been in search of that elusive calm after the events that had preceded earlier. As he relaxed he took in the crowd around him.

They all seemed content in silence to watch the musicians perform and it filled Tomasz with joy. The person sitting on his right, a young man, reminded Tomasz of his cousin. As he looked at him he noticed something peculiar. From a certain angle, Tomasz was able to look completely through him. It was as if part of the young man was missing.

He figured it might have been some sort of glitch and continued to listen to the music.

Without even thinking Tomasz glanced again to his right. The space inside the man persisted. He figured it was an error that would go away, but no. Tomasz once again forced himself to ignore the gaping hole in the man. He instructed himself to put all his focus on the band. This endeavor succeeded for a total of ten seconds. He found himself once again stealing glances. It did not take long for the young man to look at Tomasz, concerned at why the stranger kept looking at him.

"Oh sorry, you remind me a lot of my cousin Timo. Thought you were him. Sorry," Tomasz added embarrassed as he turned away.

The young man smiled at Tomasz and turned to face the musicians again. About ten seconds later Tomasz once again looked to his non-cousin, and the gaping hole persisted.

"Motherfucker," he cursed under his breath. He got up, walked outside the establishment, and floated off the ground. As he did, he started to speed up and climbed higher into the sky. While the ground grew more and more distant the sky above him started to change. It was no longer a dark cloudy night, but a sunny clear day.

Tomasz floated several thousand feet above the ground. Now he could see the shape of mountains beneath him. They formed curving lines that seemed to outline a long sleeping giant. Surrounding the mountains, there were verdant lands as far as the eye could see. He floated down to the level of the trees and touched one of the leaves. He pulled on it. As he did, the branch bent forward. Once he plucked the leaf off, the branch snapped back, and he could feel his hand recoil as the tension dissipated.

If Tomasz had not been flying thirty feet in the air, there would have been no indication that any of this was artificial. The wind that caressed him felt real, the leaf he held felt real, the recoil from plucking the leaf felt real, and the tiny amount of force exerted to hold the leaf between his index finger and thumb felt real. But he knew it was not. He let the leaf fall and saw it swaying, falling to the ground. Then a gust of wind came by, picked the leaf up, and carried it off into the distance.

Tomasz flew high into the sky and looked in the sun's direction. It blinded him in an instant and he had to cover his face with his hand. He felt the sun's warmth on his skin, the same way one would feel standing outside on a warm summer day. Yet the light he was feeling, that he was seeing, was some artificial construct placed at the edge of the simulation.

It did a very convincing job of mimicking our sun. The main difference was that he could be in front of this "sun" all day and he would not get sunburnt. Besides that, the only thing that made a difference was the fact that he did know that it was an artificial world. One from which he disconnected.

The neural interface connecting to Tomasz's cervical spine decoupled. His eyes did not take long to adjust to the room. Hundreds of others sat in chairs in the room. They were all in various stages of laughter, sadness, anger, and anguish, all experiencing a virtual world. Tomasz stepped away from the device, and looked to the people in the room once more, and then at himself. He noticed his Pink Tuxedo, smiled, and started to leave.

"Already done?" the woman behind the counter asked. "You still have close to thirty minutes left."

"Yeah, I remembered there was something else I wanted to do," he said as he walked outside the building.

Once again Tomasz found himself in a city. Only this time, this was not digital, and this one was not the pinnacle of human ingenuity. This was Crow District and it lacked a lot of the charm that Tomasz would associate with Quixos. But it was currently the place Tomasz would rather be.

***

Tomasz checked the time. Only thirty more minutes until the theater doors opened. All of a sudden, his stomach started gurgling. Tomasz realized that in the entire time in Crow, he had not eaten. He looked around as he stood outside the Virtual Reality Hotspot. Crowds of people walked around him, large masses of bodies all with different purposes. Someone bumped into him and without even saying a word kept walking. He did not care, for the city held Tomasz in awe.

Now night had set in. The bright lights of Crow District shone even brighter than before. Layer upon layer in the sky swarmed with drones flying over. It made it seem as if there was a colorful ocean swaying overhead.

As they moved around the drones interacted. They created a synchronized dance of light, with various images formed at different layers in the sky. Some were advertisements: the Cahuilla Ranchers game, the latest episode of "The Real Deal April O'Neal", a live concert by the Fox Philharmonic, and even a current address by the mayor of Cahuilla City.

Whatever spot of the sky Tomasz would look at would cue up the audio inside his receiver.

"There goes T.R. Lee with a pass—"

"—Anyone do this? It's not like April—"

"Citizens of Cahuilla, as your mayor—"

Tomasz shut down the audio and continued on his way. From a cursory glance at his interface, he found Tominy Alley. It was three blocks away and full of food vendors. Tomasz hurried over. As he moved around Crow he tried his best to place himself in the thickest crowds he could find. He did not want a repeat from when he first came into Crow earlier that day.

Like much of the rest of Crow, Tominy Alley had displays plastered over every storefront. On top of one, Tomasz could see a giant holographic ring of donuts that seemed to be about thirty feet tall. On top of a sandwich shop, a hologram projected all the different types of offerings that the establishment served. The next storefront was "Meat on a Stik". To no one's surprise, it sold different types of meats all on sticks. Then there were sweets, chicken bites, salads, noodle soups, pancakes, the list kept on going. Tomasz noted one that caught his attention—"Crunchy Hops!"

"Oh, I've heard about this place before! They don't have them in Fox!" Tomasz hurried up to the seating area picked sat down and the menu popped up in his interface.

They had fried or sauteed grasshoppers in salads, burritos, tacos, sushi, fried rice, and more. Tomasz decided on the fried grasshopper noodles. Within seconds a robotic arm brought a bowl of noodles with fried grasshoppers.

He took a bite. The crunchiness and the saltiness combined for an amazing flavor profile. As Tomasz continued his meal, a group of around ten people walked up to the seating area and sat down next to Tomasz. At first, he paid them no mind and focused on his meal. But a stray reflection in his eye caught his attention. He looked over. He was instantly captivated by what he saw.

The first person he saw had both arms bare and were completely covered in metal. The man's metal arms were thick as they complimented his large muscular frame. He had silver inlays over his face, three different lines that curved from one cheek, over the nose, and over to the other cheek. The bright shiny metal contrasted with his dark skin in a mesmerizing fashion. His eyes also had augmentations and Tomasz could see the iris and pupil adjust and readjust quickly. His scalp and shoulders had many short protrusions in the form of short metal spikes. It reminded Tomasz of a cactus. The man was shirtless, displaying a solar plexus covered in metal as well. The metal plate shimmered in the light and it seemed to paint a target dead center in his body. The rest of his group also followed his unique fashion.

The woman who sat next to him was also covered in various metallic furnishings. Her lips gleamed with metal inlays over the edges shimmering with color that would vary from second to second. Her eyes did not even look human—they were a resplendent iridescent metal. Her hair shone in the light as her dreaded locks had metal strands intertwined.

She had metal studs in her cheeks in the place of her dimples. These called attention to her smile, which seemed to be a permanent fixture. From her chin, all the way down her throat was a solid band of gold. Tomasz noticed that her hands were also metallic, yet they appeared to be quite delicate.

The others that accompanied the two sported similar bionic appendages and cosmetic augmentations. One had pure black eyes, another had a metallic scalp, a woman seemed to have metallic studs protruding from her collar bones, and one man had a metallic nose. Tomasz could spend all day staring at them. They were all of different skin colors and ethnicities, they all even wore different fashions. The only thing they had in common was their vast amount of modifications.

"Wow man, what is your deal?" the first man asked Tomasz with a serious look.

Tomasz realized he was still staring at the group while holding his chopsticks in his hand and he looked away as fast as he could.

"I'm sorry sir, I was erm, just eating," Tomasz said as he went back to his food. He started tensing up. He had never come across people who looked like them, and he was not sure what to make of them.

"No no no, you don't understand. That Pink Tuxedo, there's got to be something to that, right?" The man looked around his companions who all seemed to agree.

"Oh, this?" Tomasz was still a bit wary but started to ease up. "I'm going to um, a friend's show later. And well I wanted to buy something nice, and the tailor, well she misunderstood me. Then she, um, gave me this Pink Tuxedo, and I really couldn't turn her down."

"Oh, you don't say? Your friend is putting on a show and you go out of your way to get kitted like that?" the woman with the iridescent eyes spoke in a soft tone to Tomasz.

"Umm, well, you know I want to be supportive of her," Tomasz said as he started blushing in front of all the strangers.

"So it's her, eh? Tell me, is this friend of yours attractive? Do you consider her beautiful?" The woman's smile continued to widen as she saw Tomasz squirm.

"I guess I would say that yeah, she's very beautiful. And she has an amazing personality. But you know, we're just friends! That's it." If Tomasz squirmed anymore he would fall on the ground.

"On my name, Rina, why do you have to tease my man like that?" the first man spoke up laughing.

"Don't worry, my man, I ain't seen a finer kit than that Pink Tuxedo all day! And don't you mind Rina. She did the same thing to me when we were about to start dating. I almost had a heart attack with all her questioning." The man smiled and extended his hand towards Tomasz. "Name's Trevor by the way."

Tomasz was surprised to see that his teeth looked completely normal. He reached out and shook Trevor's hand. Compared to Tomasz's hand the man's metal hand seemed almost twice as big.

"Tomasz."

They shook hands and Tomasz could not believe how soft the metallic hands felt. He dreaded for a second that the man might try to squeeze his hand, but it felt like shaking any normal hand.

Trevor introduced Tomasz to the rest of the group. Jason had a metal scalp. Molly had black eyes. Charlene had the metal studs in her collarbone. Hadrian had a completely metal jaw. Lucas had a metal nose. Terry had metal inlays running from the front of her chin, over her face through her scalp, and down her back. Joanne had a completely chrome-plated neck. Ibrahim had metal eyelids. These were the identifying features for each of them out of all their many modifications.

"So what did you order there, Mr. High Fashion?" asked Charlene.

"I got the fried hops noodles. They are good, you should try them!" Tomasz replied. Soon each of them had put in an order for the fried hops noodles and soon after that, they all were raving about the food.

"Mr. High Fashion, this was a great recommendation!" Rina said.

"So Tomasz, what does a guy like you do for fun when he is not taking the fashion world by storm?" Trevor asked him between bites.

"Well, I'm a student right now. But I guess aside from that I enjoy playing the drums. I played in a virtual show earlier. I play with a couple of bands."

"No shit, huh? What do you play?"

"Pretty much anything, but lately I've done a lot with prog metal. At a concert earlier today we started with a cover of Denial."

"By Fantasy of Rhodes?" Trevor looked astonished.

"Yup."

"Damn, so you must be pretty damn good on the drums then!" Lucas chimed in from the back.

Tomasz asked the same of Trevor.

"What do I like to do for fun? Oh man, I know it's a terrible answer, but I love my job. I am a chef at a local restaurant. I love to cook!" Trevor smiled.

The incredulity on Tomasz's face was clear since Trevor started laughing when he saw his reaction.

"Not what you expected, I see?"

"Well, no, but then again I did not know what to expect." Tomasz felt a bit embarrassed by his reaction.

"You've never seen anyone with this much metal on, have you then?" Hadrian chimed in from the corner of the table.

"No, I can't say I have. I mean, the first time I saw someone with metal appendages was a couple of hours ago."

"Really? Where are you from?" Rina asked.

"I live near Cahuilla Tech, that's where I study."

A collective "Ah" spread around the table. They did not need any further explanation for why Tomasz had never seen metal limbs.

"You must *really* like this friend if you are out here for her show," Charlene added.

Tomasz blushed and the rest of the table laughed at his embarrassment.

"So we must be the first meta sapiens you've ever come across," Ibrahim said in a way higher voice than Tomasz expected from someone as big as him. His metal eyelids shone as he spoke with glee.

"A meta sapiens?" Tomasz replied dumbfounded.

"Oh boy, now you got him started." Charlene laughed as everyone else groaned.

"Well let me start by saying I noticed you have a notch on the back of your neck, I am assuming that is a neural port, is that right?" Ibrahim asked despite knowing the answer.

"Yeah, that's right," Tomasz replied.

"Do you have any other neural or sensory modifications? Retinal displays? Language translators? Wireless data receivers? Would you happen to have some lens adjustments for sight improvement? Adjustment to audio capacities? Do you currently have any of those on you?" Ibrahim spoke with his eyes closed as if he wanted to draw attention to his metal eyelids.

"Well yes, I have all of those," Tomasz replied with a slight nod.

"Do you consider yourself a human?" Ibrahim still kept his eyes closed.

"I guess so. If I'm not then I guess I should start going to the vet," Tomasz replied. The entire table laughed but that did not deter Ibrahim.

"You see, science created these bionic limbs around fifty years ago. These were some of the very first large-scale artificial human modifications. They came before the other gadgets you have such as neural implants, retinal displays, or audio receivers, but people did not like them. Even if they improved their life some refused them, because it did not make them feel human. So scientists realized that they had to move away from metal appendages and make them more real, more of what you would consider human, which leads us to today. People can walk around with every single appendage being artificial, and you would not even be able to tell. That is fine by them because, to the untrained eye, they do not seem as other than humans." Ibrahim took what seemed like a quick scheduled pause and then continued.

"Yet these same people have eyesight that is equivalent to an eagle, the hearing of bats, and the sense of smell of dogs. They can access all of the internet straight from their brain, yet they still consider themselves human. Because they look human? Why even pretend to be something you aren't? They are not humans anymore, and they should admit it. We are not cowering in some cave anymore afraid to go out at dark. We can be in the middle of a forest on a moonless night and be able to see as clear as day thanks to our retinal displays. So why do we keep pretending that we are the same people we were thousands of years ago? We are beyond that, we are not them. We are the future, we are meta sapiens, and we are proud to display that for all to see. Even if society does not want to admit it, this is what all of us are. That is what a meta sapien is." Ibrahim finished and finally opened his eyes.

His voice never wavered throughout his prepared speech. It was obvious this was not the first time he had delivered these words.

"Bravo, Ibrahim! Bravo!" Trevor started clapping and laughing which prompted the rest of the group to do so as well. Ibrahim had a big smile on his face.

"Wow, I had never heard that or thought about it that way," Tomasz replied as he fumbled for something to say.

"Don't spin your wheels too much, kid. Some of us just like the way it looks. Sometimes things are just skin deep," Lucas added.

"Yeah, that is also true. Why be a meta sapien if you are not going to style out? You may not have any metallic implants, but you do a great job with that Pink Tuxedo," Ibrahim chuckled. The rest of the group laughed with him.

Tomasz spent the next twenty minutes with the group learning more about them. He learned about Charlene's job as a server repairwoman. Rina's former work on a Mars manned mission got gutted because of the beginning of the Conflict. He also learned how each of them had come by this unique lifestyle.

The only one involved in an accident that required bionic limbs was Lucas. He had the choice to replace them with more authentic-looking appendages several years later but he liked the metallic look more. After a while Tomasz looked at the time, realizing the doors to Monique's show were about to open in two minutes.

"Oh damn, I have to leave! I'm so sorry!" Tomasz said as he got up.

"Have a good time Romeo, and if you ever come back to the area stop by Trevor's Cantina, you got that?" Trevor added as Tomasz walked away.

Chapter 7: A Night at the Theater

Tomasz needed to hurry to make it to the theater. At his current pace, he would be there in about ten minutes. He made sure to pick the streets with the least amount of people to avoid getting bogged down. The majority of the roads he picked were server lanes that ran parallel to most major streets in any large city.

Rows upon rows of well-disguised computers would hum as they operated the city's digital infrastructure. The artificial lighting, the targeted advertisements, the block-by-block weather monitoring, the route planning ingested by vehicles, the power and water tracking systems, and anything and everything that a modern city like Cahuilla would need were computed here. To the untrained eye, these server lanes looked like small parks and gardens spread throughout the city. What one would mistake for trees and shrubs were server stacks that had a biophilic design with the aim of optimizing both heat release and human comfort. It made for a variety of semi-alien-looking plants.

They were normal enough to be recognizable as being some sort of flora, but they never actually matched any real plants. Algorithms optimized for plant detection would recognize some as cacti from Australia and others as certain firs from northern Europe. The unique look also led to people not wanting to be near them due to the certain uncanny feel they gave off. That turned out to be an added benefit since it meant fewer people would bother the servers the city relied upon.

After crossing several server lanes Tomasz found himself in the street where the Starlight Theater was. It was hard for him to spot it since every other building in the street was one type of theater or another. There was the Teatro Fenix, the Theater of the Americas, the Crow District Playhouse, and so on and on. Each of these had its marquee lights advertising the show of the night. Tomasz finally spotted a theater that displayed a massive star in front of it with the name "Starlight Theater" in orbit around the star.

"Well, there it is!" Tomasz sighed in relief.

He walked up to a display outside the theater and requested to see his reflection. When he saw himself he was dismayed at how disheveled he looked.

His hair was a mess, he was sweaty from hurrying to the theater, and he still had the gauze from the hospital. Worse off was the state of his Pink Tuxedo. It was all bunched up and wrinkled. First off, he made sure to straighten it out as much as possible. Despite all the trouble the outfit had brought him, he was still fond of it. He thought he looked pretty good in it. After that, he fixed his hair and grabbed a napkin to wipe off any sweat and dirt on him. Then he removed the gauze. The wound that had been gushing blood earlier was now completely gone. Tomasz did one final checkup. Now he was ready.

He walked up to the theater and a holographic usher appeared before him. The holograph took the appearance of a middle-aged man in a suit.

"Here to see *The Thieving Raven,* I presume." The hologram, who floated a tad above Tomasz, had a pompous air as he looked down at him.

"Yup that's right, I should have a ticket, the name is Tomasz."

"Yes, I know who you are," the hologram replied in a disinterested tone. "Your seat is B12. We are expecting a full house tonight so please make your way to your seat at your earliest convenience."

"Oh ok and when does the show—"

"Enjoy the show," the hologram cut Tomasz off and vanished.

"Well, um, ok." Tomasz felt confused as he made his way inside. The main foyer had a large double staircase with a massive chandelier dangling overhead. The walls were covered in ornate carved wood depicting scenes from various plays. Tomasz noticed a bar at the bottom of one of the staircases and approached. He scanned a list of cocktails to see what might catch his interest. After reviewing the options he came to a realization. He had no idea what any of these drinks were.

"Dry Irish Fire Tonic", "Hungarian Malted Ice", "Sweet and Soft Gin and Tonic", "Scrumptious Vodka Whirlpool", "Kinetic Mango Rum Infusion", "Cold Fusion Distilled Whiskey", the list got even more and more ridiculous with every new entry.

"What would you like?" A virtual bartender flashed into existence behind the counter. She seemed to be as interested in her job as the usher outside had been.

"Umm, can I get like a Cahuilla Straight on ice?"

The virtual bartender glanced sideways at Tomasz before replying.

"I'm sorry hon, we only serve what's on the list. We can't go out and make everything everyone wants when they feel like it, there's not enough time for that," she said without ever having looked at Tomasz.

Tomasz looked around to see who else exactly would be delayed by his not-unusual request. No one else waited behind him for service at the bar. The only other people in the foyer were all talking to each other or walking into the auditorium to be seated.

"Well, um, ok, I will have the ah..." Tomasz was having a hard time deciding.

"To be honest I don't recognize anything here, is there any drink here you would recommend?" Tomasz smiled at the virtual bartender who had so far not looked at him the entire time.

"Oh, do I have something to suggest?" the virtual bartender said as she faced him. "Oh sure, lemme pour my favorite for me, here give me a minute."

The bartender stared at Tomasz as she went through painstaking detail preparing a drink for herself. Metal arms would come from the top of the bar following her every instruction. Tomasz was not sure if he had done something wrong but she seemed intent on dragging this process out as much as possible. She measured the exact amount of alcohol, counted each ice cube, and when shaking the drink the arm shook it as many times clockwise as counter-clockwise. When the drink was finished the robotic arm picked it up.

"Cheers!" the bartender said to Tomasz as she motioned to drink.

The result was that the drink went through her and spilled on the floor. She did not break eye contact with Tomasz throughout this entire period.

"My favorite." She smiled at Tomasz. He had not considered that he might have insulted the hologram, but it seemed he had.

"What will our dashing and well-dressed guest order then?" she asked.

"Umm, well, why not what you just had?" Tomasz said in an awkward tone.

The bartender grinned and went through the exact complex process of making the drink. She put the drink in front of Tomasz and he felt obliged to try it in front of her. To his surprise, he enjoyed it very much. It tasted exactly like what Jerry had made for him earlier.

She smiled as she said "That one's on the house. It's a Cahuilla Sour. So you know for next time." Then she vanished.

With his drink in hand, Tomasz went into the auditorium. To his surprise most of it was empty. He looked at the time on his interface. There was still ten minutes before the show started. His Pink Tuxedo drew more attention from the other guests than Tomasz would have liked. They all stared at him for a second before averting their gaze. Pretending not to notice the eyes on him, he hurried over to his seat. He sat down, drink in hand, and soon he was no longer the main attraction.

In his chair, he started to look around. An uncomfortable feeling started rising in his stomach. He had never been to a show like this before, but the theater seemed so empty that he could not help but feel bad for

Monique and the other actors. He had heard from the usher that the venue should be full, but it seemed that he had been mistaken.

Suddenly, Tomasz heard a commotion start to stir in the foyer. He tried to see from his chair but he was not able to see anything beyond the doors. It did not sound like people fighting or arguing—instead, it sounded like a large group had arrived. Tomasz realized he was not the only one in the audience who had noticed. They were all wondering what all the fuzz was about. The commotion was getting closer to the auditorium. Then the door swung open. For a split second, Tomasz was sure he was imagining things.

But he realized all that he was seeing was very much happening. He was sure of it because everyone in the hall reacted to them. All the people surging into the room had one thing in common, they were all wearing Pink Tuxedos. Not only that but the person right at the head of the group was someone he recognized, Mel. She was the first to notice Tomasz and pointed him out to the rest of the group.

She was trying to be quiet as she spoke to the rest of the Thread Barons, but one of them shouted "Tommy Boy!" Shushing noises rained down from all over onto the Pink Tuxedo wearing gaggle. The offender raised his hands in the air apologizing for his faux pas. The rest of the audience glared at the Pink Tuxedo clad group, who tried their best to be quiet as they poured into the room. In what seemed to be an eternity the hall filled to the brim with a large contingent of the new patrons. Mel walked over to Tomasz and looked at the seat next to him.

"So that must be B11!" She smiled as she sat next to Tomasz. "Oh, I'm so excited!"

"How?" was all that Tomasz managed to ask.

"Oh please I know people all over the place," Mel replied. Tomasz did not doubt it.

"Besides you did say we were welcome to come here. If you want us to leave, we'll be out of here in no time."

"No, no of course not. That's not an issue. It was well, um, a surprise," Tomasz said.

"How about this seat? Is this B13?" a familiar voice beckoned Tomasz.

He looked up and recognized the doctor from earlier, Satya Bose. Only this time he was not wearing a white doctor's coat but was sporting a Pink Tuxedo.

"You!" Tomasz yelled.

More shushing came from all over the theater aimed at Tomasz. Some of the other Thread Barons joined in scolding him.

"You know how much trouble I got in because of you?" Tomasz muttered to Satya as he sat next to him.

"Are you kidding me? You're the one who brought a bomb to my hospital!" Satya made sure to be extra quiet when he said the word bomb but sounded furious while he whispered.

"Besides how could I have guessed that you happened to be wearing the same outfit that we had decided on? Out of the thousands of tailors in Cahuilla, you happened to go to the same one we all did! And you did not even have the nerve to tell Angelica you did not like the outfit. After all the work she put into these!" Satya's whispered with fury at Tomasz.

"I never said I did not like it! It caught me by surprise is all."

"Hey play nice, ok? I don't want your little argument ruining my show, I've been looking forward to it for a while." Mel cut in.

"Had you even heard about this show before you met me?" Tomasz asked confused.

"No, but after you told me about it, I found it very intriguing. *The Thieving Squirrel* sounds like fun." Mel added as she made herself comfortable in her seat.

"It's *The Thieving Raven*!" Tomasz interjected.

"Oh right." She smiled as she stared at the stage.

After about a minute of the rest of the Thread Barons arriving the lights in the theater dimmed. A clear indication that the show was about to start. Tomasz looked around the hall once more and this time there were no empty seats. The majority of the people were all in Pink Tuxedos, just like Tomasz. To anyone who had no idea what was going on, it definitely would have caused a lot of confusion. Even Tomasz was not sure what was going on. But the fact that the theater was packed made him happy. Moreover, he felt proud of the fact that it was his group that was out in support.

My group? Tomasz thought to himself.

The spotlight shone on the stage and the red curtains were the only thing visible. This snapped him out of his train of thought. Tomasz could see the lights beaming in from a massive lamp above. He had never seen such a low-tech theater before. A low rhythmic percussion started to pick up as the curtains opened and lights above the stage illuminated the set. Tomasz could tell that the set pieces were handmade. These were not holographic projections. They were too crude to be digital. But the fact that they looked so crude added to their charm. The set showed a row of buildings with a massive building in the center that overshadowed the rest. It seemed as if all the attention should be placed on the center building.

As the snare beat continued progressing a string-led melody began and the first performer walked out on stage. This one was digitally created and it was a large black raven swooping down onto the stage. The raven starts to walk across the stage, and the melody picks up a curious tone. While the raven walks around he looks at each of the buildings, picking up items in all of them, but none catch his interest. As he approaches the large center building the music starts to shift to a more playfully devious melody.

The raven takes his time looking around the large building. Picking an item here, another there, until he enters a large room. In this large room, there is a box in the corner that shines brighter than everything around it. The music picks up whenever the raven gets close to it, and slows down when he moves away from it. In a moment he notices the box and the music quickly starts to speed up. The raven opens the box, and slowly dips his head down, the music building in intensity, nearing a crescendo. He slowly picks up a gleaming necklace, so shiny that in a night it could be seen from miles away. Once the raven picks it up the opening music reaches its climax, the raven looks at the audience and winks. This elicits great laughter from all the audience and the first piece of music comes to an end and he flies away with the necklace.

At this moment the first person made their way onto the stage. It was Monique dressed in a beautiful blue dress. As she walked on stage the light moved toward her shining bright. She took a moment to look out over the entirety of the hall. Tomasz felt a sudden pang in his stomach. He worried that the appearance of an entire crowd dressed in the same clothes might have surprised her and affected her performance. But if that was the case he was not able to tell. Before she started to sing a slow sad wind harmony started.

During the musical Monique's character, Renee, is given the stolen necklace by the raven who loves her singing. She wonders whether she should keep it, sell it, or return it to its owner. She decided to return it to the owner, an old woman who had no one to spend time with her. Renee met up with the woman with help from her new raven friend, returned her necklace, and formed a bond with her.

Every time he saw Monique on stage, Tomasz could not help but hold his breath. Her performance left him speechless. As the show progressed, he noticed that it was not just him, but the other Thread Barons were also engrossed in it. At different times he heard Satya sobbing. Tomasz himself got choked up for a few moments. At the end of every song, all of them cheered as loud as they could. Before Tomasz realized it, the musical had ended. The last two hours seemed like they flew by in a single breath. The entire cast, with Monique in the center, lined up on stage.

As the cast faced the audience the entire theater got up and gave a standing ovation. The loudest cheers were coming from those in the Pink Tuxedos. Tomasz could see Monique's face gleaming with joy. Monique found Tomasz in the crowd and locked eyes with him. She waved at him with a big smile.

"Oh, look at you there, Romeo," Mel said as she elbowed him hard in the ribs.

"Is that the Monique girl you kept mentioning when you were passed out?" Jerry asked from behind Tomasz.

"Um, what?" Tomasz said without taking his eyes off her.

"Oh, I bet it is. I can't blame him though, that girl is gorgeous!" Mel responded in his stead.

Tomasz acted as if he did not hear what they were talking about and focused back on Monique.

"You were amazing!" Tomasz shouted at her. He wasn't sure if she heard him through all the noise, but her smile showed her appreciation.

Monique pointed at him and then to the rest of the crowd. She pointed at her clothes.

Tomasz laughed and shrugged his shoulders. As Monique looked at Tomasz she saw that the rest of the cast members started to bow to the audience so she followed suit. As they did the curtains dropped. The cheering and clapping lasted for several more minutes.

"That was beautiful," Satya said sobbing once the music had died down.

"That was a great show! Thanks for the invite," Jerry added.

"You're welcome?" Tomasz replied.

"Wow, that lady of yours is so talented!" Mel added.

"She is not my lady! She is just a friend," Tomasz clarified.

Mel and Jerry looked at each other and burst out laughing.

"Well, your friend is very talented," Satya said now that he had composed himself.

"Thank you. I know she will appreciate all of you being here to support her show. I had no idea you guys were coming, but well, you know, thanks," Tomasz said.

"Wow, that must have been the most painful thanks I have ever received in my life," Jerry chuckled.

"We told you earlier, Tomasz. We support our own," Mel said with a smile.

He locked eyes with her and couldn't help but smile back.

"Classic Tomasz! Besides it's not like we endured torture for two hours. That was an amazing show!" Satya added.

"Classic Tomasz? I just met you earlier today! Besides, when I first met you, you were berating me for not knowing what the hell was going on with you guys! Classic me!?" Tomasz replied.

"Come now Tomasz, don't get too grumpy. Let's not ruin the atmosphere after this breathtaking show. And yes, I may have overreacted a bit earlier. But in the end, did you not make it to your destination undisturbed thanks to my advice? I think I deserve some gratitude for that," Satya said.

Tomasz stared at him bewildered.

Several of the other Thread Barons came in to join in on the conversation while the theater emptied. The majority of them came to Tomasz to congratulate him on the spectacular show. He kept reminding them he had nothing to do with it. Amid the rancor, a staff member on stage spoke to the gaggle of people.

"Hello! Excuse me, please I need your attention!"

The group went quiet as they all stared at the woman talking to them.

"Yes, is there a Tomasz in the group here?" she asked once everyone had quieted down.

Everyone turned their heads towards Tomasz.

"This here is Tomasz," Mel said as she patted him on the back.

The woman on stage seemed confused about the outfit situation going on in the crowd.

"Yeah, I'm Tomasz. Is there anything you need from me?" Tomasz asked as he moved ahead.

"Monique has asked to see you in her dressing room, will that be ok with you?" As soon as the woman finished talking the entire room erupted into cheers.

"Yeah, Tommy Boy!" "Go get her" "Tommy! Tommy! Tommy!" "Yee-yee-yee-yee!" Cheers erupted all over the place.

Tomasz started to feel light-headed. He walked up to the stage as everyone cheered him on.

"Hey, Tomasz you and your lady friend should swing by the bar, later on, you hear!" Mel shouted as he walked away.

He nodded and was soon led backstage by the staffer. They ended up at a door where he was told to wait.

"Monique, Tomasz is here." The staffer spoke at the closed door.

The door swung open and Monique appeared. She was out of her stage costume and now dressed in a tie-dye t-shirt and jeans. There she stood, the girl that he was desperately in love with.

"Oh, thanks, Tina!" Monique said as she grabbed Tomasz's hand and pulled him into the room, closing the door behind them.

"So what did you think?" She blushed as she asked.

"What did I think? Honestly?"

She nodded as she waited.

"That was amazing! Way better than I could have expected! And it's not like I thought it wasn't going to be good, I don't want you to think that…. But I couldn't believe it! Your singing was just out of this world! The music was great! The raven was hilarious! And did I mention your singing? It was phenomenal!"

"Yes, you had," Monique laughed.

"Well, I'll say it again because the show was great and you were marvelous! And the rest of the group out there, they could not stop telling me how much they enjoyed it! I mean everyone loved it and they all said how astonished they all were!"

"Really! Oh, that makes me so happy! But I did want to ask…" Monique started with slight hesitation.

"You want to know why I and a lot of the people in the audience were wearing the same Pink Tuxedo?" Tomasz replied.

"Well, I mean, yes? I thought you weren't going to bring anyone and then you show up with a massive group. It's not that I mind, I don't want you thinking that!" Monique interjected.

"No, don't worry I understand. I am not going to lie, it is quite a long story. And it might not make much sense. You sure you want to hear it?" Tomasz asked, unsure of whether Monique would believe his tale.

"I'm all done for tonight, so I have all the time in the world." Monique smiled as she sat down and patted the chair next to her, indicating that Tomasz should sit next to her.

Tomasz told her the entire set of events leading up to tonight. It started all with the invitation to the musical. He needed a nice outfit so he went to Angelica. That led to the Pink Tuxedo. Then came today's request for him to deliver an item. This of course led to more questions, since Monique was not even aware that Tomasz did deliveries as a side job.

He recounted meeting Mickey, and how he got the battery, although he left out the part about it being a bomb. He didn't want to go down that rabbit hole now. He recounted how he got hit by a tram in Crow District. How he woke up in the hospital in a faux interrogation room since the cops were asking about his gang affiliation. Monique was more concerned about Tomasz's well-being than anything about a gang. This filled his heart with joy.

He continued with how the doctor who was tending to him helped him escape. The same doctor who was sitting next to him at the show. How he made his way to Lowray Street. How the same bar the doctor had pointed him to had turned out to be the place where his package was supposed to end up. How upon entering he had seen them all wearing the same outfit, for a special outing that night. No specifics on what that was. How they welcomed Tomasz into their group without any hesitation, just because he was wearing the same Pink Tuxedo. He ended by explaining how he ran into them at the theater again where he did not expect to see them.

Monique was silent for a while after hearing that.

"Sounds made up right?" Tomasz felt beyond mortified now. He was sure that she was going to call for security to kick him out.

"I mean, it sounds so unbelievable that I have no choice but to believe it! Sounds like you have had quite the day." Monique seemed to struggle to come up with anything else to say to Tomasz.

"Yeah I don't know how but I just keep getting sucked into these weird situations today. I'm pretty sure you might be thinking that I am making this up, but that is all there is to it."

"So you only met them earlier today?" Monique asked surprised.

He nodded. "Never had seen a single one of them before tonight. I mean, I did tell them they were more than welcome to come to the show, but I never actually thought they would decide to show up."

"And why do you think that is?" Monique asked.

"Um, I, I really, I don't know." Tomasz knew exactly why. Mel herself said so. But Tomasz still did not grasp what she was getting at. He felt as if he couldn't bring himself to say it out loud.

"I guess since they considered me one of them they wanted to support you?" Tomasz added trying to sound as nonchalant as possible.

Monique's eyes widened. "Did you even say anything about me?"

"Oh well, I mean, your name might have slipped out at some point. And I did mention I was going to see a friend's show."

"I see. It just happened to slip out?" Monique replied while looking at Tomasz. Her look intimated the fact that there was something Tomasz was not sharing.

"Um, yeah? I guess I was talking about something and your name came up. Which makes sense. I talk about all my friends. So why wouldn't I talk about you as well? Since you know you're my friend! I mean, I consider you my friend, so I speak of you as my friend. See?" Tomasz smiled as he finished.

"Hmm, ok. So are you ever going to see these friends again?"

"Oh, will I? I have to be honest, I don't know. They did tell me that I could stop by their bar after I finished talking to you, but I didn't know what I was going to do. I mean I just met them right?" Tomasz laughed.

"Oh, well good, I have some time before getting together with the rest of the cast. I was looking for something to do and now it's settled!" Monique said as she got up.

She grabbed Tomasz's hand and started leading him towards the door. He was equal parts confused and happy.

"Umm, wait, what are we doing? Is everything ok?" Tomasz asked. He was not sure if he was dreaming or not, with Monique still holding onto his hand.

"Oh Tomasz, please. I have patience but enough is enough. Look, I will be honest. I did not invite you here because I wanted you to see a musical. I invited you here because I wanted you to see *me*! Does that make sense? I invited you here because I like you. Are you telling me you went through all this trouble of getting this Pink Tuxedo, which you look very handsome in, just because you are my friend? Is that it?"

"Oh, what? I mean, I umm, I like you and—"

"It's yes or no Tomasz. This is not orbital mechanics," Monique interjected.

This quieted down Tomasz for a quick second. He took it all in. This was not a dream. The woman he was in love with had told him she wanted to go out with him. Now all he had to do was reply.

"Oh um, of course. Wait." Tomasz stopped himself.

"Yes! I mean hell yes. Yes! Of course. I've been meaning to tell you for so long!" he replied with gusto.

"Alright, good. That took forever and a day!" Monique smiled. She gave Tomasz a quick kiss. It was bliss.

He stood there stupefied, now questioning again whether what was occurring was reality or not.

"So are we going or not?" Monique asked Tomasz, waking him from his dream-like state.

"Going where?" Tomasz replied, confused about what was going on.

"To see your new friends." She opened the door waiting for his response.

"Oh, sure. Whatever you say!" He smiled as he held her in close and they both walked out.

Chapter 8: Blossom

Bliss. That was the simple word that Tomasz could have used to describe the feeling that welled up within him. He had pictured this scenario in his head so many times that he had never even considered how it might come about. But now it was happening. He was with the most beautiful woman he had ever seen in his life, and she felt the same way for him that he felt for her. The minutes passed by so fast that it almost seemed unreal. Tomasz and Monique had a destination, but they took their sweet time.

They walked down the many weird roads of Crow District. They saw things neither had ever thought of before and with every mutual discovery a new shared moment between them came into existence. As they each wandered into different stores they never let go of each other's hands. As if the second they let go an invisible current would separate them, casting them off into the far reaches of the world, from which they would never be able to find each other. They held onto each other as if this was the last time they would be able to.

Tomasz loved seeing Monique's reaction when he pointed out something to her that would interest her. One of the things that caught their attention was a holographic art installation in the middle of an otherwise empty server lane. The holograph was of a person that would always face away from the viewer. No matter which angle the viewer approached the person from, their back would always be facing them. The installation served as a memorial to those who never returned from the Conflict.

It reminded Tomasz of Mickey and his uncle. Tomasz looked over to Monique. By the way she arched her right eyebrow and scrunched up the right side of her face he could tell found it interesting. He had seen this face many times before, when she would hear a question that puzzled her, or when she was deep in thought. But no matter how many times he had seen it, he still loved seeing how she scrunched up her face.

They continued meandering down several other blocks. It wasn't long before something else caught her attention. Before Tomasz was able to see what it was he knew it had to be something hilarious. When Monique found something funny she tended to try to explain what about it made her laugh so much. The result was that nothing she said was intelligible. Tomasz of course loved this and he enjoyed the effort it took to try to decipher what she was saying. While she attempted to form a sentence Tomasz looked at where she was pointing.

At the corner of a street, there were two women involved in some sort of performance. Tomasz could tell that one of them was a magician and the other was her assistant. The magician seemed to be struggling to attach her assistant's head back to her body, which was running around on its own.

"Well um, everything is going as expected, you know, we are um, about to get this head back where it's supposed to go!" The magician struggled as she held the head in one hand and ran after the headless body.

The bodyless assistant, who wore a blindfold, acted as if she had no idea what was going on.

"Wow, I feel so light! It feels as if my whole body is missing! I did not know that is how it would feel after getting my bottom half sawed off!" The assistant sounded very excited.

The headless body ran around the gathered street audience, every so often bumping into people. This led to a lot of screaming and cursing for those unaware of what was going on. This also led to a lot of hysterical laughter from those watching the show.

"I guess some people have never seen a headless body before!" The magician quipped, running after the headless body. Tomasz found the entire act hilarious. He wondered how they were able to make it look so realistic.

"What? There's a headless body out there? I want to see it. Can you take off my blindfold? Please!" the cheerful head chimed in. More laughter erupted from the audience.

"Umm, can you do me a favor and wait for a second?" The magician asked the head, and without waiting for a reply put it on a table.

"Umm ok, wow my neck feels so cold! Everything ok out there?" the blindfolded assistant asked.

At this point, the magician got a hold of the body and wrestled it to the ground. She tried to put it into a headlock, which failed and got everyone laughing even harder.

"Oh yeah. Everything is going great! Nothing to worry about here!" the magician replied as she grunted and struggled with the headless body.

She finally managed to tie it down with a rope, which elicited a lot of clapping from the crowd. She brought over the body to the head and covered the head in a towel. She put the covered head on the body, recited some magic words, brought the body up, and took the towel off.

The whole crowd laughed even harder. The head was facing the wrong direction.

"Wow, I feel my body again! You are great at this!" said the blindfolded assistant.

"But something feels wrong. Can I take off my blindfold?"

"Nothing is wrong! You should feel fine! But just give me a second, ok?" The magician tried to play it off as if everything was ok and put the towel once more over the assistant's head.

"Well, am I ok?"

"Well, of course you are! Why wouldn't you be? You have your head back on your body! What more could you want?" the magician added as she recited her magic words again.

"Was my head not on my body!? And why am I tied with ropes?" the panicked assistant asked as the magician kept trying to reassure her.

She once again took off the towel, and this time the head was attached correctly. She presented her assistant to the crowd and everyone clapped.

She proceeded to loosen the rope and take the blindfold off as everyone kept laughing and clapping. Monique had been struggling to catch her breath the entire time.

"Wow, I feel a bit light-headed now!" the bubbly assistant added.

"Well, losing your head will do that to you," the magician replied.

"A hand to my great assistant, Clara, everyone!"

Tomasz and Monique clapped along with everyone then continued their stroll, never letting go of each other's hands. They glided through the crowded streets of Crow District. There were throngs of lights swirling around and above them, masses of people around them, messages flying from all different directions trying to catch their attention. Despite the two of them being in the same streets as the rest of the people, they felt as if they were off in their world.

Tomasz could not explain it. He did not have to explain it. He just knew it. The same way one can tell deep in their stomach when something scares them, the same way one can tell when they are in a safe place, Tomasz knew he was not in the same place as everyone else. To the outside world, it looked like it, but he knew it wasn't the case. He and Monique made their way through the crowded streets, arriving at Lowray Street after some time.

Lowray Street was still abuzz with people, although less crowded than before. Monique seemed intrigued by what she was seeing. Tomasz let her know this was the place where the old subway he had taken earlier had brought him. People greeted the two of them with kind smiles. To them Tomasz and Monique were not strangers, not others, but rather fellow human beings, people like them.

Monique greeted them in turn. She saw a woman cooking a stew who offered her a quick taste. Monique tried it and let her know how delicious it was and thanked her. Tomasz was taken aback at how amicable and personable Monique was.

He never took her for being an unkind or uncaring person, but this went beyond that. This was an interaction with a stranger as one would treat their closest relatives. Not that Tomasz needed any more reasons to do so, but he felt himself falling ever more in love with her. Something he did not know was possible. He still could not believe that someone as amazing as her would be interested in him, but here they were. They made their way to the one building with the functioning sign—the Thread Barons' local hangout spot.

Monique eagerly went ahead of him and opened the door. The scene that greeted them was a raucous sight to behold. The lighting inside was bright, so it was easy to see. Unlike earlier there was now a mix of people in different outfits, not just the Pink Tuxedos.

With conversation all over, Tomasz noticed that now there was a group singing on the stage as well. Although they belted out their song with great enthusiasm it did not seem as if many in the bar were paying attention to them. Once again, as when Tomasz came in last time, little by little the bar's patrons started noticing the new arrivals. Only this time they were not greeted with hostility, but as if a celebrity had walked in their midst. Tomasz realized it was not him they were all smitten by, but Monique.

Mel rushed over to them.

"Hi, I'm Monique!" Monique introduced herself gazing at the friendly new face.

"Oh, we don't need you to introduce yourself, young lady!" Mel said with a big smile. She towered over both Tomasz and Monique.

"You were amazing earlier! We were telling everyone about the show, I mean your show! When we decided to go, we all thought it was going to be barely tolerable, but you guys blew us away!" Mel added.

"Well, I'm glad you guys enjoyed it." Monique beamed as she spoke.

"We loved it!" a random voice boomed from the back.

"Yee-yee-yee!" The bar erupted in unison.

"Tomasz, you did not tell me you were bringing this lovely lady here! I would have made proper arrangements! And why are you waiting here at the door? Bring her inside and get her something to drink!" Mel chastised Tomasz and he hurried to escort Monique to the bar.

Monique laughed at seeing Tomasz so frazzled. At the bar Tomasz and Monique both got water. Monique drank it all in one sip.

"I sort of forgot how thirsty I was," she laughed.

"I bet! You were out there singing your heart out for close to two hours! I don't think I'd be able to do that even for five minutes," said Jerry the bartender as he filled up her water again.

"Oh thank you! That means a lot to me! But it wasn't all me! And I had a lot of practice that helped for sure! But it means a lot to me that you all loved the show!" Monique replied with a smile as she had a sip.

"Well, that is true you were all impressive. Although I'm sure some of us here were more interested in your performance compared to others, right Tomasz?" Mel added.

"Umm, well, I mean, I thought the whole cast did great," Tomasz replied, trying not to trip over his words.

"Really Tomasz? What did he say to you about the show?" Monique asked Mel.

"Oh, that he was looking forward to it for a while, got the Pink Tuxedo because he wanted to look nice. As soon as we saw you on stage we all figured it was because of you pretty quickly."

"Is that so? Well, I had to ask him out earlier because, after months of giving him hints, he would not pick up on them! I have patience but enough is enough. I had to go and do something to get his attention! If I had kept waiting, I don't know how long he'd take to ask me out," Monique spoke as she grabbed Tomasz's hand.

She leaned in for a kiss and Tomasz blushed but was more than happy to reciprocate.

"Good, good on you. I'm amazed at how blind some guys can be," Mel said, shaking her head. "It was the same way with my husband. After my third attempt at giving him a hint, I asked him what in the hell he was waiting for and if he was ever going to make a move. To this day I still have to drag out decisions from him."

"You're married?" Tomasz blurted out.

Mel and Monique gave him dirty looks.

"I'm sorry, I didn't mean it in any negative way. I just met you earlier today, ok!" Tomasz added trying to salvage the situation.

"I'll have you know that yes, I am married. His name is Henry, and although he is not here at the moment, he does participate in our little expeditions now and then. But he has a family emergency so sadly he has to miss our outing later today," Mel explained.

"There's an outing?" Monique added confused.

Mel was about to reply but Tomasz decided to cut her off.

"Well anyways Mel, now that I think about it, what else don't I know about you? What do you do for work?" Tomasz asked trying to change the course of the conversation.

"Oh me? Well, I am a personal injury attorney!" Mel oblivious to Tomasz's attempts at changing the conversation was more than happy to answer him.

"Oh wow!" Monique replied.

"Yup, been doing it for about five years now," Mel said, smiling. "But that's my most recent job. When I first started in law I was an associate attorney at a big firm in the city, Dogan & Sorash. Back then I was working copyright cases."

Tomasz recognized the name. Their offices were only a short distance away from Cahuilla Tech and he had walked by their building on an almost daily basis for the past three years. They were one of the most well-known law firms in the entire city.

"I worked there for close to a decade. And let me tell you I was good at what I did. All the cases I worked on dealt with questions of intellectual property. We had a framework for those cases. Some random person decides they want to become famous, so they start flooding the internet with different content—songs, dances, different recipes, stories about their lives, and on and on. Now and then one of those would catch enough people's attention and then boom, they would make it big. Once they had enough clout, some big companies would go and use their content for advertising. But of course, they would do so without asking. This led to a majority of the creators suing the companies. They expected that since it was their content they deserved some sort of compensation. Makes sense right? Seems like it would be an easy win for whoever uploaded the content. But do you know how many times they won? Out of six hundred and thirty-seven cases?" Mel stared at both Monique and Tomasz as she asked.

Tomasz shrugged his shoulders and Monique replied "Fifty?"

"No, only two."

Tomasz and Monique both looked wide-eyed at each other.

"One of the 'wins' was a settlement. In this case, this person was always streaming their life at all hours of the day. Even when this guy was in the bathroom, sleeping, or taking a shower, he had a camera on him. Since there was a video of him creating his content it was hard to use our 'collective intellectual property' approach. The other was a complete mishandling of the case on our part. Not my fault, mind you. But as I said, the way we would always win these cases was by invoking 'collective intellectual property'."

"What is that? Something to do with being influenced by what others post?" Monique asked, intrigued.

"Yes! You are right! See, we would scour the internet for anything that seemed even a bit like what was being argued about. If it was a book, we would look for some fanfiction that had something similar in it, even if it was decades old. For a song with a catchy chorus, we would search for a previous song that had a similar melody. Regardless of what media we were arguing about, there was always something similar that we could find. And to prove that the content was not completely original, we produced something similar using algorithms trained on the data we found. Those algorithms would then produce media very similar to what the plaintiffs had created. Therefore we would argue that these content producers probably used one of millions of available algorithms to produce their content. With that we could argue that it fell under 'collective intellectual property' and so the company was free to use the content how they wanted. Worked without fail." Mel paused to take a sip of her drink.

"Well, one day one of these cases comes by, and it's a video from some pre-teen girls in some poor neighborhood doing some silly funny dance. This is the first thing they ever uploaded and it becomes a viral hit in like a week. Then some company decides to use that as part of their advertising campaign. But they don't bother with telling these girls anything." Mel paused and took another sip.

"A while later the company called us because of course, they were being sued. The girls' uncle was the one who started the lawsuit and was well prepared to argue on their behalf. He argued how the girls had spent years in different dance classes. He gave evidence of many dance recitals they had attended. He mentioned how they had always wanted to pursue dancing as a career and that this would be a big break for them. This would effectively change their lives due to their poor background. But all that preparation did not make much of a difference. We found some random video with around one thousand views that were posted about fifty years ago. Within a matter of hours, we were able to replicate the girls' dance almost exactly with another algorithm. That was the end of that. The case was deliberated for a total of one hour. I walked in to deliver the news to the family." Mel paused but this time Tomasz could see pain in her face.

"That was the first time I saw these girls face to face. When they saw me walk into that room I don't think they knew who I was. They seemed happy to see me. They probably thought I was bringing them good news. I looked at their uncle and told them the truth. The judge had ruled against them. They had no grounds for claiming it was their intellectual property and that they should cease all claims against the company. The uncle started getting into a fit, but I just walked out. But before I did I heard the two girls sobbing. In my entire life, I had never seen two people go from being ecstatic to completely heartbroken that fast," Mel added in a somber tone.

"It was the first time I felt any sort of regret for anything I had done. I had worked on so many similar cases, but I don't know. That was the one that did it. I quit the week after that. For a while, I wasn't sure what I would do, but somehow, I ended up here in Crow. Then I ended up opening my law practice. Now I specialize in cases where people have been injured by automated devices. Anything from vehicles, cleaners, attendants, valets, AIs, you name it. I make it a point to prioritize cases for those who do not have anyone stand up for them. Some of these are attendants at hospitals, hotels, and restaurants, people with low-wage jobs, who get injured on the job and then try to get stifled. Most of them are seldom savvy in technical matters. Therefore, it is very easy to convince them that their injuries were due to their carelessness. That's where I come in, and that's where I've met some of the people right here. Like Raul, one of his friends was one of my clients. Poor guy got both legs cut off clean. At least it was painless," Mel mused as if talking about the weather.

"I haven't been as successful as I was in my previous job and it sure doesn't make up for all that I did, but I try," she concluded and smiled.

Monique seemed to be at a loss for words. Tomasz as well. Meanwhile, the bar had reverted to its original raucous atmosphere.

"How about you Monique, is your dream to be a singer? Or do you have different aspirations?" Mel asked breaking the silence between them.

"Me? Oh, the truth is that I don't know!" Monique answered thoughtfully.

Tomasz was curious too—he knew that she was in school with hopes of becoming a surgeon one day, but he was not sure how singing fit into that.

Monique continued, "To be honest I have never decided what I wanted to do for a job. And now that I am in school, I still feel like I don't know. I started school to become a surgeon, because, well, that's what I grew up surrounded by. My parents met each other at their first job, both surgeons at a CMC hospital, close to here actually. So when it came time for me to decide what I wanted to do, I figured I would also pursue medicine. I never cared for it, but I thought I would grow to like it. But that still hasn't happened. I feel like I am so far along now that there is no point in changing my mind. So I figured I would try something new this year." Monique paused.

"And?" Mel asked.

"Oh, yeah, well I met up with some local theater kids in our school and they let me know that they were going to be putting on a musical in Crow. They invited me to audition. Music wasn't new to me. Throughout my childhood and into my adolescence I played piano. I even played in various concert halls, so being in front of a crowd wasn't new to me. I also took some vocal lessons. But compared to what I just went through they were completely different."

"Really?" Mel asked.

"I'm sorry I'm sure that doesn't make sense…" Monique laughed as she trailed off.

"I get it," Tomasz interjected as he placed his hand on her shoulder. He knew what she was referring to.

"Well, it's hard to say. I had played so many times in front of crowds, but all those times I felt like I had to do it. I wasn't doing it because I wanted to, but because I was expected to. After a while playing music in my head became associated with something that I did out of obligation. So when I heard about the musical I was conflicted. I felt like it would be more of what I had already gone through. A soulless experience that I had to do, with no real emotion in it. But when I auditioned, I realized that I was afraid for no reason. I loved every second of it. I went in with no expectation of having any part in the musical. I wanted to see how it would feel. Next thing I know they're offering me the lead role! I didn't even hesitate!" Monique paused and took a sip of her drink.

"It was the first time I can remember feeling so excited about something. I was so nervous. But it was such a good feeling! During my piano recitals, I didn't feel anything. No excitement, no joy, no anxiousness, nothing. And since those performances were only me, I didn't feel any pressure to not mess up since it would only look bad on me. But here if I messed up, I could ruin the entire rest of the show. When I was getting ready to step on stage tonight, I was so nervous! But as soon as the show started I felt as if I was in an empty hall, with only me and the rest of the cast members. I didn't even notice any of you until after the show ended!"

"Wow! I really can't believe that this was your first musical. You were so composed up there I sure thought you had been doing this your whole life. They made a great choice choosing you to be their lead," Mel said.

"Yes, you were incredible out there! If you had not told me this was your first show I would have thought you had been doing this for years!" Jerry chimed in from behind the bar.

"So does this mean that we can expect to see more shows with Monique as the star in the future?" Maria asked as she got to the bar.

Monique looked at her surprised.

"I'm Maria by the way. Nice to meet you and I loved your performance!"

"Oh thank you," Monique said as she greeted Maria.

"But will I do more shows? Maybe? I don't know. It's all so sudden. A year ago, this was not something I was even considering. And now I just finished my first show. It's a lot at once," Monique replied.

"Well, you don't have to decide anytime soon. But when you do decide on your next show you better invite all of us!" said Mel.

"How about you Tomasz, I don't think we have any idea of what your plans are. Will you continue smuggling contraband as a career for the rest of your life?" Jerry laughed.

Tomasz replied with a nervous laugh at Jerry's remark. Monique still was not aware of the device that he had transported.

"Well, my answer is a lot more boring. I like computers so I decided to study programming and that's what I plan on doing. My dad and all his siblings are programmers, so I figured I should do that as well."

"So where does transporting stuff fit into all of this?" Mel asked.

"Well, I started this because I wanted to help my cousin. His dad was over in the Conflict and he had some, well, unique ideas on how to raise a child. And eventually, my cousin bought into some of that and became a contratech. I started by getting him some things he was missing from outside and from there it kind of grew."

"A contratech?" Monique asked.

"Oh, I'm sorry, a tech contrarian. In general, contratechs isolate themselves as much as possible from any type of digital technology. It's ok if it runs on electricity, but they do not want anything that connects to the internet or has any sort of computer. Since so much of the infrastructure around here is online it is hard for them to get access to things that are not bare necessities. In Cahuilla, there is a large group of contratechs in Fox District, called Cunha. It was started by some finance billionaire who had some sort of epiphany about the corrupting nature of tech. He started with only a handful but now there are hundreds of them. They are an interesting group for sure, anytime I go in there they ask me to turn off all data streaming. At first, I thought it was bizarre but they are all some of the nicest people I've met. They all seem content with their lifestyle. When I started bringing things in for my cousin, others in there asked me for help. So little by little I started doing deliveries for more people until I ended up here, I guess."

"Wow. You two are not a boring duo," Mel replied.

Tomasz blushed at the suggestion. "Oh I'm nothing like Monique, she is the insanely talented one, I deliver stuff and now and then wear great fits."

"Oh, you're being too modest." Monique smiled as she put her hands on Tomasz's.

A great warm feeling overcame Tomasz, an unrivaled bliss that he still could not fathom.

"If only you had some musical talent, you guys could make a great duo," Jerry said to Tomasz.

"Oh, Tomasz is talented musically. He is one of a kind at the drums!" Monique interjected. Tomasz could feel his face get beet red as he flushed.

"No way?" Mel replied.

"Well, one of a kind might be a stretch. I've been playing drums for a good amount of time, so I guess you could say I'm somewhat decent."

"Somewhat decent? I've seen you in some of the concerts you've played, you stole the show in most of them!" Monique insisted.

"Wait. You have?" Tomasz looked at her in astonishment.

"Of course! When you said you played in some virtual concerts I of course had to see for myself. It sounded like there were three different people playing drums at the same time! You are probably the best drummer I've ever seen play! " Monique replied.

He was speechless and beaming.

"Ok, I have to hear this," Mel said. She turned towards Monique and then to the stage. "May I?"

Monique looked to the stage and understood. She nodded as she giggled. Mel got up and grabbed Tomasz's hand.

"Umm, what's happening?" Tomasz asked as she started guiding him towards the empty stage. He noticed that it was equipped with a guitar, a piano, a bass, and a shiny unoccupied drum set.

"Oh, man." He knew what he was being set up for.

Mel reached the stage and got up on it with him. She got everyone's attention.

"Everyone, listen up. Earlier you all heard a great performance from the beautiful lady in the back, Monique! Let's hear a round of applause for her!"

The entire bar erupted into clapping and once more "Yee-yee-yee-yee!" was shouted from all corners.

"Well, I have another surprise for all of you. I have heard on good authority that our new friend here, our unwitting new member, Tomasz has been hiding something from us. He is quite a talented drummer. Who here would like to hear him perform?" Mel asked.

"Yee-yee-yee-yee!" The cry repeated without hesitation all across the bar.

Tomasz looked in the back and even saw Monique join in on the fun.

"So what do you say, Tomasz?" Mel asked.

Without a word, Tomasz took off his suit jacket and handed it to Mel. This brought the entire bar to more cheers.

Tomasz walked over to the drum set. It was a large set with seven cymbals and eight different drums. He sat down and adjusted the positioning of the cymbals and drums to his liking. He noticed a pair of drumsticks on the floor and grabbed them.

He started with a simple beat on the bass pedal. A constant rhythmic thumping. He transitioned to incorporating the different cymbals. By view alone, he knew what they ought to sound like, but he needed to hear them himself. The bass continued. He started to find the rhythm he liked.

He moved on to the floor toms now. *One two.* They sounded nice and heavy. *One two.* This time faster. *One two,* incorporating the cymbals now. He started incorporating the different drums, still not interacting with the snare. He would wait for that until the end. The bass pedal kept on beating; the pulse steady. He kept a quick one-two pace for a bit, the bar silent in anticipation. Then he hit the snare, the pace quickened, and the pulse started to increase.

The interplay between the bass pedal, the cymbals, and the drums was a rapid-fire progression. The bass pounded at a furious pace with no cessation. The drums and cymbals offered an unrelenting stampede that kept amping up in intensity. Tomasz kept increasing the pace as if there was no limit to where he could go. But just as he brought it a near machine-like cadence, he was able to slow it down. The transition occurred fast, but with such a natural feel to it that all those listening to it could not understand how complex that was. Regardless of whether they knew how difficult it was, they showed their admiration, as Tomasz could hear loud cheering from the bar.

He felt a smile creep up on his face. He was not expecting that. When was the last time he had played for an audience and enjoyed it? Well, that could wait until later. Now Tomasz focused on transitioning to a quick, but light interplay between the floor tom and the hi-hat. The pace stayed constant as he incorporated different drums and cymbals. The cheers kept coming in and Tomasz loved it.

Tomasz continued to play for another ten minutes. In the end, he sat drenched in sweat. When he got up, once again, the entire bar erupted into cheers. Monique was one of the loudest.

"Tomasz you killed it up there!" she squealed as she hurried onto the stage.

"You think so?" Tomasz asked.

"Of course! The fact that you improvised all of that is incredible, you did great!" Monique said as she smiled. This was the only person whose praise he wanted to hear. She kissed him which sent the entire bar into loud hollering and more cheering.

"DU-ET! DU-ET! DU-ET!" The chanting began from the crowd. Monique and Tomasz looked at each other.

"What do you say, do you want to give them a show?" Monique looked at Tomasz.

He looked at her and then back to the crowd. He grabbed his drumsticks and sat back down at the drums. The whole bar erupted into cheers. Monique sat by the piano and brought a microphone with her.

"Well, what do you all want to hear?" Monique asked.

There was a second of silence in the bar.

"Sunday Sunset!" someone yelled from the back.

It was a song Tomasz knew well, a classic love song that was around two decades old. Tomasz and Monique looked at each other, and nodded, and Tomasz started with a quick count. During the entirety of the song, Tomasz and Monique locked eyes. They were more playing for each other than for the audience in front of them. The audience did not care one bit, they enjoyed the show all the same. Monique's voice sounded as beautiful as ever and her skill on the piano was amazing.

Once they finished that song, requests started pouring in from the crowd. All the attention focused on both Monique and Tomasz with the audience singing along. If Tomasz had enjoyed his previous solo performance, nothing could compare to this unexpected duet with Monique. She would provide the vocals and the melody and he would provide the percussion.

After about twenty minutes of playing music, Monique made a quick announcement.

"Alright, this next one is going to be my last one," she said.

A collective "Aww" broke over the bar.

"I know, I know, but I haven't had much rest! But this one will be special. I want to give my partner a break so I'll take this one by myself is that ok?" she asked the audience.

Tomasz was surprised to hear this but everyone started clapping, interested in seeing what Monique was going to do.

"First of all, let's give my handsome bandmate a hand! Tomasz, you were amazing!"

Tomasz sat up and waved to the crowd. He had a smile plastered over his face that he could not get rid of. He had not enjoyed playing for an audience this much in a long time. He sat back down and watched Monique.

"Alright, this is one that I would be surprised if you have heard. It's close to ninety years old so it might sound very different to what we've been playing, but I swear you all will love it."

The audience replied in cheers.

"Ok good, I like what I'm hearing. You know this song holds a special place in my heart. This was the first song my mother taught me to play on the piano. She told me the words helped her get through some of the hardest moments of her life. So now anytime I'm struggling I like to listen to these lyrics and sing them. I wanted to share them with you all. And I hope that if you ever find yourself struggling or need some motivation this song will help you."

"Yee-yee-yee-yee!" the crowd erupted.

"Alright, here I go," Monique said. The crowd quieted down as fast as it had erupted.

Monique started the melody and started singing. This time she was not singing for anyone but herself. The entirety of the bar stood in silence, experiencing the performance with bated breath. From his vantage point, Tomasz could only stare in awe. He had seen her perform with such energy, but this time the energy originated from somewhere else, a place of vulnerability. This performance came from her very essence. Every word uttered was a fragment of her being, a chance to peer into the person on stage, a reflection of a beautiful soul. To express herself in such a way took courage.

The song came to an end and the entire bar was silent.

Monique said in a soft voice "Thank you all I hope you enjoyed it, and I hope you liked the words."

The entire bar was still speechless.

"IN-CRE-DI-BLE!" Maria shouted.

The entire crowd erupted in cheers and applause.

Monique smiled as she stood up. She went up to Tomasz and grabbed his hand, brought him to the front of the stage. Tomasz followed her lead and bowed along with her. Then he grabbed her and kissed her, which the audience loved. He felt such a rush of joy that he almost could not believe himself.

Mel got on the stage and gave them a big hug.

"Guys that was one of the best shows I have ever seen in my life."

Tomasz could see that Mel was overcome with emotion. She hugged them once again.

Mel turned to the crowd and spoke. "OK guys, don't worry, we will get these two back here as soon as possible to play more music for us, ok?"

The entire crowd applauded. Tomasz and Monique bowed one more time before getting off.

"Let's do that again!" Monique smiled at Tomasz as they made their way to the bar.

"You don't have to tell me!" Tomasz replied without even thinking.

As Tomasz sat down he was still enraptured in a feeling that he could not describe. It seemed as if the last hour or so had been some sort of dream.

"Hey Jerry, can I get a Cahuilla Sour?" Monique asked the bartender. This snapped Tomasz out of his dreamlike state.

"Of course." Jerry got to work on the drink.

"Oh, that's right! That's what you made me earlier! I didn't even know the name until the weird bartender in the theater made one too. They must not be well known," Tomasz said.

"Not well known? They are one of the most popular drinks in the Crow District," Monique replied as she smiled.

"You can't be serious," Tomasz said, surprised.

"You need to get out more often." Monique laughed.

Maria approached Monique and started speaking with her.

"That was great! I've always wanted to learn the piano! And I loved the lyrics! But some of them didn't make much sense. What was it 'Even when I'm a mess, I still put it to rest?'" Maria asked with excitement.

"Hah, no I'm sorry. It goes 'Even when I'm a mess, I still put on a vest'. " Monique explained.

"So I heard you do deliveries to the contratechs?" Raul spoke behind Tomasz.

Tomasz turned around and saw the short stout man.

"Oh yeah. Although it has been quite a while since I've been there," Tomasz replied.

"My sister moved there several years ago. I haven't had time to go visit her there, especially with all the restrictions they have. But I feel like I should go there sometime soon," Raul said.

Tomasz and Monique spent the rest of their time in the bar chatting up the other people in the bar, stealing glances at each other from time to time. Even though they knew neither had left the reassurance of seeing each other brought them joy. After a while, Monique approached Tomasz.

"Hey I'm sorry but I'm meeting up with some of the people from the musical soon. Wanted to let you know before I head out," she said.

Tomasz having lost track of the time checked his interface, 11:42 PM.

"Wow, it's late," he said out loud.

"I'm assuming you're going to be staying? Unless you have plans?" Monique asked.

"Do I have plans?" Tomasz wondered aloud. At the moment he had forgotten if there was anything else for him to do in Crow District. The only two things that he came to do were to deliver the package and see Monique perform.

"Oh, we're all having a group outing later on at three AM! We invited Tomasz here," Jerry mentioned.

"An outing at three?" Tomasz blurted out confused. He looked behind Jerry and saw the package. Now he remembered. It was the whole reason Tomasz had met up with the Thread Barons in the first place.

"Oh, the outing! You mean at Yurok Park?" Tomasz said.

"That's the one!" Jerry smiled.

"Oh dear," Tomasz muttered. He grabbed his drink and gulped it all in one swig.

He looked around at the bar. All the other people in the Pink Tuxedos like him were laughing, cheering, and completely present in the moment. Those people he had met only hours ago. Those people seemed to relish his company for some reason. And Tomasz also felt the same way.

Everything in his mind was telling him that was it. He had more than accomplished what he wanted for today. He had gone to see Monique's show. After the show, Monique confessed her feelings for him and they became a couple, what he had been wanting for months now. But that wasn't all that had occurred, far from it.

He had met this weird group of people who seemed to be looking to cause trouble. Yet despite how completely crazy it might sound he had loved every second he had spent alongside them. It was not because they were out to get people, or because they committed felonies, or because they liked to wear good fits. None of that mattered to him.

What mattered to him was how committed they were to each other. The fact that they cared for each other is what he loved. Being amongst them was something that Tomasz was not used to. It was as if he had found something that he never felt possible. He found a group that he could belong to.

Tomasz's brain kept telling him to get out of there, but something else inside him was not sure about what he ought to do.

"Oh, the outing. I heard a bit about it. Tomasz were you planning on going to this?" Monique asked him. She either did not notice his apparent internal conflict or did a great job of not showing it.

"I- I don't—" Tomasz started. Once again he looked around the bar.

Tomasz felt a hand on his. It was Monique's.

"Well, you don't have to decide right this second. If you are unsure, then stick around for a bit! I'm sure you'll have fun. I know that whatever you end up doing it'll be fine." She got up and kissed him.

He once again thought about it. Should he leave now, stay for a bit, or go to this crazy thing they were planning on doing later?

He got up with Monique and walked her to the door. They stood there for a while, due to Tomasz's indecision.

"Look Tomasz, you don't need to leave if you're not ready. I'll be busy anyways, so why not spend some time with these guys," she said.

They kissed once more and Tomasz smiled as Monique walked away. He had no idea what exactly he would end up doing.

Chapter 9: Jakey

Time seemed to fly by while Tomasz was at the bar. He talked with so many different people. He learned that Raul had also attended Cahuilla Tech earlier in his youth. He was asking Tomasz if some of the same professors he had when he was studying there were still teaching.

He spoke to Maria who kept mentioning how as a young girl she started practicing violin but gave it up once and never picked it up again. Watching Monique and Tomasz play so well earlier made her want to start learning music again. Throughout all these different conversations not once did Tomasz ever feel tired of them.

After a while Tomasz found himself speaking to two massive muscle-bound guys who towered above everyone else in the bar. They too wore Pink Tuxedos. The one on the right, Fred, was dark-skinned and had a cleanly-shaven head. His head was so shiny that for a second Tomasz thought he might have some sort of scalp modification. The other thing that stood out about him was the fact that he seemed to always have sunglasses on. Tomasz had noticed him earlier in the day and at no point had he seemed to take them off.

The man on the right, Oscar, was olive-skinned and had long hair in a ponytail with a well-trimmed beard. If they were not dressing in the same Pink Tuxedo everyone else had, Tomasz would have thought they were security for the establishment.

"So you met Mickey earlier today, right? What'd you think?" Fred asked Tomasz.

"Yeah, I did. Well, all I can say is that he was a unique guy for sure. He was so calm and collected, such an easygoing guy. To think he was making, well umm you know."

"Bombs?" Oscar chimed in laughing.

"Um, yeah, I guess." Tomasz shrugged.

At that, both Fred and Oscar laughed. The two of them had a deep booming laugh that seemed to make the ground shake every time they exhaled.

"Yeah, I'm glad to hear he hasn't changed. We've known Mickey a looooong time. But let me tell you, if you needed something blown up back in the day, there was no one better. If we needed to get people somewhere and there was something in the way, Mickey would clear that shit out in record time. He was like a rat. But that sounded too mean for him, so that's why we stuck him with Mouse," Fred explained.

"When Mel brought up what she wanted to do, we knew who we needed to reach out to. We didn't give him too many specifics, but it didn't matter. The guy's an artist. You give him a bit of detail and the next thing you know he paints you a goddamn masterpiece. Kinda like you and your girl with music," Oscar added.

"But with bombs?" Tomasz asked trying not to say the word bomb too loudly.

"Yeah exactly!" Oscar laughed as he replied.

"Not surprised he seemed calm even when giving you explosives. Mouse never felt the squeeze. We could be in the most fucked up situation and he would just be his usual self. Focused on the task at hand. It was quite amazing to see," said Fred.

"I mean, if it wasn't for him neither Fred nor I would be here," Oscar added.

"Really?" Tomasz replied.

"Oh yeah, for sure, he got himself a distinguished service cross for that," Oscar said.

Tomasz wasn't sure what that was, but it sounded nice.

"Oh ok." Was Tomasz's response, both Fred and Oscar could tell he had no clue what they meant.

"It's a big deal in the Army. It means you saw some shit go down in combat and stepped up. You know, hero stuff, but above and beyond, like there were several times where I was sure he wasn't coming back alive," Oscar said.

Tomasz could see Fred and Oscar's somber expressions. Although he didn't know the specifics of what they meant he could tell it was something of great importance to the two of them.

"Wow," Tomasz said.

"Yeah one thing you can say about him, he is that guy. If I ever had to pick two people to go with me into a combat zone I'd ask for Mickey and someone better clone him and give me another Mickey," Fred added.

"But you would never know it. He rarely talks about his time in the Conflict. He's ok hanging out with his cat, Pedro, and teaching his yoga lessons. Still an awesome guy though, would walk into a machine gun nest if he was there with me," Oscar mused.

Tomasz had an inkling that Mickey must have been in combat if he was in the Conflict. But he would have never guessed that he was in such danger and was some sort of decorated war hero. Hearing both Fred and Oscar talk about Mickey, who they would tower over, made Tomasz respect the guy so much more. Tomasz could not help but wonder how would he react if being in the same position.

Mel walked over to them. Behind her she had around twenty other people in Pink Tuxedos, all focusing their gaze on Fred and Oscar.

"Seems like we need to go out for a walk, boys," Mel said to Fred and Oscar.

The friendly expressions they had a couple of seconds ago disappeared.

"So we going out in force tonight?" Oscar asked.

Mel nodded.

"What are we expecting?" Fred asked.

"Word is the gray shirts are pulling out there harassing people, you know the norm. Communications on the wire are flaring up with discussions on a group of shits in gray shirts that stopped by Luca's joint about twenty minutes ago. Smashed up the windows, and harassed some of the customers and employees. Standard piece of shit behavior."

Fred and Oscar were now fuming.

"So are we going?" Mel asked.

"Of course," Fred said and started to go. Oscar followed.

Tomasz started to follow, completely lost about what was occurring. Before he could get too far, Mel stood in front of him.

"Tomasz. I said earlier I don't want to lie to you and I don't. So I'm going to get straight to chase. What we're going to do isn't pretty. This has been a long day for you and I don't know if you are going to be up for this," Mel said as she put her hand on his shoulder.

Tomasz looked at the hand on his shoulder and then her face. He could tell by her look that whatever was happening was serious.

"Don't, Mel. Let him come," Fred interjected as he stood next to her.

She gave him a puzzled look.

"That's right. He can make up his mind. Let him see and if he does not like it then he can leave. But if he's going to be with us, then he needs to see us here, and then out there as well. Hiding the other stuff isn't much better than lying," Oscar added.

Mel looked at both of them, let go of Tomasz, and threw her hands in the air.

"Alright Tomasz, I only want you to know, it might get violent. You can stay here if you'd like, but if you come with us you might see some stuff you might not like."

Fred and Oscar looked at Tomasz. Tomasz looked at Mel, at Fred and Oscar, at the rest of the people in the Pink Tuxedos that had gathered around. What exactly was going on?

Earlier in the day he had gone to a musical with them. Then he spent the rest of the day playing music for them and enjoying their company. And what did they say now? That it might get violent? That did not seem to make any sense. This must be some sort of joke.

He looked at the group. They were all on average as big as Tomasz or even bigger. And unlike earlier they did not have smiling expressions of joy. They seemed ready for something, well, unpleasant.

Tomasz knew this was not some sort of weird prank they were pulling on him. They were dead serious about going out and finding some other group, and it might get violent. His gut recoiled, a deep sensation of doubt starting to fill inside of him. He didn't know how he would even handle violence. If he relied on his gut feeling he would have decided to stay, but there was something else that he could not shake off.

In the short amount of time that Tomasz had spent with the group he had been treated as one of their own. All he had done was waltz into their bar wearing the same clothes and they had accepted him. But he felt as if he had not done anything to prove himself to the group. Even though they had not asked him for any sort of proof of his loyalty he felt as if he owed it to them to show that he was willing to be with them, even at the worst of times. He wanted to show them that he would be willing to stand with them not just when it was singing and good times, but when things go serious. He needed to show them he was dedicated.

"Alright, I'll go," Tomasz replied.

Without waiting for any other word the group started to head out. Mel hurried to the front of the group to lead them.

Fred stayed behind next to Tomasz. The two of them walked out of the building.

"Tomasz, if things start to get out of control, get out of there as soon as possible, do you understand?" Fred spoke to him with an intensity he did not expect.

"It's ok man, I'll be fine, don't worry about me," Tomasz said as he kept walking.

Fred put his hand on his shoulder. Tomasz froze in his tracks.

"No, you don't understand. I'm not asking you. I am telling you. As someone who does not want to see you get hurt. If a problem breaks out, you will leave. Is that understood?" Fred asked.

Tomasz stared above him, at the towering man. He understood that there was only one acceptable answer to this question.

Tomasz nodded resolutely. Fred stared at him for a split second and then let go.

Tomasz steeled himself and followed.

***

Tomasz was following along with the group, unsure of where exactly they would end up. They had already crossed several blocks but their pace never slackened. Everywhere they went they made sure to walk in the middle of the lane. They wanted others to notice them. Tomasz was the smallest among them. This was something that he was not used to. The carefree attitude the group had earlier disappeared the moment they left the bar. No idle chatter came from those in Pink Tuxedos. They went out with a singular goal in mind.

Oscar was in the back, right next to Tomasz. He was paying no mind to him, instead, his eyes scanned all around them.

"You ok there?" Oscar asked aloud, never looking at anyone in particular.

Tomasz did not respond.

"Tomasz. You ok there?" Oscar asked again, still not looking at anybody in particular.

"Oh me? Oh yeah, no issues here." Tomasz tried to portray an air of confidence. That was the furthest from the truth. He was grateful that no one else was paying attention to him.

He decided now would be a good time to get more information on their mission. "So these gray hoods—"

"Gray shirts," Oscar interjected, still not looking at him.

"Right, gray shirts, umm, who are they?" Tomasz asked.

This time Oscar looked straight at him.

"You never really spend any time in Crow District, do you?"

"No, not really," Tomasz replied with mild embarrassment.

"Well, the short answer is they are assholes. You want the long answer?"

"Um, sure." Tomasz wanted to know what exactly had his new associates so worked up.

"Well if we are splitting hairs here they do not go by gray shirts. Everyone calls them that because that is what they wear. A gray buttoned long-sleeve shirt, with a gray tie, gray slacks, and shiny black boots. They officially call themselves the Voluntary Order of Urban Security, or VOUS. The guy who founded them is a veteran of the Conflict. He calls himself Colonel Arnold. Mind you he was never actually a Colonel and his real name is Nolan Smith. Anyways, he says that our government betrayed veterans with the Treaty of Washington Place. Which forced him into turning traitor, like Benedict Arnold from the American Revolution, so he says. He wouldn't shut his mouth after the Conflict. It didn't take long til he found some like-minded people and started the movement."

That rang a bell for Tomasz.

"Oh is that treaty the one from like fifteen years ago? The one that led to a lot of soldiers getting thrown in jail because of all those towns they destroyed, all that land that we had to cede back and the no-fault statement on their end?" Tomasz asked.

Oscar once again looked at Tomasz. He was trying to hide his displeasure, but that only made him look even more terrifying.

"I'm sorry I didn't mean it like that," Tomasz added as fast as he could.

"No, you don't have to apologize. What you said, well, it's not inaccurate. And besides you had nothing to do with." Oscar interjected.

"Anyways" Oscar continued, "like I said, the treaty left a bitter taste for a lot of people. All the death and destruction that happened and the best both sides come up with is to pretend those years were not real. Once neither side could go on, they decided they had to stop and neither was going to give up anything. So this meant going back to the status quo and calling a truce. The reality was that short of launching a full-out nuclear assault, the Conflict was at a stalemate. Depends on who you ask, but it seems like many times we almost got to that point. I don't know how true that is, but it doesn't matter."

The group quickly halted which brought Oscar to a pause. Without words the group continued and so did Oscar.

"But anyways, there was no way one side was going to get the upper hand. Both sides had exhausted their ability to wage war about a year and a half into the Conflict, not even a quarter of the way through. By the time the peace accords were signed both sides lacked most bare necessities. So there was no way to prolong the Conflict. But then there came the trials. The majority of the fighting had been overseas. Most civilians affected were not our citizens, so the blame for whatever atrocity befell them, fell on us. I know for a fact that is not an inaccurate statement. That is what made it in the text of the Treaty. Most people were happy after the treaty was done. They were sick of the constant news cycles with nothing but death, and they were glad to not have to worry about an impending nuclear Armageddon. But for some, especially those who had been in the Conflict, this was worse than being killed in action. This was betrayal by your own country." Oscar emphasized that last sentence.

"So then this idiot, Colonel Arnold, shows up. He felt that the government had betrayed its most basic tenets and should be overthrown. He started small. He talked to former military buddies, those he knew were already predisposed to disliking the government. From there he used his connections to find disaffected groups within the military. Pretty soon his movement was massive. He had groups in many major cities. He held rallies that had massive counter-protests but his gray shirts served as security for him and other high-ranking VOUS members." Anytime Oscar said the word "gray shirts" he said it with vitriol.

"The gray shirts protected the VOUS higher-ups from violence by attacking those who disagreed with them in every possible manner, whether physically, online, or whatever it was. But a close encounter with a gray shirt group led by Colonel Arnold and a senator went bad, and the senator was killed. Since then Colonel Arnold has gone into hiding. That was a decade ago. But the movement is still strong, and everyone is sure Arnold is still running it. They target a lot of businesses run by Asians of any kind, regardless of which ethnicity they are targeting. Because you know they're idiots and think that people whose families have been in this country for generations had anything to do with how the war played out."

Tomasz was silent for a while. It was a lot to take in. He remembered a story from when he was younger about a senator from New York being murdered during a protest. He felt ashamed to not even know that it had anything to do with this larger movement.

"Sorry if I dumped all of this on you kid. I understand it's quite a lot," Oscar added.

"No, no need to apologize. I mean, damn, I kind of remember this senator dying during a protest but I don't know much about the rest."

"You're not the only one. You rarely hear about groups like these in the news. The Conflict is something everyone wants to forget. Anything that reminds them of it, they pretend is not real. They pretend that if they ignore it, it never happened. They'd rather go to a virtual city and get drunk than have to face the reality here. Sometimes I can see why."

"Damn. But these gray shirts. They're not only in Cahuilla?"

"Nope, they're still going strong in most major cities. A lot of young men who lost parents or older siblings in the Conflict make up the bulk of their recruits. And there are a shit ton of those. And those kids are angry. Their loved ones died and all they see is that they were being called criminals. That's where the gray shirts come in. They tell them, 'Your dad was a hero. But if you don't fight back they will always be labeled criminals. Are you going to let them do that?' Works every time. They get those kids worked up to the point that they'll smash businesses, disrupt events, beat up people, and sometimes even kill them. It's fucked up on so many levels."

"And you guys—" Tomasz started asking but he saw the group ahead of him stop.

They stopped at a wide half-lit server alleyway. On either side, the walls shot up straight to the sky. Everyone was staring straight ahead, Oscar included. Tomasz followed their lead.

It seemed like looking at a reality-bending mirror that reflected an alternate dimension. On his side of the mirror, there was a large group all dressed in Pink Tuxedos. About thirty feet away from them was a group of about the same size in gray uniforms, just as Oscar had described them.

They all wore ironed buttoned long-sleeved gray shirts, a gray tie, and long gray trousers tucked into tall black shiny boots. Just like Tomasz's side, the opposite side stood like statues focused on his group. Between the two groups, there was only silence. Tomasz scanned the faces of the people across from him. Most seemed to be young men, early in their twenties, like Tomasz. He noticed one of them staring straight at him. Tomasz disregarded this person, but a split second later realized something. The eyes looking straight at him belonged to someone he had not seen in a while. He struggled to remember who it was.

"Jakey?" Tomasz muttered to himself.

Tomasz kept staring at the young man. He looked away, pretending not to have recognized Tomasz. But Tomasz was now sure it was Jakey.

"Jakey!" Tomasz shouted as he made his way through the Pink Tuxedos.

He felt a hand try to stop him, but Tomasz pushed it aside. He kept walking until he was between the two groups. All by himself Tomasz stood in no man's land, shouting to the young man he once knew.

"Jakey, I know it's you, don't look away!"

The young man now stopped looking away. His face burned with emotion, a mix of melancholy and rage. He stared straight at Tomasz as he tried to restrain himself.

"Do not call me that!" the young man shouted back.

Those five short words sent shivers down Tomasz's spine. It felt like a gut punch. This boy he knew once, this kind soul that would always tag along with his group. The one that would always be smiling. He was the spitting image of his older brother. The brother he idolized. That young boy stood only a couple of feet away. But he was no longer a young boy, and he did not smile. All Tomasz could see in the man in gray was hatred in his eyes and anger in his voice.

Tomasz composed himself, unsure of what exactly he was trying to do. He once again tried reaching out.

"Jakey, what are you doing here?" Tomasz's voice quivered in confusion.

"I told you not to call me that!" shouted the man again.

"Trooper Morell, do you know this man who is with those traitors?" A tall man walked to the front of the group looking straight at Tomasz. Like the rest of the gray shirts, he was clean-shaven and had short-cropped hair. In the sporadic lighting, he and the rest of the gray shirts could be mistaken all for identical copies.

"Squad Leader Hines, he is an outsider, someone of no significance, sir," said the young man. He did not break eye contact with Tomasz.

Tomasz started to walk towards Jakey but did not get very far.

From the opposing side, someone shouted "Halt!" at Tomasz. At the same time, someone behind Tomasz screamed "Stop!" at him. As he turned his head in both directions to see who was addressing him, he felt something hit his head.

Suddenly he was losing his balance falling on the ground on his knees. He put his hand to his head, feeling a damp spot. He looked at his hand and noticed a large red stain all over it. Staring at his hand he saw out of the corner of his eye that no man's land was no longer desolate. All around him, he saw a rash of chaos ensue. He was pushed to the ground and felt blows rain down on him from all sides. He tried as best as he could to cover his face, but the blows did not stop. The chaos surrounding him only intensified. Tomasz was sure he was about to die here.

He felt a tug on his shirt collar, a sharp and sudden pull that raised him. Standing up he could see a mob of people doing everything possible to inflict as much pain on the other side. As fast as he got pulled up, the same force pulled him away from the melee. Before he could react he felt his back hit a wall. A light flashed into his eyes, almost blinding him.

"Ow goddamn, what the fuck!" Tomasz shouted, finally coming to his senses.

The light moved over to his other eye, blinding Tomasz once again. He could feel something against his temple where his head throbbed. Once the light had turned off Tomasz saw who had tossed him around like a rag doll. It was Fred. He pulled something from his pocket, a white cloth and a gel gauze bottle. He used the cloth to clean Tomasz's head and the rest of his face and sprayed the gel gauze on the large wound. The burning pain in Tomasz's head started to subside as Fred looked at him.

"You with me?" Fred asked.

Tomasz nodded, unable to say anything. He had heard what Fred had said. He had understood it. But it seemed as if his brain was still trying to process other events.

"Well, let me say, you either got the biggest cojones or you're the biggest idiot I've ever seen. Still unsure. But I'm sure that hurt like hell. Your face is not looking good, not the worst I've seen though. I got that nasty cut to stop bleeding, but you got nicks and hits all over. But nothing seems too terrible. I could be wrong, but we did tell you there was going to be violence, right?" Fred started.

Tomasz stared at Fred.

"It's not your fault," Fred sighed. "I was the one who said you should come. But look at it this way, you got your first several battle scars. And you ain't dead. Anyways I gotta go in there and lay waste to some assholes."

Tomasz nodded as Fred got up. Before he left Fred handed Tomasz the can of gel gauze that he had used and some extra cloth.

"Don't worry I have plenty," Fred reassured him.

Without hesitation, Fred turned around and headed straight into the heart of chaos. Tomasz was still unsure if the violence occurring mere feet from him was real. It was not the first time he questioned what was going on around him that night. He had felt that same way when Monique had told him how she felt about him. But in that case, he could not believe his luck. He was on top of the world then. That was not even two hours ago.

Now he lay against a wall clutching gel gauze and a white cloth. As he did so, he did not look towards the brawl. But he didn't need to look at it. He could hear it. Yet he still could not convince himself that it was occurring. Could this be the same people he had earlier been having such a great time with? He took his eyes off the can. He turned his gaze to the carnage next to him.

There was nothing but pure madness perpetrated by both sides. One of the gray shirts was lying on the ground, being pummeled by two Pink Tuxedos. Near them, someone in a Pink Tuxedo was being choked from behind by a gray shirt. Tomasz could not tell whether the person was conscious or not. He saw someone in a gray shirt swinging a metal rod around. Tomasz could not move. He did not even know what he should do.

Should he jump in and fight? Tomasz did not even know the first thing about actually fighting someone, what would he do? Should he run away? On some level, he felt some guilt at the thought of leaving the Pink Tuxedos behind. That is what they told him to do. But he thought they were exaggerating. He could never foresee such a chaotic scenario. Tomasz sat still, trying to make sense out of a senseless situation. He saw someone in a gray shirt fall on the ground. The man covered his head as he tried to protect himself. All around the man others would wail on him if they wore something different from him. It was Jacob.

Without thought Tomasz ran up to the edge of the crowd. He grabbed Jacob by the arm. As soon as he did Tomasz felt someone grab the back of his shirt. Tomasz looked back. The man grabbing his shirt raised his fist to strike Tomasz. As he readied for the fist to hit him, the man stumbled and fell.

"Get him out of here!" a voice shouted at Tomasz.

Tomasz recognized the voice as Oscar's. He did not hesitate to comply. Tomasz started dragging Jacob away. He could feel him struggling. It was hard for Tomasz to drag him as he struggled but he refused to let him go.

"Stop it! I need to get you out of here! I don't want you getting hurt!" Tomasz shouted through gritted teeth.

Tomasz wasn't sure if Jacob had understood him or even knew what was occurring. He continued trashing but it did not deter Tomasz. With whatever meek strength Tomasz could muster he kept pulling the injured man. He was a much bigger person than Tomasz both in height and weight. But Tomasz was able to get him away from the commotion and to an unoccupied offshoot of the alley.

There he propped Jacob up on a wall and collapsed in front of the young man. His heart was racing so fast that he thought it was about to burst from his chest.

Jacob finally looked up. Tomasz had a hard time recognizing the young man he had seen a couple of moments ago. His face was all cut up and bruised. He had a gash above his left eye that was spilling blood at an alarming rate. His right eye was completely swollen shut. His lip bled as a deep gash ran across the middle. His nose had a shape that was indistinguishable from a regular nose.

Tomasz got the cloth and tried to clean whatever wounds he could, then used the can of gel gauze on the cuts Jacob had on his face. Jacob did not move a muscle. He sat there, looking beyond Tomasz.

"Hey um, Jacob, are you with me?" Tomasz asked after a while.

He got no response, only a blank stare.

"Hey Jacob, I'm not a doctor or anything but I need to know if you are ok. Can you at least say something?" Tomasz put his hand on Jacob's shoulder, who still did not react.

"Can you at least nod if you are ok?" Tomasz started to get concerned for his friend. He had no idea where they were or where the nearest hospital was. Tomasz was sure that he did not have it in him to drag him much further.

Jacob looked at Tomasz and nodded. Gone was the cold look of pure rage. Now all Tomasz could see were deep pools of sorrow. Those eyes conveyed hopeless defeat. Tomasz remembered that look. It was the same one he had seen the last time he saw Jacob, at his older brother's funeral.

"Jacob, do you want me to get you to a hospital, call you an ambulance?"

"I'm ok, Tee," the young man replied in a soft sad voice. He now looked down at his hands.

Tee. It had been a long time since Tomasz had heard anybody call him that. A distant memory came storming into his mind. A young Jakey followed Tomasz, Rui, Andres, Felix, and Joshua on his bike as they darted through a thick forest on the outskirts of the city. Joshua, Jakey's older brother, was their de facto leader.

From the very first day Tomasz had met him, he had a way of making others follow him. Fearless, daring, and bold, he was always at the head of the group, even though Joshua was younger than Tomasz, Rui, Andres, and Felix. This meant everyone always struggled to keep up with him. Tomasz would be the only one who waited for Jakey as he struggled to keep up with the older boys. He would come huffing and puffing behind the others, but he was always smiling. Even though he always struggled to keep up, Jakey never complained about the other boys leaving him in the dust. He never once questioned the petty tasks the older boys asked him to carry out. He was happy to be part of the group. The memory caused Tomasz to reel with a clash of emotions. He felt a sudden lump in his throat and his vision started to get blurry. He used his sleeve to wipe his face and looked at the young man's hands.

Jacob's knuckles and the backs of his hands had cuts all over them. Tomasz grabbed the cloth and cleaned his hands the best he could. He applied the gel gauze without restraint over the entirety of Jacob's hands. He hoped that the topical anesthetic would help with whatever pain Jacob felt. Jacob never showed any discomfort if he felt it.

"Jacob, can you walk?" Tomasz asked the young man.

Jacob nodded. He put one hand on the ground and the other on the wall to support himself. He groaned as he got up and held onto his abdomen. Tomasz was going to reach out to hold him but Jacob extended his hand to let him know that he was fine.

"We should get out of here, Jacob," Tomasz said as he could still hear the sounds of the brawl. He had no idea what was going to happen but he did not want to be around to find out.

The young man took a deep breath. He tried his best to hold himself upright but struggled and fell back on the wall. Jacob steeled himself to try once more. Tomasz held his hand out. The young man looked at it and then at Tomasz. Jacob reached out and grabbed Tomasz's hand.

"Let's get out of here."

***

Tomasz and Jacob now sat across from each other. They had made it to a desolate park. There they found an empty metal table with four metal stools around it that floated two feet above the ground. They had been at the park for around five minutes. In that time all they had done was try to catch their breath. They must have seemed like quite the odd couple. Two bruised men, one in a bright Pink Tuxedo, the other in a muted gray outfit, sitting across from each other without saying a word. Tomasz knew what he wanted to ask. But he did not know how he would even start. He looked at Jacob. He could tell that whatever he was grappling with was not easy.

Jacob finally broke the silence. "I know you want to ask me, so go ahead. You're probably going to ask me what the hell is wrong with me, why did I get myself mixed up with those people, right?" The look of rage that Tomasz had seen earlier started to flare up once again inside his eyes.

"I, umm, I don't know what to say, Jacob. The last time I saw you, the last time I spoke to you, that was over two years ago," Tomasz replied in an offhand manner. He had tried to be more tactful about it but had failed.

"Well, you weren't the only one who didn't reach out after that. Rui, Andres, Felix, none of them ever bothered to reach out. So don't feel like you're special. You're another asshole who only cares about people when everything's great. I've had my fill of people like you, fucking hypocrites." Jacob's ire started to build up again and he got up from the stool.

"Are you being serious?" Tomasz raised his voice, his temper flaring up now.

Jacob stopped and looked at Tomasz.

"I saved your ass from a massive beating! You were getting your fucking lights kicked in while your asshole buddies left you for dead. I was the one who stepped in! And this is the thanks that I get?"

"Well, I remember it was one of your friends punching me in the face and throwing me to the ground. Do you want me to thank you for that too?" Jacob replied.

"Well, your friends had been going around smashing up businesses and ganging up on people, you think that's ok? Should we have let you keep doing that? You're lucky that you got away from that with only some bruises, you fucking asshole!" Tomasz shouted.

Jacob seethed with rage. He started to walk towards Tomasz. Tomasz thought for a second that he would have to fight Jacob. Tomasz's heart started pumping again and he balled up his fists. But as he got to the table Jacob stopped short, rage in his eyes.

"I don't have to explain myself to you. Thanks for getting me out. But that's it. You can go back to not giving a fuck about me," Jacob spoke and turned around.

Tomasz wanted to lash out again, say something hurtful, do something, anything to make Jacob hurt. He balled up his fist again.

He started to walk towards Jacob, he had no idea what he would do when he got to him. He knew that when he got to him he would have it figured out. Then Tomasz tripped over one of the floating stools. He caught himself before falling. He stared at the ground for a second composing himself. As he prepared to stand up, he breathed in deep and unclenched his fists. He stood up and looked at Jacob.

"Wait, Jacob!" Tomasz shouted.

Jacob didn't respond.

"Please, Jacob. Please, can I talk to you?" Tomasz pleaded.

Jacob stopped.

"Look, all I'm asking right now is for you to listen to me. After that, if you want to go on hating me, I'm ok with that. But please let me talk to you. Can I talk to my friend?"

Several seconds passed in silence. Then in an instant, Jacob turned around to look at Tomasz. Tomasz sat down as an overture. Jacob followed suit and sat down across from him. He crossed his arms waiting to hear what Tomasz had to say.

"Look, I know I haven't reached out to you in a while. There is no excuse for it. But I want you to know that I think about that time. I think about that week a lot, you know?" Tomasz paused struggling to think of what next to say.

"I still remember when I first heard about Joshua, about the accident. I couldn't believe it. It just seemed too unreal. I convinced myself that I had misunderstood something. That somehow this would all sort itself out. I thought that at some point I would wake up and it would have been some weird but terrible dream. It only sank in when I saw him lying there. When I saw him, when I realized I was wrong, I felt scared. An irrational fear took hold of me. I knew people died all the time, but when it happened, it somehow made sense. The first death I remember was my grandmother. At the time I was twelve and although it hurt, it wasn't a surprise. We all knew it was going to happen any day. But when Joshua died, … I just, I mean, young people like him? Like you and me? We don't just die like that. And if something like that did happen, it's always somewhere far away. It feels more like a statistical anomaly than something real. All I knew, what I felt, was that something like this wasn't supposed to happen. I mean, I still remember the last thing I talked to Joshua about. It was something to do with a new area opening up in Quixos. We were both excited to go. That's not a conversation you have with someone before they die. But then two weeks later, I was told about the accident. It didn't make sense. It wasn't fair."

Jacob stared at the table; arms still crossed.

Thomas continued "Then came the funeral. When I last saw you, Rui, Andres and Felix together. By that point we rarely got together, barely spoke to each other. After we all graduated, none of us put a lot of effort into staying in contact. But Joshua's passing settled it. I have always wondered how they felt about it all. I wonder if they felt the same as me. If they felt the same fear. But I never bothered to ask them about it. And then there was you… If I couldn't even reach out to them, what was I supposed to say to you? I didn't know. I was so scared about what had happened and so worried about finding the right thing to say that I let the moment pass. But I shouldn't have done that. I should have tried to be there for you, and I wasn't. Now I know, saying anything, doing anything, that would have been better than the nothing I gave you."

Tomasz paused but Jacob never moved his gaze.

"You're right Jacob, you don't have to explain yourself to me. I have no right to demand anything from you, but I want to tell you. I'm sorry. I can't even imagine what you have gone through…but this? What I'm seeing here? This isn't the same kid I remember who was always following us around with a smile, regardless of what we were up to."

Silence ensued. Tomasz could see that Jacob was deep in thought. He felt it best to let the young man think. Finally, Jacob spoke.

"Everybody told me they couldn't imagine what I was going through back then. And yeah, they were right." The anger on Jacob's tone was palpable.

"It wasn't just the fact that Joshua was gone. That in itself hurt more than anything I've ever experienced. But it was seeing what that did to Mom and Dad. That was too much for me. Those two were never the same after Joshua died. They tried their best to hide it, but there's only so much you can ignore when you walk into the kitchen at midnight and hear mom sobbing over old pictures. What the hell was I supposed to do then? What was I supposed to do when my father stopped being the person who would try to lighten the mood? When he instead became a shadow that would wander around the house, waiting for his turn to die? I couldn't stand being in that house anymore, Tee. I couldn't. I would make excuses for why I was going out. I would tell them I was going to see you guys, anything to get out of the house. That brought a bit of joy to their lives. I know they were struggling. I wanted to be there for them. But I couldn't even help myself. And no one was there for me."

Jacob spoke in a slow cadence. The last sentence cut deep at Tomasz. It hurt more than he thought it would have.

"It was around a year ago I first met one of those guys. I had gotten into a fight with someone in Crow District. It was some dumb thing that shouldn't have escalated into a fight. But I didn't care. I was looking for anyone to take my anger out on. I got my ass kicked but I didn't care. Afterward, some guy came to talk to me. He spoke to me as if he knew exactly what I was going through. He could tell I was angry. I only had rage. He asked me who it was. Who was it that I had lost? I told him to go fuck himself. He laughed. He said that if I didn't want to keep getting my ass kicked that I should at least go meet his group. Said there were a lot of guys like me, that I would fit right in. The place he told me to go to was some old vet's house. That was fucking weird but I had nothing better to do. I decided why not. At first, I didn't care for anything they said. They kept going on and on about the government and their rights. Kept going on about the Conflict. I don't remember much about that. But they made a real effort to look after you. It was nice to feel that I wasn't alone anymore. After spending enough time with them I felt like I belonged again. I felt like I had a purpose. They were there for me when no one else was, Tomasz. A lot of people might judge me. But none of them stood next to me when I was in my darkest moments. So why did I care what they had to say about me?"

Tomasz was quiet. He did not know how to respond. He could not pretend that he did not understand what Jacob had explained. He felt very conflicted about the Thread Barons he had only met earlier today. He knew that what Jacob was saying was true, there had been no one else there for him.

"Jacob, do you remember when we stumbled upon that old abandoned house, the one by Taipan Street?" Tomasz asked.

"Of course I do. It was your idea to go inside," Jacob replied.

"Yeah. I was a bit too much into adventure movies back then. It seemed like such a great opportunity. A great adventure for the five of us. I could tell that you and Rui didn't want to do it. But that didn't matter. Joshua didn't hesitate to jump at the opportunity to go in and that meant we were all going. Do you remember what happened when we went in?"

"Yeah, we saw fresh food, clothing, and all kinds of random stuff. The kind of things an abandoned house does not have. Felix was the one who figured out someone had been squatting there for a while. That was when Rui said we should leave. After we left there was this big argument. What was it about?" Jacob stared into the sky waiting for the answer to come to him.

"Oh yeah, that's right! Andres wanted to tell his dad about the house. With his dad being a cop, Andres knew that was illegal and how much of a problem it had become. All those Conflict vets started squatting around town and it was getting out of hand," Jacob added.

"But do you remember why it became an argument?" Tomasz asked.

Jacob hesitated. Tomasz could tell he remembered.

"Yeah, it was Joshua. He didn't see it that way. He asked why we should tell on some random person living in an abandoned house. If they're not hurting anyone, why should we do anything about it? Joshua told him that we would only be hurting whoever was there. He even insisted on coming back with some supplies for the people there." Jacob answered.

"That's how Joshua was. I don't understand where he got his sense of righteousness from, but man he could be a pain sometimes. We did come back with a lot of stuff. I hope it got used and didn't go to waste." Tomasz said.

Tomasz hoped that his message had the intended effect. He gave Jacob a second before he continued.

"Jacob, I'm sorry. I really am. I'm sorry that I wasn't there for you. I know that saying sorry is not enough. But I also know that you or Joshua would never hurt others. I don't know what you have gone through in these past two years. And I know there are a lot of things I could have done differently. But I am asking you, to please let me help you move away from this group. I don't know them too well, but I know this isn't you. I know this is a big ask from someone you haven't seen in a long time, but please give me a chance. I want this to be the first step in making this right. Because I hope that one day, you'll once again think of me as your friend," Tomasz finished.

Jacob rested his chin in his hand as he stared at the table. Although he was quiet for only several seconds it felt like hours had passed. He looked up and got up from the table. He turned around. Tomasz started feeling desperate, thinking of what else he could do to try to convince his friend not to walk away.

Jacob loosened his gray tie and let it fall to the ground. He then unbuttoned his shirt and dropped it. He took his boots off and left them on top of the pile of clothes. All he had on was a white shirt and the gray pants.

"Thanks, Tee. To be honest I never liked fighting. Mom will be happy to hear I ran into you. Don't be surprised if you see the gray shirts again soon. They don't like others standing up to them. Talk to you soon." Jacob spoke in a calm voice and walked away.

The desperate feeling that had started to take root inside Tomasz washed away. He knew the road ahead would not be easy. But he was glad to have the opportunity to take it.

Chapter 10: Missed Messages

Tomasz sat by himself for a while. His mind couldn't stop racing. All he could think about was what had occurred mere moments ago. He checked the time. 12:30 AM. Two and a half hours until the fateful moment. He felt crazy about the fact that he still contemplated participating in the bombing of a statue in Crow District. At best it would be a very extreme case of vandalism. At worst it would some might call it a terrorist attack.

His recent activities with the Thread Barons also gave him much pause. Going out in a gang, looking for another group to fight. Tomasz could not see himself doing that ever again. From what little he knew about the gray shirts he did not agree with what they were trying to do. But to go out in force to fight them?

He always thought that he would never shy away from a fight if need be, but when he found himself in that same situation that's not what happened. He was on the ground and getting beat before any real fighting began. It did not seem like an encouraging start to his street fighting career if that was ever going to be a thing. He sat down his head drooping low. He thought about what others would do in that situation. Others like Fred and Oscar.

Both of them helped Tomasz in the middle of the fight, and all he did was run away. He felt terrible about it. He wondered about Mickey. How would he have handled that situation? The same guy that was cozying up to his cat earlier. The same guy who had a lot of first-hand experience with violence from his time in the Conflict. The same man he had promised to contact whenever he found out what the Thread Barons were going to do with the delivered item.

"SHIT!" Tomasz shouted out loud. He had completely forgotten to call Mickey. Tomasz was so used to communicating via interface that the thought of using the separate device he had been given had not occurred to him.

He took out the small cell phone and looked at it. He flipped it open and the screen turned on. The message displayed on the screen notified him: "16 Missed Calls". Tomasz hurried as he dialed the number that had been trying to reach him. Tomasz felt awkward as he held the device as he had seen in the movies. It felt uncomfortable to hold a piece of cold plastic against his head. How people did this for hours on end he would never understand. After two rings the call connected. The voice on the other end sounded frantic.

"Tomasz? Is it you? Please tell me it's you. If you've abducted him, I swear I'll make you pay!" Mickey spoke at a frenetic speed. Tomasz did not think that he could get so worked up.

"Hey, yeah, it's me. Nobody abducted me. I'm sorry it took me so long to get back to you. I'm ok," Tomasz replied.

"Oh thank goodness." Mickey sighed. "I thought the worst had happened! I thought you were dead or something!"

"I'm sorry. Things have been crazy since I last saw you. I lost track of time and completely forgot to check this phone. It's been one thing after another here."

"Are you still in Crow District?" Mickey asked, surprised.

"Um, yeah I am," Tomasz replied.

"This late? Well never mind. I came down to Crow District because I started getting worried when I didn't hear from you. I've been going all over the place looking for you, or traces of your remains. Let me know where you are so I can meet with you," Mickey said. In the background, Tomasz could hear a lot of noise.

Tomasz looked around. He had no idea where he currently was.

"Well about that. I am in the middle of some random server park. I don't know how I got here or how I can guide you here. So I'm sorry about that."

"But you're ok?" Mickey started sounding worried again.

"Oh yeah, I erm, I just needed some open space, nothing to worry about."

"Ok, well here's what I'll do. I'll send my location to your interface, and we can see where to meet up. Does that sound good to you?" Mickey asked.

"Yeah, that should work."

Within five seconds Tomasz could see Mickey's location in his retinal display. He was walking down a street that was about ten blocks away from Tomasz. At the same time, Tomasz sent Mickey his coordinates.

"Oh wow, you are in the middle of nowhere," Mickey replied.

"It's a long story," Tomasz said. He didn't have the energy to explain anymore right now.

"Alright well, I'm not too far away from a spice lounge, it's called Padilla's, you ok to come out here?" Mickey asked.

Tomasz looked up in his interface the location.

"Alright got it, on my way."

With that, Tomasz was once again on his own going through the sprawling streets of Crow District. Despite his misgivings about the place it seemed like he could not leave it.

***

Tomasz made it to Padilla's Spice Lounge as fast as he could. Before going in, he looked at himself in a display. He still had some blood on his face, and there were several cuts over his face. He did his best to clean himself up. Once done he approached the door to the lounge. The holographic bouncer gave Tomasz a thorough once-over but relented and opened the door for him.

Inside the establishment, the air was thick with smoke from the different spices burning. This made it hard for Tomasz to see. The aromas all mixed in to make Tomasz feel as if he were in a sort of wood-themed perfume parlor. His interface pointed out Mickey's direction, somewhere to the right inside the lounge. After walking several steps Tomasz saw a short man waving enthusiastically over to him. Mickey was glad to see him and showed him the spot he had reserved for them. Instead of the bathrobe he'd worn earlier Mickey was dressed as if he had gone out for exercise.

He had long pants and a tight-fitting shimmering shirt that accentuated his sculpted physique. In his hand, Mickey held a stem from a waterpipe and he was blowing smoke as Tomasz approached him. It seemed that Mickey was quite familiar with this place. Once Tomasz got up close to him, Mickey's face turned from one of relief to one of worry and surprise.

"Brother? What the hell happened?" Mickey asked as Tomasz sat down in front of him.

"Well for starters you gave me a bomb and didn't tell me anything about it. A bomb which I carried across the entire city unaware of the fact that I could have blown up at any second!" Tomasz snapped.

Mickey was quiet for a second.

"Well when you put it that way, it does kind of make me sound like a low-mint guy, right?" Mickey replied in a soft tone. He offered Tomasz one of the stems from the pipe but Tomasz was not feeling it.

"Well, how else would you put it?" Tomasz replied as he waved his hands in the air.

"Well, for starters I would say that I gave you a rigorously tested device. So no worries that it would blow up. And it is only supposed to work when it should! Before I gave it to you I took it out to a forest on the outskirts of the city. There I put it through various tests to see if it would blow up and not a one of them made it go off! See? I'm all about safety. Safety is my number one priority! Do you think I would hand you something that would blow up at the slightest touch? I mean I am sorry you think I am a low-mint guy, which you have every right to do brother, but I don't want you thinking that I am not amazing at my craft!" Mickey exclaimed a bit too loud for Tomasz's taste. He proceeded to inhale some more of the smoke from the sweet-smelling spice.

"Besides what else would someone pay you ten thousand sweet monies to transport across a city? Cookies?" Mickey asked while he laughed at his joke.

"Nom! Nom! Nom!" Mickey added as he mimicked eating cookies. This made him laugh even more.

Tomasz could only stare in response to Mickey's nonchalant attitude. Mickey realized Tomasz was not enjoying his jokes as much as he was.

"Look, I'm sorry that I lied to you man, I am. Any other time I would have done this myself. But given that group's history of questionable behavior and my background, any direct tie between the two of us would raise suspicion. They suggested a third party and I felt bad about having to lie, but how else am I supposed to bring it up? 'Hey guy I met with the cool fashion sense; would you mind carrying a bomb across the city for me?'" Mickey asked as Tomasz still sat quietly.

"Look, when I say I took this thing out for testing, I mean it. I did everything I could short of actually activating the thing to see if it would go off. I would have never given anyone this if I thought there was any danger to them. I understand if you are angry at me, but I mean it when I say that I am glad to see that you are ok. And hey you got paid ten thousand dollarinos! Not a bad deal for picking up a heavy battery and just dropping it off somewhere else in the city, right?" Mickey once again tried his best to smooth over tensions with Tomasz.

Tomasz threw his hands up in the air in a gesture of defeat.

"You know what? Out of all the things that have happened today, transporting a bomb across the city is not even the craziest or the worst, so I'm not going to keep arguing over it. You're right, I did get paid for it and it's done," Tomasz replied as he relented.

"Well, I assume part of that involves how you got those nifty nicks on that face of yours?" Mickey asked with a mix of concern and curiosity.

"Yeah, you're not wrong about that," Tomasz said. Mickey perked up as if waiting for Tomasz to finally get on with his story.

"Well it's a long story, you sure you want to hear it?" Tomasz asked him.

"Oh, I would say this is one that I want to hear. I can tell a high-mint person such as yourself must have some pretty good stories to share!" Mickey replied with a smile.

Tomasz told Mickey what had occurred since he last saw him. From the moment he left his apartment, his meeting the Thread Barons, his encounter with his old friend, Jacob, and their ensuing conversation. Throughout the entire time that Tomasz spoke, Mickey was completely silent. He would only move to inhale from the pipe, but his gaze never wavered.

"And well now I'm here," Tomasz grumbled as he gestured around him.

Mickey shook his head as if waking up from a stupor. "Wow."

The next second a robotic arm dropped a glass in front of Tomasz and one in front of Mickey. Both glasses were filled with drinks. Tomasz picked up his glass and took a sip. It was a Cahuilla Sour.

"You earned this," Mickey said.

Tomasz drank the rest in one quick swig. Mickey did not hesitate to get him another one.

"First off, cheers to you and your new girl!" Mickey raised his glass and Tomasz obliged him. It was still hard for him to believe that Monique felt the same way about him. But after all that had gone on since the last time he saw her, it was a bit hard to focus on that right now.

"But their target is the Madame Sonali statue huh? In about umm..." Mickey checked the time. "Two hours?"

"Yup."

"Well, I don't want to miss that!" Mickey replied with giddy enthusiasm.

"You're going to go see that?" Tomasz asked in disbelief.

"Well yeah! I love seeing stuff blow up! And for such a massive ugly statue? With my explosives? That's like the gift that keeps on giving! If I had known that was their intended target this whole time, I probably would have done it for free!" Tomasz had yet to see Mickey so happy. The idea that his explosives were being used to demolish that statue filled him with a childlike glee.

"How about you?" Mickey asked. "Are you going to be there for it?"

Tomasz fell quiet.

"Hey, you've had a long day, man. It's completely normal for you to feel, well, any way you feel right now, man. If you feel angry, sad, happy, confused, whatever it is, you are completely justified in calling it a day."

Tomasz appreciated the comment. But he thought Mickey was being nice for the sake of it. Mickey could tell.

"I'm serious, man. I have gone through some crazy stuff in my time, but what you went through, well that is up there." Mickey laughed. Tomasz couldn't help but smile with him.

Tomasz felt a certain kind of comfort in speaking to Mickey. His easygoing personality was disarming, and it seemed like there was no experience too insane that he would not be able to relate to.

"Well, I find that to be high praise. Because according to Oscar and Fred, you are some ultra-mint combat hero," Tomasz added.

"Really? They told you about that, huh? Mickey the hero! That will never stop sounding silly to me. I think their heart is in the right place but they're blowing things out of proportion. I did my job that was it," Mickey said in a casual tone.

"But didn't you get a medal or something? Like an honor medal?" Tomasz asked.

Mickey gave him a serious look and burst out laughing.

"No, I did not get an honor medal or a medal of honor. It was a service cross, which was nice. But honestly, it's overblown. I was doing what I went there to do. Nothing more to it. It just so happened that I was best positioned to help us get out of a debacle our platoon leader got us into. It was not his fault, he was following the route mapped out for us. But I'm sure if Oscar or Fred or any of the other guys in the platoon were in the same position they would have done the same." Mickey took a quick swig from his drink.

"That I guarantee," Mickey added with such emphasis that Tomasz was taken aback.

It seemed as if there was something else that underpinned Mickey's feelings on the matter. Tomasz himself was not sure he knew what that was. He could only think back to his encounter earlier in the night. He felt like a coward, thinking about how he was helpless and needed to get dragged out from the pile of people. How after that he froze up and wasn't able to help the other Thread Barons and just ran away.

"How were you not scared?" Tomasz blurted without a thought.

"Scared? Hmm." Mickey paused.

"Well you see, sometimes shit happens so fast, you don't have time to shit yourself. Fear can be something that builds up in anticipation. You think about some random scenario that has almost no chance of happening, but you tell yourself that it will happen. And that when it does everything will go wrong. But when you are going to a designated location and then you're surrounded on three sides and you have no idea what you walked into, you have one of two choices. You can follow your training or freeze. You really don't know how you are going to behave until you're in that situation. I mean when it all happened I hesitated for a second. But I knew that I had to do something, so I did my best to make sure I and the other guys came out of it alive. Once I went into action that was it, just kept at it until it was done. But once it was done, well that was a different story. After that, I thought about all the different ways I could have died. That bullet that shattered the tree stump several inches from my face. The round that got stuck in my upper back plate that would have cut through my spine with no effort. Those explosives that went off on a mound half a minute after I had gone over that same spot. So many things that could have gone any other way and I would have been some red mist on top of someone else. Even though that's all in the past it still scares me sometimes. "

Tomasz did not know what to say, but he couldn't help his boiling insecurity. The fact that he had been unable to react was not something that sat well with him.

"Did anyone who completely froze, did you ever see anyone who did that ever overcome it?" Tomasz looked Mickey straight in the eyes.

Mickey stared at him for a second and then started nodding as if realizing something.

"I see, this is because of the exchange of the fisticuffs that you went through. Is that where this is coming from?"

Tomasz nodded.

"Brother, you are being too harsh on yourself. If someone came up to me right now and knocked me to the ground I am going to be disoriented too. Especially if I have a mob of people fighting on top of me right after. If what you expected to do was to get up and single-handedly take every one of them fuckheads out with some nice hand-to-hand combat then I have news for you. The only one who can do that is Mister Jeremiah Stonefist from the amazing film series 'Blood Merchant'," Mickey finished.

"Besides man, let me tell you something, and of course, this is Mickey's opinion alright. But are you ready to hear my opinion?"

Tomasz looked at Mickey, curious about what the man was about to say.

"Going up to someone and beating them up, any fuckhead can do that, that's not bravery. But putting yourself in danger to try to help your friend? Brother, in Mickey's opinion, that is some hero shit right there. If there was a Mickey Medal of High Mint Heroes that I could award, you would get it."

Tomasz smiled at Mickey's response.

"Well, now I feel silly," Tomasz replied.

"See! Now you know how I feel!" Mickey added with glee and started laughing once again, he could never get enough of his cleverness it seemed.

"But the VOUS huh? Those gray shirts are some very low-mint people in my opinion," Mickey said, no longer brandishing his usual amicable smile.

"So you know about them too?" Tomasz asked.

"It's hard not to if you were in the Conflict. When I first heard about this Colonel Arnold, I thought it was a joke. Nobody was happy with the shakeout of the treaty but I didn't think anyone wanted to rehash any of that shit. It was in the past, it was done. The world was ready to move past that. Then this guy comes out and starts out opening a lot of wounds that people were not ready to revisit, not then and perhaps never. Talks about how contemptible the peace deal we made was. How we were so close to victory, one last offensive and we would have finished this on our terms. But how many more people would have died during this offensive? And for what? It was so fucking stupid that I ignored it, and I thought others would too. But then I saw other Conflict veterans agree with that shit. It just blew my mind. I mean did they want to start the killing again? Did they want to overthrow the government? Shouldn't they be happy that the war was over and that we didn't have to go on with senseless killings? Did they want something out of it that made it seem as if that whole conflict wasn't for nothing? " Mickey asked Tomasz as if pleading for an answer.

"I- I really…" Tomasz started but he was at a loss for words. "I'm sorry." Was all Tomasz could think to say.

"Sorry? Nah man you don't have to be. You didn't have anything to do with this. This here is Mickey and his endless quest for the meaning of life. You don't have to worry about what kind of inane thoughts come into my head." Mickey laughed again, but Tomasz could tell he forced it.

"I see. I mean I can't understand how you feel, but hey at least you're here. That must count for something right?" Tomasz said.

Mickey looked at Tomasz. He was quiet for a second.

"At least I am here," Mickey repeated the words back to Tomasz. It was as if he did not understand them the first time he heard them.

"Brother, you go above and beyond." Mickey laughed.

"You are correct once again. There were so many instances where I thought I was not going to make it out alive. But I did and I'm glad I'm here to say that. And when I think about all those people who don't know what to make about the Conflict all I can think is, I'm just happy there's no more killing. Some say the cost to achieve that was too high. But to me, not having to see stories about entire cities vanishing, and millions dying regularly, well, I say all that stopping was priceless. " Mickey said.

Mickey continued, "But then you have those grayshirts that disagree. I've talked to a couple that have joined them, some that used to be good friends of mine. At some point, they turned into people I could not recognize anymore. Everything with them turned into a real black-and-white world. It was either you were in their group or you were not. Constantly bringing up old battle wounds, stuff that I'd left in the past, just to try to rile me up. And it was so easy to fall into that other group, the ones against them. I tried talking to them, you know, doing the tough love thing. Telling them that they got their heads filled with stupid shit and that they were being real pricks to everyone. But it didn't work. They started seeing me as the other. As one of the many traitors. Me. The person they had known for years. The person who was with them in our darkest times. The one who cried with them when we lost Moore. I was a traitor compared to a group of people they had met only months earlier. That pissed me off. I told them to go fuck off. They were dead to me. It was not my proudest moment, and while it felt good at the moment it accomplished nothing. Haven't talked to them since." Mickey paused.

"What you did was the right thing. If you want to get someone out of that mentality you can't beat it out of them, you have to pull them back a bit at a time. Like someone deep in the ocean, you can't just drag them out. You have to slowly bring them up. But that's the hard part. Now you have to make sure you follow up with him and pull him out of that crap. Make sure he doesn't keep sinking. Because if he gets down too deep there is no way you'll be able to get him out. But if you're there for him, he has a chance of finding his way back."

Mickey's candor brought Tomasz a level of comfort he had not felt since he had first seen Jacob earlier. It was by no means a guarantee that Tomasz would succeed. But the thought that he could reconnect with his friend again, that he could pull him back from such a path gave him hope.

Tomasz and Mickey were both quiet and sipped on their drinks while the swirling smoke in the room ebbed and flowed around them. They both were taking in the entire environment around them. The dim lighting. The holographs above them that would create ephemeral figures that would show up on the ceiling displaying all sorts of odd patterns and symbols. The hazy air. The low pulsating music and the chatter of conversation could be heard all around the room. For the first time since they both sat they were content to experience the moment.

"So what will you do now?" Mickey asked after several minutes of silence.

"Well, I will reach out to him and try to make sure that he does not go back to those VOUS people. I know I got a lot of work to do on that front, but I'll do my best," Tomasz said.

"Oh no, I mean what are you going to do right now!" Mickey clarified as he pointed to the display on the wall.

It read 1:32 AM. Less than ninety minutes until the group would head to Yurok Park.

"I mean do you even think they'll be back out there?" Tomasz asked Mickey.

"Oh yeah, they're not going to miss it. Not because they got tangled up with some lowlifes out in the city. Trust me, these guys first reached out to me about this package months ago. They've been working on this for a while and they're not going to let this opportunity pass," Mickey stated with certainty.

The display now read 1:33 AM. Tomasz felt a knot in his stomach. It would be so easy for him to get up and say his goodbyes. Then he would go back to his apartment ten thousand dollars richer and wake up tomorrow as if none of this had happened.

He could try to ignore the whole delivering a bomb across a city, and loving the time he spent with the Thread Barons, both by himself and with Monique. During that time, he felt not like an individual but as part of something bigger. He felt as if he had a place. But if that was all then he wouldn't feel so conflicted right now. There was also the violence with the gray shirts. That too was part of what had happened tonight. It was not a part that he could stomach.

"Hey man, I don't want to pressure you into doing something you'll regret, ok?" Mickey said, bringing Tomasz out of his thoughts. Mickey once again was smoking from the pipe.

"You've had a hell of a day already and nobody would expect any more of you. So if you are ready to call it a day no one would hold it against you," Mickey added.

"Yeah, I guess you're right," Tomasz replied with a half-smile.

He once again looked at the clock. 1:35 AM. Tomasz did not know where he was going to go now, but he felt that he knew what he had to do.

"It has been a long day. Thanks for the drink, Mickey, and I hope to see you again," Tomasz said as Mickey blew out a thick cloud of smoke.

"Tomasz, brother, we need to hang out again! I don't even need to say this, but keep being high mint!" Mickey added with a smile.

Tomasz walked through the hazy smoke, out of the establishment, and into the dark of the night. As he stepped outside he knew the truth. He had made up his mind. He knew that his association with the Thread Barons was over as of that moment.

Chapter 11: The Parasocial Network

Tomasz wandered with no set destination through Crow District. The streets were so well-lit that it was hard to believe that it was the dead of night. Yet these same streets that earlier in the day bustled with unending waves of people were now silent and empty. As he made his way to the train station a familiar sensation hit him. The pang of hunger. He had not eaten since before the show. That was over five hours ago and he was now famished. Upon scanning the nearby places still serving food at this hour Tomasz saw one with a familiar name: Lokos Tacos.

With no other choice, he made his way there. Once inside the restaurant, his interface lit up with the menu. He got the first item on it. He looked around and did not see a single person. He was glad there were no human servers on staff at this hour. He knew how much attention he would bring covered in cuts and bruises and a bright Pink Tuxedo.

As he sat down to wait for his food, he brought up his visual interface. He was looking for any type of entertainment to distract him from everything that he had gone through. Inside the interface, he entered a virtual plaza.

It served as a hub for a variety of entertainment options he could access. As he moved around in the interface he could see various things on display. Some rerun shows. Some movies. A video game tournament was occurring. A live wrestling match occurring in some Central Asian country. He skimmed through the various options but nothing caught his eye. He started scrolling through what was being streamed live.

One of the only things on was a conversation between a man and a woman sitting across a bonfire from each other. There was an empty spot reserved next to them. Behind them, in the distance, Tomasz could see tall mountains dotting the landscape in the night. Tomasz decided to enter the room.

When Tomasz entered, he saw his name announced as a new addition to a long-running chat box that hung suspended in the air between the two people.

"Hey, Gunther Roadies, it seems a new member has joined the conversation! Let's all give Tomasz a nice warm welcome!" The woman announced as Tomasz found himself seated between the two people.

Tomasz saw the chat box in front of him flood with hundreds of messages along the lines of "Welcome to the clan!" or "Welcome to the Gunther Roadies". The sudden rash of welcome messages that Tomasz received was confusing to him.

He didn't even know what kind of content these two people produced. Normally when he entered a live stream he did so only as an observer. He never had a desire to be a part of their conversation. But now that he had been introduced, he felt as if it would be too awkward to leave.

"So, Tomasz, what brings you into our family get-together today?" the man asked with a smile.

"Peter, we haven't even introduced ourselves and you are already asking our guest questions!" the woman chastised the man, who Tomasz assumed was Peter.

"Oh goodness gracious Molly, you are right! Where are my manners? Well, my apologies there Tomasz, but my name is Peter Gunther and this is my sister Molly Gunther. We run this channel here called Gunther's Adventures." Peter stopped as Molly waved at Tomasz.

"We go to different parts of the US and talk with our friends out across the country about what crazy things we've seen. Right now we are visiting Utah and have been hiking around the Salt Lake area. We were telling the Roadies about how beautiful this state is. And not only virtually but showing them as well as we've met with some of the Gunther Roadies here. Oh, that's what we call our friends out in the different states that meet up with us. Do you think I missed anything, sis?" Peter turned to Molly.

"Well, we don't only go travel and show off. We do other things that are even more important, Peter. While we hike we try to bring up different topics of interest to our Roadies. And also talk about any struggles that any of us might be having and try to bring our community together to help each other. We also meet with interesting people who might have awesome things to share with our Roadies. Last week we met with the most intriguing man. He is a doctor of Nothing! Can you believe that? His name is Dr. Nullo, and he had more to say about nothing than anyone I have met before! I know it sounds crazy, but I am serious, that was his specialty and it was fascinating." Molly added while Peter nodded in the background. As weird as it sounded Tomasz did agree. Listening to Dr. Nullo talk about nothing was indeed fascinating.

"Thanks, Molly! But yup, that's about right. Right now we are hiking near Salt Lake. This trail is the feared Bear One Hundred Ultra. It's a pretty long hike so we are taking breaks to talk to our Roadies to get refreshed and ready for whatever we have to face tomorrow. We are excited to show you all what we accomplish and show you in the meantime that you're able to do it as well!" Peter finished with an enthusiasm that did not feel forced at all.

There was a short silence afterward. Tomasz was not sure if they expected him to say something.

"Oh ok," Tomasz responded.

He saw his words appear in the text box and the faces of Molly and Peter as they read his response. He felt awkward and tried to think of something else to say.

"Well, what part of the country are you coming to us from Tomasz? What is going on in your little corner of the world?" Peter asked enthusiastically, trying to continue the conversation.

"Oh me ok, yeah no problem. I am, umm, I am in Cahuilla City. In Crow District, specifically. If you don't know much about Cahuilla that's one of the two districts. But umm, well right now, I am hungry, so I am waiting to get a loaded burrito. It is very late and there are not a lot of other open places. I saw your channel in the interface and decided to hop in. Yup, and my name is Tomasz. Oh right, you already knew that."

Both Molly and Peter read what Tomasz had to say. It took a while for them to respond. Every fiber of Tomasz's being was telling him to leave this livestream but he could not bring himself to do so.

"Great! Thanks for the intro, Tomasz! I hope you enjoy your loaded burrito! That sounds like something that we'd love to have up here, right Peter?" Molly chirped.

"Oh, yeah, right! And of course, the best thing is that we have a new guest join our group! Right, Roadies?" Peter added.

Once again the chat box populated with hundreds of messages saying stuff like "Great to meet you Tomasz", "Loaded burritos are my favorite!", "Crow District is awesome!", "Glad to have another Roadie!", "My name is Thomas, but I like the way yours is spelled!" on and on.

"Thanks," Tomasz replied.

"Alright Roadies, as we were telling you earlier, we were having some issues around the feared fork in our hike. But we came prepared and Peter brought out—can you guess what it was?" Molly asked with a sly smirk.

"The beans of swiftness?" a user wrote.

"Nope," Molly replied.

"The nectar of the gods?" another comment.

"Nope," Peter replied.

"The high-quality H-two-Oh?"

"Not that either!" Molly replied.

"The dried fruits from THE garden?"

"Getting closer." Molly laughed.

"The mixing of the trails!" Hundreds of messages started pouring in.

At this time a robotic arm dropped from the ceiling bringing Tomasz his food. At least he could eat now as the bizarre stream unfolded.

"Ding ding ding, we have winners!" Molly laughed again.

Right on cue, Peter brought out a bag filled with various nuts, dried fruits, and small candies. The commenters went wild. "The mixing of the trails!", "All hail the mighty mix of trails!", "I had some earlier today and it was delicious!"

Tomasz was amused at how enthusiastic these viewers seemed to be about a bag of trail mix.

Peter took out a handful and stuffed it in his mouth. As he chewed on it, Molly spoke in cadence "Crun-Chy! Mun-Chy!" Without even missing a beat the comments all repeated the same "Crunchy Munchy!" in sync with Molly as Peter ate the trail mix.

"It was a hard one today, Roadies. The weather was much warmer than we were expecting. We set out to do around twelve miles, but halfway through we weren't sure if we were going to get eight! Peter and I sat down and decided to take a break. At first, we thought about cutting it short. But we decided that if we took a long break then we would be able to muster our strength to get to twelve miles. After that, it wasn't too hard until we got to mile ten. The terrain started to get steep and we were starting to feel the burn on our legs, but we knew what was at stake," Molly recounted in a determined tone.

"One week for Gui." The comments popped into view at lightning speed.

"That's right, we knew that to raise awareness for treatment for Roadie Gui we need to finish this in one week. If he is struggling hard with his illness, then how can we complain about our issues? We looked deep inside us, brought out the mixing of the trails!" Peter said as he held up the bag.

"Mix of the trails!", "For Gui!", "Gui Roadster!", "We're here with you Gui!", the messages read.

Despite his empty stomach, Tomasz was having a hard time focusing on his food instead of the stream.

"That's right guys! You all know that we are not doing this for ourselves! Me, Peter, all of us, we are doing this for Gui, one of our original Roadsters! If you have yet to reach out to the family to try to collect funds for Gui's treatment, please do so now! Remember all donations need to go to Gui's page at funds for medical care dot com! That is under Guilhermo Abreu's funding page! Let them know the amazing story of our Roadster Gui, who's been with us now for over three years! He's been our rock since we began this journey and we couldn't have gotten here without him!" Molly added.

A single message came in after that.

"Thanks, guys! You and the rest of the Roadsters mean everything to me. It has not been easy these last four months after hearing about my diagnosis. But having your support has made all the difference. I want to let you guys know how much you mean to me and that I know I'll get through this because I have you guys. For now, I am enjoying some high-quality H-two-Oh!" The message was sent by Gui.

More and more messages came into the chat room stating their support for Gui. Tomasz read the messages as he nibbled on his food, skeptical about what he was seeing. It was not that it confused him. He understood what was occurring. It's just that he was not sure how authentic it all was. The exaggerated expressions seemed too much, but at the same time, it seemed as if they all meant what they were saying.

"So after today, we have four more days to go. In those days we need to cover around fifty-five more miles. We've already covered the hollows that we dreaded, but we still have a lot more to go through. It will not be easy!" Peter added with a big smile.

"Yeah, I think we will need a big break after this, what do you guys think?" Molly asked as she stared in the direction Tomasz sat in.

The chat box was filled with a random assortment of locations. One kept popping up "Omaha!", "Yeah try Omaha, I hear they like you guys there!", "Why not Omaha again? What could go wrong?", "I hear Omaha is lovely this time of year."

"You guys never change!" Peter replied, laughing.

"I thought our Roadies loved us? Last time we went there we almost got run over four separate times! How is that even possible with all the technology we have? You're more likely to get hit by lightning five times in your life than get run over four times in your life! And this all happened in a week! What did we do to Omaha?" Molly said as she laughed.

"Hahaha!", "Omaha does not like roadies!", "We apologize on behalf of Omaha!", "Kidding! Just kidding!", "2Funny." Although he found it completely bizarre, Tomasz found himself enjoying the back-and-forth banter between the siblings and their online group.

"How about Cahuilla?" Peter suggested.

"Oh yeah, we can ask our new friend Tomasz about it!" Molly replied.

There was a brief silence as Tomasz wondered who they were talking about. While waiting for a reply, he decided to grab a bite of his burrito. It was at the moment when his mouth was full that he came upon a realization: He was the new friend from Cahuilla named Tomasz. He had forgotten that he was not only a viewer but also a possible participant.

"Oh, that's me! I'm sorry I completely forgot for a second what you guys were talking about," Tomasz said in between bites. His muffled words were for the most part misunderstood by whatever voice-to-text model was being used by the program. All that could be read was

"Oh [unintelligible]. Sorry [unintelligible] forgot [unintelligible]."

The siblings laughed as the text populated.

"Just [unintelligible] second"

Tomasz finally finished swallowing his food and cleared his throat.

"Sorry guys, I had a bite of my burrito in my mouth when you mentioned me and I was caught a little off guard."

"Oh, that reminds me of that time we tried that place in San Antonio. It was the worst place for us to do a stream when we constantly had food in our mouths! Was it Insane Burritos?" Molly replied.

"Lokos Tacos!" the response was resounding.

"Damn, I'm at Lokos Tacos right now," Tomasz replied without a thought.

Upon seeing his response the chat box lit up with a litany of messages.

"Roadie!", "Those are the best burritos!", "Loaded loko tacos are the best!", "The best place to have a mouthful is at Lokos Tacos!", "You better be careful with those takos there! They will take your breath away!"

Tomasz could not help but laugh at the inanity of the situation. The thought of bonding with strangers on the internet over a well-known Tex-Mex chain brought him unexpected comfort.

"Well alright, now that I am done eating I can shed some light on Cahuilla. One thing I will say is that as a lifelong resident of Cahuilla, I still find things that I have never seen before. Most people know of Cahuilla due to its two very different districts, Fox and Crow. Even though they are about the same size, Crow district has around ten million residents whereas Fox only has two million. I have lived in Fox District my entire life and have rarely gone into Crow District. Of course, Fox always gets all the attention. It is home to the world-famous Zhao Daiyu art district and the lithography corridor which is known for its high-tech manufacturing facilities. Despite that, I would say that Crow has as much to offer as Fox. In my time today in Crow I have discovered many amazing things here. If you guys have never come to Cahuilla I think you would enjoy it very much. And I would tell you to explore both Fox and Crow districts, not only Fox."

Tomasz saw as Molly and Peter read his reply. They seemed very enthusiastic as the text filled up the screen. The first one to speak up was Peter.

"So what's the social scene down there? Molly and I love hanging out with big crowds and talking to as many locals as we can. Do you happen to know where we could go and meet lots of people?"

"Oh yeah, actually earlier today I ran across this one group that I'm sure you'd love to meet. They love meeting new people and having a great time. Even if they just met you they'll treat you like one of them. I mean I had the time of my life with them. I'm sure if you came by you would really—" Tomasz stopped himself.

It was almost as if he had forgotten who he was talking about, the Thread Barons. These were the same people he had decided to cut ties with. The same people he knew he could no longer see himself even in the same room with.

"Are you ok, did we lose you Tomasz?" Molly asked, half concerned.

"No sorry, I lost my train of thought. Like I was saying I recommend Cahuilla. I think you guys would have a great time if you came here."

Molly and Peter seemed content with Tomasz's reply. Maybe they understood there was something there that Tomasz did not want to delve into. But they were not the only voices in the room.

"What about the group you were talking about?", "Yeah those guys! You were just talking about some group!", "Maybe the loaded burrito had something more in it than what he ordered?" Tomasz felt a knot in his stomach as he read the chat messages. There was what Tomasz wanted to say and then there was how Tomasz felt.

"Yeah no sorry, I was thinking about some childhood friends and got it mixed up with this group I saw a musical today. Sorry, it's been such a long day that I can't even keep my head on straight. But anyway you should still come to Cahuilla and explore both districts. I know you'd love it!" Tomasz replied trying his best to salvage the situation.

"That sounds great, Tomasz! We always love meeting Roadies! I think we found ourselves the next place we want to visit once we are done here!" Molly said as both she and Peter smiled.

"The next adventure spot is now determined!" Peter crowed.

"Adventure Time!" The messages flooded in.

Tomasz was glad that with Peter and Molly leading the conversation the rest of the group focused on whatever topic they moved on to.

Tomasz found he had lost his appetite. He decided it was time to go.

"Alright guys thanks so much for um, being so friendly! If you do come by Cahuilla let me know! I'd love to show you around!" Tomasz said.

He did mean it. The sibling duo seemed nice enough.

"Say bye to our friend!" Molly replied.

As Tomasz got ready to leave he saw the messages on the chat box popping into view. "Goodbye, Roadie!", "Welcome to the family!",

"Roadies forever!", "Is anyone else confused about his story from earlier? Like it didn't make much sense right?"

He was out of his interface now.

Tomasz looked at the time: 2:03 AM. Less than an hour now. The thought crept into his mind, but he brushed it aside. He had other things to focus on. He was going to head to the station and head home.

But out of pure curiosity, he looked on the map to see where Yurok Park was located. It was only a ten-minute walk away. Alright, good to know. Now he would be getting ready to go home.

The determination he had felt less than an hour ago about forgetting about the Thread Barons had started to wane. Tomasz was going to go back home. But first, he would take a nice stroll in the night.

Chapter 12: Nothing Redux

Tomasz meandered as he made his way to the station. In no particular rush he found an empty bench that faced the Cahuilla River and sat down. Across from it, he could see Fox district. At this time, in the middle of the night, all that could be seen was the great din of lights from the high rises. All so elegantly crafted, all so exquisitely planned. Their beautiful light reflected in the still waters of the river, creating a unique and mesmerizing sight.

As he sat he buried his head in his hands. He needed to focus. To determine what exactly he ought to do. Deep in his thoughts, he went. He remembered his first encounter with the Thread Barons. The first time he heard from them was from the two cops who were questioning him, and from what the cops said they did not sound trustworthy. So when Tomasz finally met the Thread Barons he could not help but be wary of them. But after they had bonded over their shared attire, the musical, the night at the bar with Monique, he not only felt as if he had found a group that accepted him, but who was happy to see him flourish.

And it extended beyond him to include Monique. This was a feeling that he was not even aware he yearned for. If things had ended at that point then Tomasz would have no cause for pause. He would be more than happy to join the Thread Barons to go blow up a statue, regardless of how questionable that might be. But it did not.

The violent encounter with the gray shirts was still too raw in Tomasz's mind. He was not a person accustomed to violence. The sight of violence in movies made Tomasz feel queasy most of the time. So the idea of going to such a group again was hard for him to grapple with. But then again, the gray shirts were going around being assholes by ganging up on people and causing trouble wherever they went. So weren't the Thread Barons justified in trying to stop them? Would he be wrong if he were to join them?

Tomasz tried to reconcile his feelings, but something interrupted him. He felt something graze his hand and felt it get wet. He raised his head and within seconds saw the culprit, but he was too slow to stop what happened next. Before he could react a large Great Dane licked Tomasz from his chin to his forehead. His face was now completely covered in slobber.

"Hey, stop that, Ginger! How many times have I told you that you can't lick whoever you want?" a man's voice called out to the dog while Tomasz used some of the towels given to him by Fred to clean his face.

"Are you all right there young man?" the voice called out to Tomasz as he got the last of the slobber off his face.

"Hey, weren't you at my lecture earlier today?" the man asked Tomasz. Tomasz focused on the man and recognized him almost in an instant. It was Professor Gerald Nullo. Although it had only been several hours since Tomasz had seen him, he felt like it might as well have been weeks or months.

"By the way, sweet Pink Tuxedo you got going on there, I am thinking I might have to incorporate that into my wardrobe in the future," Professor Nullo said.

"Oh, thanks! Yeah, I was at your lecture earlier. I, umm, thought it was very entertaining!" Tomasz replied.

"Hey kid, let me ask you something?" said Professor Nullo.

"What?"

"You're not thinking of becoming an actor, are you?"

"Umm, no, wasn't planning on it?" Tomasz replied, confused.

"Oh ok good, because I don't think anyone would believe what you said." Professor Nullo laughed as he sat down next to Tomasz.

"I'm sorry, I didn't mean anything by it, Professor Nullo." Tomasz started feeling flustered about having insulted such a respected scholar.

"Oh don't worry, kid. I'm not mad, I'm teasing. By the way, Professor Gerald Nullo, Doctor of Nothing, and regular old Jerry walking his dog at two in the morning might as well be two different people. I don't mind if my talk isn't exactly for you. Besides, the entire time I was talking, I only saw you looking over at a girl there. I hope you asked her out or something."

"Oh well, it turns out she asked me out." Tomasz grinned as he replied.

"Really? Well good for you! I bet it was the Pink Tuxedo that finally convinced her to give you a try?" Jerry smiled as he spoke to Tomasz.

"Well, it seemed like she liked it! Even if I ended up getting it by happenstance."

Jerry got a little more serious as he said "I do have to ask something and I hope I am not prying. To me, it seems as if someone has used your face as an outlet for their frustration. Or maybe several people did. Are you ok? Do you need me to get you to a hospital or something?"

Tomasz looked at Jerry and could see his genuine concern.

"Oh this, I got it treated fast so it looks worse than it feels." Tomasz tried to laugh in a show of bravado, but again his acting was subpar.

"Ah of course of course," Jerry replied. It was clear he knew that Tomasz did not want to continue discussing the topic.

He settled in to look at the Cahuilla River next to Tomasz. The two of them were silent for a bit.

"You know, I normally don't encounter many people when I walk my dog at this hour. I like to call this my Nothing Hour. I was quite surprised to see someone out here, especially someone I had met earlier in the day. Now again, this is not my business, so feel free to tell me so, but I can tell that something is bothering you. While it may not seem like it, I do try to help people whenever I can. So if you would like someone to talk to feel free to talk to me." Jerry turned to Tomasz with an earnest smile on his face. Next to him, Ginger also looked at Tomasz. But she had more of a curious look.

Tomasz thought for a second, trying to decide what to say. Should he confide in this person, a stranger? It did seem as if Jerry was earnest in his concern.

"I don't think I could even begin to explain what my problem is, or if it is even a problem, so I feel like I would just be saying a lot of nonsense," Tomasz replied.

"Is it bothering you?" Jerry replied without hesitating.

"Oh. Um, well, I guess?"

"Then it isn't nonsense and you should talk about it."

Tomasz stared at Jerry.

"Something tells me you won't let me say nothing here, will you?" Tomasz said with a laugh.

"Are you kidding me? I walk my dog at two in the morning and come across someone in an amazing Pink Tuxedo and covered in cuts and bruises. Of course, I want to hear what is troubling you! Think of it more as a favor to me if that helps!" Jerry smiled.

"Well, you asked for it. I don't even know where to start. I guess for a while now I have been feeling… I don't know…lost maybe? I don't know if that's the best way to describe it. Or maybe it would be better to say like everything kind of sucks? Just going through the motions daily, expecting I don't know what to happen. But today, something did happen. A lot happened. It has been such a fun and crazy day that I don't even know how to feel anymore. It all started when I met this group of people. It was a complete happenstance. But even though they had only met me, they welcomed me with open arms. And honestly, even crazier is that I loved hanging out with them. Later on, I brought Monique over to spend time with them and we even had a better time with them. Oh, I forgot to mention but Monique is that girl that I kept staring at during your lecture," Tomasz clarified for Jerry.

"Oh, I figured, no worries," he replied without missing a beat.

"But then later on I went along with them for something else and umm, you see that's the thing. I just, I don't know. I saw some stuff I didn't agree with. Maybe not why they were doing it, but how they were going about it. I mean I keep trying to tell myself that it was one weird evening with a bunch of strangers and that that's all it was, not worth me worrying about it anymore. It's in the past and that's where I should leave it. I should focus on Monique and myself and everything will be fine," Tomasz finished. Jerry's gaze was fixed on him.

After some silence, Tomasz decided to speak up.

"I'm sorry, I'm sorry. I know I did not make much sense with what I said, but I did try to warn you."

"No, it is not that. Not that at all. Do you think that what you are experiencing is something unique? Something that no one else has gone through? Feeling lonely? Isolated? Feeling like nothing makes sense? Like the only thing that makes sense is nothing? Do you think I would not understand that?" Jerry the professor spoke to Tomasz.

"Of course, you feel that way. It is in your very nature to feel as if you do not have anything larger to strive for. The world in which you live is not the world your mind evolved to exist in. You live in a world where you can digitally manifest a person in your head, where you can exist in a vast virtual city many times larger than any city in the history of humanity. Where you can have a virtual experience with thousands of strangers in an arena and never even leave your room, this world that we live in is in many ways alien to us. Yet despite all these amazing connections that we now have with other people, we feel more and more isolated. We feel emptier, we feel nothing. This is what motivated me to start studying nothingness. I wanted to understand how there could be so much in the physical world and yet we still felt so empty on the inside. It was maddening at first, this inverse relation. The more you have access to, the more you can get, the more you obtain, the emptier you feel. How could it be that we, the pinnacle of human civilization after hundreds of thousands of years, with so much around us, feel nothing on the inside? That is when I came to a realization." Jerry spoke in a precise and quick manner. It was clear he knew every single intricacy of this topic. Tomasz was hanging on every word. He wanted to know what it was that Professor Gerald Nullo, Doctor of Nothing, had discovered.

"I realized that all these things that aim to revolutionize our lives are trying to replace things that were often fine as they were. It's fine that I can virtually visit Prague from my apartment in Cahuilla at any moment. But deep down I know that is not the same thing. When I talk to someone in a different city, I do not feel the same breeze they feel, smell the same aroma, or experience the city as they do. The way my brain is wired is being fooled into thinking it is the same, but I know it isn't. If I want to talk to my sister across the country I can do so in a second. I can beam myself into her living room and pretend I am there with her and her kids. But I cannot hug them. I cannot hold them up and feel how much bigger they have gotten. I can't peer behind the curtains when they ask Uncle Jerry to play hide and seek. I cannot taste the sweet potato casserole she learned to make from our mother. And sure, if I am bored I can find a group of people online that I can talk to about my interests. I can commiserate about how the Cahuilla City Ranchers lost another game and unite in grief with them. But these are not people I know. I cannot talk to them about how proud I am of my niece being accepted into Caltech. I can't gripe to them about how the local bar no longer has that new Cahuilla Red on tap. As we advance and technology becomes more integrated into our lives, we have all on a physical level become more isolated. That is not how humans evolved to interact. Our needs are very simple. Shelter, food, security, health, and a strong social sense of belonging. That sense of belonging is hard to replicate in an online fashion. There are groups out there that try, but in the end, they always resort to meeting in person. Because there is an inherent level of disconnect between what you present online and who you are. When I look at a virtual avatar, I see what a person would like to represent. Most would like to represent someone always happy, healthy, and without problems. But if that is what you show to the rest of the world how will I know if you are sad, hurt, or need help? I can't. And since no one shows any sort of struggle it only perpetuates the virtual façade that people raise. We create a cycle where everything on the outside looks perfect, but on the inside, we feel more and more isolated. "

Tomasz had listened with all his attention. He could tell Jerry was not done yet.

"But this does not mean that I believe that we should abandon technology and move back into caves. It does not mean that technology has degraded our way of life, or has made us into lesser beings. Before the digital age, there were still wars and conflicts, atrocities still occurred regularly. And I cannot ignore all the amazing technological feats that we have accomplished in the modern age. We can cure diseases like polio, HIV, and many others. We can communicate with people around the world almost instantly. Without modern societies these technologies would probably never have evolved. Yet despite all our advances, we should not think there is nothing to learn from our ancestors. I think that in our rush to move on from those societies, we shed parts of ourselves we found useless. A strong sense of belonging was one of those. In the grand scheme of things that might seem meaningless, but you and I both know that it isn't. You and I both know there is a deep chasm within us, a pit of nothing, that we don't know how to fill. But I think that if we surround ourselves with people that we care about and we know to care about us, we might gain some of that back, we might be able to fill the nothing within ourselves." Jerry the professor concluded, rubbing Ginger's head.

Tomasz considered what he heard. The professor's words elucidated how Tomasz felt. The emptiness that Tomasz could not explain. The nothingness that had pervaded his soul. It was as if he had been ill for years with no idea of what it was. And now he found someone who could identify it and tell him it was real. Tell him that he was not imagining how he was feeling.

"But how, how are we supposed to know if this group that we might need is good for us? What if I join some crazy death cult and end up hurting a lot of people? How would that be different from what you described?" Tomasz asked. He felt so close to being reassured. He needed to know the answer.

"The truth is that it isn't," Jerry said bluntly.

Tomasz recoiled. He'd felt as if he was on the cusp of something great, something that would help him understand, only to be pulled back from the brink.

Jerry explained further. "In reality, most people would like to join a group that aims to help society positively. To join a group to effect change in a way that they agree with. But there are certain groups, or rather certain people, that know that very well. They know that there are those out there yearning for a connection, for a group to call their own. So they sell them on these high-minded ideals, on a mission greater than any a single person could accomplish. That mission could be to recruit you as an aid worker in an impoverished country. Or it could be to enlist in some army to go fight wars in a place you might have never even heard of. Or you might end up joining a group, or a cult, that could end up hurting a lot of people. So if that is the case what are you to do about it? Well, all you can do is to ask yourself if you think that the actions of the group are acceptable or not. If you do then that should be your answer, and well your choice to join them or not."

Tomasz internalized the words from Jerry the Professor. Hearing this all brought some clarity to his situation, but he still struggled with his decision concerning the Thread Barons.

Both of them were quiet for a while. Tomasz sat silent for a while until a different question popped into his head. A nagging question.

"Well I did zone out during your talk earlier, but I don't think I ever heard you mention any of this." Tomasz asked.

"You got me! You are correct that I didn't mention any of that." Jerry said with a guilty expression.

"But why?" Tomasz asked.

"The truth is that it just does not interest the general populace as much. While my main interest in nothing was in studying how people have been becoming more isolated, most people are interested in fun mangled popular trivia bits about the study of nothingness. About how studying nothingness might help them navigate the stock market. How thinking about nothing might help them eat less and lose weight. Or how it might help you achieve a mindset that is more in tune with ancient Far East mystics. So I decided that I would pursue that path since it has more commercial appeal. Now close to thirty years later I am writing all these books about who knows what and going around blabbering about nothing." Jerry tried his best to smile.

"Well, at least you didn't become an actor," Tomasz replied.

Jerry laughed at Tomasz's remark.

"Do you regret what you did?" Tomasz asked.

"Do I regret what I did? Hmm." Jerry sank into silence for a few moments.

"No, I don't. Where I started and where I ended up was not anything I had planned. When I started the only thing I had in mind was to do what most interested me. That meant a lot of risky decisions. Some of those I succeeded at, and a lot of those I failed at amazingly. Despite that, even when I did fail, I was glad I took the risk. Because doing so allowed me to get to a place where I can sit here in the very early morning and talk to people like you."

Tomasz was confused as he looked at him.

"When I talk to people like you," Jerry continued, "it reminds me why I got into this in the first place. It reminds me of what was that little push that made me so determined to study this great field. When I meet people who talk to me about their issues, I try my best to reach them, and I think I have helped a considerable amount of people this way. So I have to say,

I am happy with how things worked out. I don't regret what I ended up doing," Jerry finished as he stared off into the distance, looking at Fox District across the river.

Tomasz also stared off across the river to Fox District. Fox District where his whole life was. His apartment, his school, his family, all of it was there. It would be very easy for him to go to the nearby train station and go home.

He could be going back to his usual life with this day receding into the past. In the future, this day would become a memory so buried in his consciousness that it would only resurface now and then. But even if he went back now, he knew the life he once led was not going to be possible. Even if he tried to pretend that in Crow he had only seen Monique in a show and became a couple, that was not all.

He could not forget the feeling he had when surrounded by the Thread Barons, how he felt as if he had become part of something bigger, how it contrasted with that other feeling—the emptiness, the nothing so well described by Jerry the Professor. He knew this nothing inside of him would continue to fester and grow like a cancer until his whole being was consumed by it.

Tomasz kept staring across the river, still undecided.

"You know, I walk my dog here every night, at the same hour. There are many reasons I come out here by myself. One is the fact that whenever I do go out during the day sometimes, I get surrounded by too many people and I don't feel like talking most of the time. I know that might seem surprising to you. Another is the fact that I travel so much that I have a messed-up sleep schedule. I can only take short naps and if I am awake in the middle of the night, I figured I might do something productive. But the real reason, do you know what the real reason is?" Jerry asked while still staring into the distance.

Tomasz who had been so focused on his thought process at this point, had no clue what the real reason might be. He glanced around trying to figure something out. As he did he looked up and saw the fake Milky Way Galaxy in the sky above them.

"Umm, is it the fake galaxy?" Tomasz asked confused.

This remark made Jerry turn his gaze upward. As he did, so did his dog Ginger. As he looked at the faux galaxy above them Jerry laughed.

"No no, it is not because of the artificial lighting we have here to simulate the Milky Way. It is because of *that*," Jerry said as he looked straight ahead and pointed at Fox District.

Tomasz shifted his focus to the high rises of Fox District. They both stared in silence at the awe-inspiring structures that towered over the Cahuilla River.

"When I look at those I feel inspired by what we can do," Jerry explained.

"We?" Tomasz asked.

"Yes, we. Such a city was built by the collective labor of millions of people, all of whom shared a dream. Did you ever hear this story?" Jerry asked.

"Oh of course I did. I was raised here in Cahuilla. The story goes that the founders of Cahuilla came together close to half a century ago to try to build a model city. This city was founded to create a more equitable society to serve as an inspiration across the nation. Their vision drew in millions of people. That led to what we know today as Cahuilla City. Kind of a funny story if you consider the state of disparity between Crow and Fox districts."

"Yes, that is half-true. The founders of Cahuilla did share a dream, but it was more than just to build a more equitable society. They wanted to build a city where people could thrive together, a city founded on the idea of brotherhood. You do bring up a good point. It is ironic that when people think of Cahuilla and its greatest achievements, they think of Fox District. The part of the city that is known for its higher class of society. But I think the founders would likely have viewed Crow District, with its more dense and interconnected population, as much closer to their dream. A city that thrives because of its shared consciousness."

Once again they both fell silent, admiring the view across the river.

Tomasz checked the time. 2:47 AM. He got up. He had made up his mind.

"One more question before you leave," Jerry said to Tomasz.

"What?" Tomasz looked at him as he prepared to go.

"Your decision?"

Tomasz hesitated as he looked towards the Fox district, the place he called his home. The place that would have to wait a little longer before he would return.

"I am going to go look for my tribe."

"I am going to go look for my tribe."

Chapter 13: In the Air Tonight

Tomasz knew he had enough time to get to Yurok Park but he still hurried. He was unsure of how exactly the Thread Barons were going to carry out their plan. As he made his way across Crow District, Tomasz noticed something different about the city itself. He noticed a change in the city. There was nothing specific about Crow that had changed. It was he who had changed.

Earlier when he saw the sprawling towers, the lights overlayed on the buildings, the detailed server lanes, everything that defined the city, he only saw it as a collection of details. But now he could see how all these amazing things that came together to form such a resplendent city were only possible through the work of millions of people who had come together with a singular goal. It was one of the many testaments in this world to the work that can only be achieved in concert with others. This new appreciation filled him with pride in what had been accomplished, but also of hope. The hope that whatever comes in the future will be even more grand than the heights they had already attained. While deep in his thoughts Tomasz's heart almost leapt out of his chest when he heard someone behind him.

"Tomasz! Hey, slow down a second!" Tomasz stopped dead in his tracks. He recognized the voice before even turning around to look.

"Monique? What are you doing here?"

As he turned he saw her face turn from joy to shock as she looked upon his roughed-up visage. She hurried over to him and started caressing his face.

"Tomasz, what the hell happened? It hasn't even been that long since I last saw you," Monique asked bewildered.

Tomasz put her hands in his and tried to best prepare himself for what he was about to say.

"Look Monique, I'm sorry but I need to tell you something. I wasn't completely honest earlier when I spoke about what this outing was or how I even ended up meeting these Thread Barons," Tomasz replied in a somber tone.

"Are you about to tell me how these guys are planning on blowing up that statue in the park?" Monique replied.

"Umm, yeah how did you find out?" Now Tomasz was confused.

"Tomasz, I know these guys by reputation. When I heard who you were spending time with, I figured something questionable was going to be happening. Also, while we were at the bar some of the more outspoken members were saying how they can't wait to see 'the fireworks'. Those were the subtle ones. The other ones were just saying 'Can you believe we're about to blow up that statue in Yurok?'. So yeah, those Thread Barons are not the most discreet. I mean you see how you are dressed right?" Monique said.

Tomasz looked down at the Pink Tuxedo. Her point was not lost on him.

"Ok, fair. But still. I'm sorry. I should have told you earlier what they were planning. I mean I had no idea what to even say, but that doesn't excuse it and I'm sorry about that."

"It's ok Tomasz, I will make sure I bring this up in future arguments, deal?" Monique smiled as she spoke.

"I will take that deal in a heartbeat," Tomasz replied, feeling relieved.

Tomasz and Monique stood there holding hands for a while. It was so nice that Tomasz had forgotten why exactly he was out in the early hours of the morning.

"But Tomasz, what happened to your face?" Monique added, sounding concerned again.

"Ah yeah there is that," Tomasz replied.

He told Monique what had happened exactly after she had left, how the Thread Barons had gone out to look for the gray shirts and his encounter with Jacob. He also mentioned how he had spent the last two hours away from the Thread Barons. He did not know whether he would go back and join them.

"You know, as I say this out loud I realize how crazy all of it sounds," Tomasz added.

"You are right, it is crazy," Monique replied in a deadpan manner.

Tomasz was taken aback.

"First off you learn that a group of people were planning on bombing a massive statue in the middle of the city. Then you take me to join them for drinks after my show. Then the same group of people tell you they are about to go out on patrol to beat up some assholes. You join them and get beat up by the raging assholes and you still decide to join them to blow up a statue? Of course, that sounds crazy! It is some of the craziest stuff I have heard of in a long time! So if it is so crazy why are you so determined on going back to them?"

"Because I want to," Tomasz said.

"Of course you do! Do you think I don't know you? Now we need to hurry up before we miss this!" Monique said with a smile.

"Wait you are coming?" Tomasz asked in shock.

"Tomasz, you think I would miss this? This sounds like the most insane thing that I have heard of happening in the city. This is something that will be talked about for decades. Of course, I'm not going to miss this!" she continued with the same enthusiasm.

She grabbed Tomasz's hand as she started to get them going but came to a sudden stop.

"But one thing before we go mix up with them," Monique mentioned to Tomasz.

"What?"

"I don't want to encourage fighting, but fuck those gray-shirt guys. They went to the coffee shop that belonged to my friend's mom broke all the windows and harassed the customers. So don't feel bad about getting tangled up with those assholes. They are always looking for trouble, but do try to be careful in the future. And as for your friend Jacob, you better make sure he stays on the straight and narrow because staying with them will not end well for him."

"You don't have to tell me twice! No way in hell I'm looking for more fights."

***

Tomasz and Monique made their way to Yurok Park. Upon getting there they found a sea of people in Pink Tuxedos and Tomasz's heart skipped a beat in excitement.

As he walked up to them, the Thread Barons acted overjoyed, as if they had not seen Tomasz and Monique in ages. They were more than eager to greet them into the fold. Some of the first to greet him were Fred and Oscar. They had a third person in tow, the much smaller Mickey.

Fred put his hand on Tomasz's shoulder. His hand was about the same size as Tomasz's head. Even though he towered over Tomasz he could not bring himself to look him in the face.

"I am so sorry about what happened earlier. If I had known what was going to happen I would not have told you to come with us. Please know that that was never my intention," Fred said without raising his head.

"I'm glad I went. You were right. I needed to see what you guys were about. The good times and the bad times. But don't blame yourself for what happened. It's not like you knew I was going to try to get in the middle of the two groups and talk to those guys." As Tomasz spoke Fred raised his head.

For the first time, Tomasz got a good look at his and Oscar's faces. Now he could see that they too had some cuts and bruises from their earlier encounter. Part of Oscar's Tuxedo was torn around the neck area. Despite their tattered appearance they acted as if nothing was amiss.

"He does have a point, Freddie. I mean what kind of lunatic walks in front of a group of violent assholes and tries to break bread and bring peace? That's why I love this guy! High mint character right here!" Mickey came in with his usual jovial attitude as he put his arm around Tomasz.

"And you must be the lovely Monique everyone here is raving about? The greatest singer since Ms. Annette Baker graced the stage half a century ago," Mickey mentioned without missing a beat.

"They've been talking about me?" Monique blushed.

"Have they? Oh, these people have been raving about you since I got here. And honestly, I have been hearing about you even before then! First when this guy came around with his amazing outfit, telling me all about this amazing performance he was going to see. And here everyone is talking about *The Thieving Raven* show and then the encore in the bar. I must see you perform soon because from what I have heard it will be the experience of a lifetime." Mickey smiled.

"Well, it wasn't all me," Monique added.

"Oh, you're right. I hear this guy right here is some sort of maestro on the drums. Fashionista, courier exceptional, the voice of reason, an amazing musician and he is high mint on top of that? These kids these days are just too talented. How is the old generation like ours supposed to compare?" Mickey laughed, along with Fred and Oscar.

Oscar came up to Tomasz.

"So your friend, Jacob. Were you able to talk to him?" While Oscar spoke Mickey stepped away. He started speaking to Monique near Tomasz.

He recounted to them what happened after he left the brawl with Jacob. He also let them know what had happened the last time he had seen him.

"Of course. I'm not surprised at all," Fred said with a hint of anger.

"That's what they always do. They always go after the young guys who are going through a shit patch," Fred added as the anger swelled within him.

"They always look for the most vulnerable ones. They go out where they know they'll find them. Bad neighborhoods, bars, and any local joint where they know there's trouble. There they keep a constant lookout for those they know will fall for their bullshit. Those who are struggling, the isolated ones, the ones that for whatever reason don't have anyone to rely on. It makes sense your friend would fall for their whole thing. Losing his brother and then having to deal with it on his own. He's still an adult and he should have known better but now he has an opportunity to make it right. But it's not all on him, you also need to make this right. Honestly, when I went out there, I had nothing in my mind but to make some faces eat pavement. When I saw you walk out in front of us and then start to talk to them, I was so surprised that I completely froze. I had no idea what to do."

Tomasz was surprised at Fred's words. They brought him a certain level of comfort, but also guilt. He knew he had abandoned Jacob when he was at his most vulnerable. But now he had a chance to make it right, and he would not let that chance slip.

"Yeah, we all froze," Oscar added.

The thought that they also might freeze in such a situation was not something Tomasz thought even possible.

"I mean we've been in our fair share of fights, so it takes a lot to surprise us. But what you did? I mean we had no idea what to make of it," Oscar said.

"I thought you had snapped or something," Fred said.

"But let me tell you something. That was the right thing. To go out in front of a group like that and try to reach out to them? That was brave, man. There's only one guy that I've ever met that has ever gone and done something as crazy brave as that. And neither Oscar nor myself would be here if it weren't for him," Fred said as he motioned behind Tomasz.

Behind him, he saw Monique talking to Mickey. He of course looked interested in whatever it was that Monique was telling him. Now and then his raucous laugh could be heard.

"When we saw Mickey earlier, he told us how he had met up with you after our encounter. He thanked us for helping get you out of the brawl, we were relieved to hear you were alright. But honestly, we should be thanking you. It's not like we're going to go out there to sing songs with those guys in the future. But maybe there's something different that we can try," said Fred.

"You guys give me too much credit," Tomasz replied.

"There he is!" A loud voice boomed behind Fred and Oscar.

As Mel sauntered over to them Tomasz could see that although not as bad as the rest of them, she too had some scrapes on her face.

"I see your pretty face did not make it out unfazed huh?" Mel said as she approached Tomasz.

"So is everything in place?" Mickey asked as he walked up to her.

"Oh yeah, thanks for that. I was going to set the bomb at the base and hope that it would take it down and that it would topple into the lake. But I like your idea much better," Mel replied as she held the battery in her hand, waving it around like it was some harmless random brick.

Mickey looked to Tomasz.

"I told Mel that to maximize their chances of making sure the statue falls into that lake over there she should attach a blast diverter at the base. It ensures all the force in the explosive gets directed in a very specific direction. That way when the statue topples it will go where you want it to instead of crashing into those trees or that building over there." Mickey pointed to each of the landmarks he mentioned.

Around the statue, Tomasz could see a lake to the left, some trees behind it, a clear path in front of it, and far to the right an old-looking building.

"Yup, all I got to do is place this thing in that container there, press the button on the detonator and POP! She goes stumbling!" Mel's enthusiasm was overflowing as she spoke.

"But please remember to have everyone behind this line," Mickey mentioned as he pointed down.

Tomasz looked and saw a painted yellow line that ran perpendicular to the statue in the distance.

"Oh of course I'll remember. I'm not gonna let my guys get crushed by that dumb statue."

"Well, I hope so."

"That wasn't part of what I delivered was it?" Tomasz asked puzzled.

"No not really. I mean I wasn't sure what the bomb was going to be used for, so I brought some things to either help it or unhelp it. But when I heard what the target was I got to work on it personally! I don't get to participate in these anymore so I wanted to make this early morning spectacle extra special. I also brought a remote detonator so that you don't have to press a button and run like crazy. I can't wait!" Mickey laughed. He brought out the remote and put it in his pocket.

Tomasz could not help but laugh at Mickey's enthusiasm for explosions.

Mel looked behind Tomasz for a second and seemed confused.

"Did you bring your girlfriend?" Mel asked.

Tomasz turned around and saw Monique standing behind him. He had not considered whether Mel would be ok with Monique coming. Now he started to worry.

"Monique, why are you back there, come up here!" Mel said, pushing Tomasz to the side.

Monique came up to her and they both seemed overjoyed at seeing each other.

"I'm so happy you came! I didn't know that Tomasz was such a romantic to invite you to a special early morning statue bombing!" Mel added with glee.

"Oh well, I didn't come because of Tomasz. I was going to come here whether or not he came. Once I heard the people in the bar talking about blowing up this statue I knew I had to see this myself! This is like a once-in-a-lifetime kind of thing! People are probably going to be talking about this for decades," Monique replied.

Tomasz felt kind of hurt at what Monique had said. But in all fairness, he had not told her about the plan at all.

"Oh, I guess you have a point. I hadn't considered what a momentous occasion this would be," Mel said.

"You know I was thinking a lot of what you were talking about earlier. Your work as an injury attorney. For a long time, I have been struggling to decide what I want to pursue as a career. But hearing what you said made me rethink what I can do when I finish school. I want to do what you've done and help people!" Monique said and Mel seemed taken aback.

"Wow, well I don't know what to say to that." Mel paused. "I will be honest though; I am not an ideal role model. I am sure I have done way more to hurt people than to help them. I appreciate the compliments, but I am not the person that you think I am," Mel added with a weak smile.

Monique shrugged. "You might see it that way, but that's not how I see it. I didn't get to meet the Mel that you are talking about, I met the one right in front of me. The one that tries to help others. And that's the one I want to try to be like."

Mel was silent once again.

"Wow. I appreciate those words. I do. I am flattered, I am, but I think you have the wrong impression of me," Mel replied.

"Are you kidding me, Mel? Our favorite singer here is right Mel, you are someone that we all look up to. Do you think there is anyone else that we would listen to if they told us to go bomb a statue in the middle of a city? We'd be crazy to listen to anyone else that suggested such a thing," Oscar interjected.

"I mean you guys are pretty crazy," Mel laughed.

"Well true. But still, the girl's point stands," Fred added.

Mel turned towards Mickey.

"So you have it?" she asked him.

"Right here," Mickey said as he padded his chest.

Mel looked around at everyone gathered. She then looked down and made sure to step exactly on the yellow line on the ground.

"Everyone, gather round."

All the Thread Barons started to form a circle around her, with Mickey standing right next to her.

"No come on guys, we talked about this. I need you behind the yellow line. Come on, we don't have all day!" Mel sounded exasperated as the rest of the Thread Barons mumbled and moved around. She waved them into formation with the explosive in her hand as if she were directing traffic. After a minute or so the group rearranged in a semicircle in front of her.

"Alright, finally!" Mel said.

"Wait for me!" a voice cried out from the corner.

It was Jerry. He was running over from the bushes.

"Sorry guys I had to go to the bathroom!" Jerry added as he ran to the group and positioned himself.

"Ok, so we are all here!" Mel said and paused. There were no interruptions this time.

"As I was saying. We are all here and we are about to blow this stupid statue into the water. As many of you are aware we have been planning this event now for close to a year. So why do this? Why bother toppling a statue of a woman who is safe and secure in her position in this city? This action will not affect her at all. She probably could afford to have a hundred statues made exactly like this one. So why does it matter to us, if it does not even matter to her? Because every time we see it we are reminded of the apathy the people in Crow District have to live with every single day. To them, this is a constant reminder that city hall does not care about their wants or their needs. After years of struggling with city hall to have this simple location granted they had to put this stupid statue up here. As a reminder of who holds the power in this city. But although we know that at the end of the day, all we accomplish is toppling one single statue, the message we send will be much louder. We speak on behalf of Crow and the injustices perpetrated against its citizens daily. Our voice is loud because it's not only ours. It's louder than those idiots in City Hall. It speaks louder than all the money that Madame Sonali can throw at people to make them do whatever she wants." Mel took a quick pause at this point.

Some of the Thread Barons were cheering her on, but the majority watched in silence, so entranced by her words that they did not want to interrupt a second of it.

"That's why we are all here tonight. You all, like myself, have spent many hours and days speaking to people who call Crow District their home. You know as well as I do their daily plight. But there is not a single person in city hall who is willing to listen to them. That is why it is so important today that we start this movement to let people know that Cahuilla is not just Fox, it is also Crow. The majority of Cahuillans live in Crow, but they might as well be invisible to city hall. But to us, they are not. And that's why—"

Somewhere in the distance, Tomasz could hear something. It started very faint but it grew at a rapid pace. The first one to notice was Mickey who turned around and without hesitating grabbed Mel by her shoulder. By the time she turned around all of the Thread Barons had realized what was occurring. An angry mob of people in gray shirts came swarming upon the Pink Tuxedos. They were approaching at an alarming pace and in an instant, the mob that was not even audible a second ago was upon them. Tomasz noticed that this group of gray shirts was larger than the one they had previously encountered. As they kept marching the Thread Barons formed ranks around Mel getting ready to meet the horde headfirst. Meanwhile, Mickey turned around and went straight for Tomasz and Monique.

"Alright, guys this has turned into something ugly. Let's get out of here," Mickey urged. Monique was following Mickey, but Tomasz stood still. He did not move an inch. He stared at the statue.

"Mickey, give it to me," Tomasz said as he pointed toward his pocket.

Both Mickey and Monique seemed confused at what Tomasz was referring to. Mickey touched where Tomasz pointed and realized what he was referring to.

"You sure about this?" Mickey now looked intrigued as he fished for the item.

"Well not really, but I'll think about it later," Tomasz grumbled.

"Alright well, just so you are aware you need to press the two buttons for a full five seconds before it detonates! Safety first!" Mickey added as he threw the detonator at Tomasz. He snatched it from the air.

Monique smiled as she looked towards Tomasz.

"I guess we can add demolitions expert to your extensive resume soon!" Mickey laughed as he and Monique scurried back.

Tomasz looked toward the scuffle that had broken out now. In the bright lights of the park, all that could be seen was a sea of pink clashing with a thick gray fog. Every single one of the people he had seen earlier at the bar, no matter how big or small was entangled in the scuffle. Tomasz could even see the tiny Maria kicking someone who was lying on the ground. Tomasz searched the crowd for two people.

One of them was Mel, whom he figured must be in the center of the brawl. The other he was not sure would be in the brawl. But he sure hoped he wasn't. That was Jacob. Peering from the outside, Tomasz was unable to spot either. He decided that he would need to dive into the middle of the chaos to find them.

As Tomasz dove into the melee, he did his best not to get entangled in any fighting. But that only lasted so long. He felt someone push him from behind and down he went. Tomasz was able to get up on one knee before someone tripped over him which once again sent him tumbling down. As he felt around the ground for somewhere for him to stabilize and get himself up, he felt a hand grab him by the collar. Pretty soon he was being dragged up. His head shot up, ready to get hit. Instead, he came face to face with Fred.

"What are you doing here? I didn't think you liked fighting?" Fred shouted at Tomasz.

Tomasz brought up the detonator. He almost shoved it into Fred's face.

"Where is Mel?" he shouted.

Once Fred realized what Tomasz had in his hands his head snapped towards his right and then he started looking around them. Towering over everyone else around them it was easy for Fred to find people in the chaos.

It took Fred about three seconds before his arm snapped out towards his left.

"There!" Fred shouted.

Fred helped Tomasz move in that direction by pushing him. Tomasz took several steps forward as he attempted not to fall and then looked up. As he righted himself, right in front of him two people fell to the ground—a gray shirt who was choking one of the Thread Barons in a rear hold. The person who was being choked out was Jerry.

"Sorry!" Tomasz shouted as he swung a kick at the gray shirt's head. It didn't connect well but it did distract the gray shirt. He covered his face with one arm to protect himself. Jerry took the opportunity to grab the man's arm and bite into it. He had a look of bloodlust as the man he bit started wailing out loud.

"Sorry again!" Tomasz shouted as he went by them. It seemed as if Jerry had the situation under control. He continued moving towards Mel amidst the chaos of the battle. At one point, Tomasz saw a black boot flying right in front of his face like some sort of missile. But finally, he saw Mel surrounded by around five other Pink Tuxedos all involved in their fights. Tomasz pushed and shoved, inching his way towards Mel. Suddenly he felt a random object ricochet off of his head.

"Ow!" Tomasz shouted as he looked around, rubbing his head.

He could not tell what the object was or where it had come from. He did not see anyone coming for him so he continued pushing past the group. When he finally got to where he had last seen Mel it took him a second to find her. She was no longer standing. Now she was on the ground rolling around as she and a gray shirt were trying their best to choke each other out.

"Oh dear," Tomasz said to himself.

"Sorry!" Tomasz once again shouted as he apologized to the gray shirt as he tried to kick him. But this time he was pushed. With one leg in the air, Tomasz lost his balance and fell forward. As he fell he flailed with his arms everywhere, doing his best not to press any of the buttons on the detonator. He fell to the ground, hitting something hard with his knee, but it did not feel like pavement. He looked downward to see what had broken his fall.

A gray shirt's head was squarely under his knee. Tomasz panicked and fell backwards looking at the man who was no longer moving.

"Oh my god! I killed a man! I'm a murderer!" Tomasz cried in panic.

Mel rushed towards the man, putting her hand around his neck.

"He isn't dead," Mel said without even looking at Tomasz. She spat in the unconscious man's face.

"Piece of shit!" She was gasping for air as she got up. Her eyes were bloodshot and she seemed to be ready to kill someone. Once she finally got herself up, she took in one deep breath, brought her leg back, and kicked the man in the torso. He did not even flinch.

Mel kept taking deep breaths. Tomasz thought that by now she had calmed down. As Tomasz prepared to talk to her, she once again shouted at the unconscious man.

"Asshole!" She kicked the man once more. She was getting ready to do so again when Tomasz intervened.

"Wait, Mel! Wait!" Tomasz shouted as he got up. Mel looked at him. It seemed as if she had forgotten there were other people around her and the gray shirt. The fury in her eyes dissipated.

Still looking at Tomasz, she wound up again and kicked the man. This time not as hard.

"Hey I appreciate the assist but I had this under control," she said through gritted teeth.

Tomasz looked at the unconscious man.

"He'll be fine. At least I'm pretty sure he'll be. I gotta get back to it, you going to help?" Mel asked Tomasz who once again found himself in a daze.

This time Tomasz was able to snap out of his stupor. He reached for the detonator and pulled it out, showing it to Mel.

Mel transitioned from a look of confusion to one of approval. She dug around her coat and pulled out a bag. She threw it at Tomasz, who felt the weight of the device as it hit him in the chest. It almost knocked him down.

"From the moment I saw you I knew you were one of us," Mel told Tomasz as he righted himself.

Tomasz felt a deep sense of pride at the compliment. He could not explain why, but he knew that this feeling that had overtaken him, whatever it was, this was what he had been looking for. Sure he had found it in the middle of a brawl between two groups dressed outrageously. Sure he was about to set an explosive and blow up an icon of the city he had lived in his entire life. Sure he had met this group of people earlier in the day. But this feeling, this was what he had been looking for. This was what—

A large body pushed up against Tomasz in his back, sending him to the ground. Tomasz crawled forward several feet until he saw another pair of pink trousers. Two hands grabbed him by his shoulders and pulled him up.

"What the hell are you waiting for? Hurry up!" Mel shouted in his face.

"Oh yeah right!" Tomasz said as he turned around and found the statue in the distance.

Tomasz pushed through the mob of people around him as he made his way out of the fray. Once he was clear of the chaos he saw he had several hundred feet to make it to the statue. Tomasz sprinted as if his life depended on it. He was unwilling to stop for anything. As he got near the statue he was taken aback by its massive height. Seeing it up close made him realize how crazy this whole thing was. But there was no going back, and Tomasz was prepared to see it through to the end.

It seemed as if he was running for an eternity but he finally made it to the base of the statue. Once there he found the device that Mickey had mentioned, where the bomb should be slotted. Tomasz realized he had no idea how exactly he should put it into the enclosure. He thought about going back to Mickey to ask him how exactly this was all supposed to work. He looked back to where he had left Mickey and Monique, but all he could see was a crowd of pink and gray all struggling against each other.

"Ah FUCK!" Tomasz yelled.

He took the bomb and struggled to insert it into the device. It did not seem to be staying in place. Tomasz tried different angles until he found one where the bomb stayed in place.

He stared at it. He wasn't sure what he was waiting for, but he figured there might be some sort of sign. Maybe a beep, or a light, or maybe it would fall out. Anything to let him know whether he had done it right or not. Tomasz stared and stared and nothing occurred aside from a single solitary thought: *This is it.*

There was nothing else more he could do. All he could do was run away now. Run away and hope to whatever that he had done it right. Tomasz grabbed the detonator and sprinted away from the statue.

"It's going to blow! Bomb! Bomb!" Tomasz yelled as he ran near to the fighting.

It took a while but people started paying attention to him. The fighting started to die down.

"Did that guy say he has a bomb?!" a gray shirt shouted.

"It's about to blow up, getaway! Bomb! Bomb!" Tomasz kept screaming as he ran through the park waving the detonator.

The Pink Tuxedos were already on the move. It did not take long before the gray shirts started to scatter too. Tomasz ran to the yellow line and came to a halt.

He stopped to catch his breath as he put his hands on his knees. He was gasping for air as he held on to the detonator and finally raised his head. In the distance he could see the gaggle of people, all staring.

Those dressed in pink stared beyond him, toward the statue. Those in gray stared at Tomasz, still unsure of what he meant by his threat of a bomb.

Tomasz picked up the detonator and brought it up, pressing down on the two buttons on the device. As soon as he did most of the gray shirts dropped to the ground. The Pink Tuxedos all kept staring beyond Tomasz. After about a second or so of no activity, the gray shirts started to look at each other. Then they looked at Tomasz. The first of them got up.

"He's fucking lying! They don't have sh—" Tomasz was unable to hear what else he said as a loud *BOOM!* roared throughout the entire park.

The man who was shouting fell flat on his back, while the rest of the gray shirts covered their heads.

Tomasz turned to see what had happened. A cloud of smoke emanated from the bottom of the statue as it spewed forth what remained of the base.

"Goddamn, I still got it!" Tomasz heard Mickey say who had appeared next to him.

"Good job there babe." Tomasz now heard Monique who came up to him and held his hand.

"But also kudos to you, mouse," Monique said.

"Well, some things you just can't forget!" Mickey replied.

The three of them went back to staring at the statue as the smoke cleared. The statue started to tilt. This brought Tomasz relief. Up until this point, he did not know whether he put the device in the right way. But there was one issue.

"Well, that doesn't look right. The lake is on the other side," Mickey spoke in a confused tone.

He was correct though. The plan was that the statue would fall into the lake to the left. But now the statue seemed to be tilting towards the right. This was not as planned, and instead of falling into a lake, it was now tilting towards an old building.

"Oh dear," Mickey said.

The base of the statue was completely shattered. Now nothing was holding the statue back as it commenced its free fall.

"Well, sometimes things don't go as planned," he added with the same nonchalance.

The statue was now going straight towards the building.

"Still I was supposed to get it knocked down, and I succeeded." As Mickey finished his sentence the statue crashed into the building.

Like the statue, the building was destroyed by the crash. Large chunks of concrete started flying everywhere. Tomasz felt a hand on his shoulder that pulled him down to the ground.

It was Mickey who was now lying flat on the ground. He had dragged both Monique and Tomasz down with him. Around them, debris from the statue and the building rained down. Tomasz closed his eyes and kept his head down, waiting for all the chaos to subside.

He could hear crashes all around him, people screaming, and a few others laughing. One of those laughing was Mickey.

But the violent storm that had erupted all around them subsided in only a few seconds. Now Tomasz heard nothing. He did not move an inch for several more seconds. Once he was certain it was over he opened his eyes. Something did not seem right.

He noticed that his surroundings were much darker than they had been before. Now he was unable to see anything. He touched his head trying to make sense of what was going on. Did he lose his vision? Did something hit his head and now he was blind? Did he die and he wasn't even aware of it?

"Tomasz are you ok?" It was Monique's voice.

He turned and saw her face, barely visible in the night

"Monique, oh you're fine! Thank god!" he exclaimed as he got up to hug her.

"What happened?" she asked him.

Tomasz struggled to think for a second, but he had no idea. He did not know why the park was completely dark.

"That my very young friends, is a power outage," Mickey spoke near them, in the darkness. "Seems that building there was more than just an empty piece of crap. Something about it must have connected it to all the power in the city because it's gone."

"Wait, what's gone?" Tomasz asked.

"The electricity, brother. We blew out a power station and now the city lost its electricity. Sometimes you get a little extra with your bang," Mickey laughed.

"The electricity left?" Tomasz asked again, failing to comprehend what Mickey was talking about.

"Yeah I'm sure this is not something you're used to, but I dealt with this a lot overseas. It sucks, but I'm sure the city will fix it soon. Too many people will be complaining if they can't watch the Cahuilla City Ranchers suck again this weekend."

Tomasz turned towards Monique. He noticed that her attention was all directed above them.

"Monique, what—"

"Look," she said as she pointed straight above.

Tomasz followed her finger and looked to the sky.

"Wait. What am I looking at?" Tomasz whispered.

He knew what it was, but it seemed unreal. This sight he was experiencing was not something he would have expected within the confines of the city. Many nights he had looked above and seen a pale imitation, but what he was staring at now was the real thing.

There were no small blobs of light scattered around the sky imitating stars. Instead, this was a broad brushstroke composed of millions of stars.

It spanned the entirety of the sky. It was so massive that Tomasz could even see the difference in certain stars. Some shined brighter, some dimmed in the background, some clustered together, and some twinkled far apart from each other. Tomasz had seen so many facsimiles of the Milky Way, but seeing it for real, he was at a loss for words.

Tomasz saw a star that shone brightest than all. His gaze was focused on it.

"It's amazing isn't it," Monique breathed, still looking at the sky.

"It is," Tomasz replied.

In the far distance, a sound started picking up. Sirens. It seemed the loud explosion and the loss of power had alerted the authorities to something occurring in the park.

"Alright, you two need to get out of here."

Tomasz and Monique turned to see Mel standing close to them.

"We can't have you guys near here, so try to find a way back to Fox," Mel added as she looked around them.

"But wait, you want us to leave you guys? After all of this?" Tomasz asked, confused.

"Look Tomasz, the rest of us will figure out something. We're all based in Crow. Besides, you and Monique have done way more for us than I would expect anyone to do. There is nothing else for you to prove. You were the crazy asshole who went and took the bomb, planted it, and blew it up! What more do you need to do? Now get the hell out of here!" Mel ordered.

Tomasz and Monique were still quiet and not sure what to do.

"Now!" Mel added as the sirens intensified.

"Guys, come with me. I'll make sure to get you back to Fox District," Mickey said.

Holding tight to Monique's hand, Tomasz started to follow Mickey. As they ran, Monique told Mel "You guys better be ready because when we come back we are going to do a duet for the ages!"

With that, they followed Mickey into the night. As they went in deep into darkness Tomasz could not help but look back. Although he could no longer see them, he knew they were there. The Thread Barons, in their Pink Tuxedos.

He had only come to know them several hours earlier, but it seemed as if decades had passed. As he left a deep melancholy overcame him. But it was a bittersweet feeling. Because he knew that the only reason he felt sad at having left them was because they had provided him with a community, somewhere he could fit in. And not only did he have a community, but now he had a partner. She was beautiful beyond his dreams, and he could revel in this community with her. Tomasz looked forward to where Mickey and Monique went because for now, he trusted that the future held something of meaning for him. His future was not filled with nothing, he now had something. He had a tribe.

Epilogue:

"Are you Tomasz?" A young woman asked him as she got near the table. Tomasz was deep in thought and took a second to remember where he was. He looked up and recognized the man and woman standing in front of him.

"Yes. That's me. You must be Molly," Tomasz said to the woman. She nodded as Tomasz stood up to greet her.

He turned to the man and said "You must be Peter."

Peter nodded as well. The siblings smiled at Tomasz.

Tomasz went and embraced the strangers. He offered them the seat across from him.

"Did you guys already order?" Tomasz asked as they got settled in.

"Oh well, we decided to get sauteed grasshoppers! Apparently, they are a fairly new addition to this restaurant! " Molly replied.

"That's a great choice. I've been coming to this restaurant regularly since we last spoke. The chef here, Trevor, is such a nice guy and an even more amazing chef. " Tomasz said.

"Well sorry it took us so long to get here. Gui's medical situation deteriorated very fast after we finished our hike in Salt Lake and after that, it's been one issue after another," Peter explained.

"Oh, no worries. I saw your updates and I understood that you guys had your hands full, so no judgment on my part. I'm just happy you guys finally were able to make it out here," Tomasz replied.

"Oh yes, we sure are too! It's kind of hard to believe that we're here now after all that's happened. When we talked to you, Cahuilla City was some sleepy Midwestern city that rarely made the news. Several hours after that, that tower in the park gets bombed and your city is the talk of the entire country. I mean even now when it's almost half a year later all we heard on our way here was about the bombing," Molly added with a certain air of astonishment.

"Yeah, our mom was telling us to be careful about where we go and who we meet up with! Hah, can you believe that? She was telling us, don't go mixing in with any strangers, you don't want to be an accomplice in some bombing!" Peter mentioned as both he and Molly started laughing. Tomasz also laughed along with them, but he found it funny for a different reason.

"And you're still ok with taking us to Yurok Park later? I mean I know you said you were going to show us around Cahuilla, but if it is going to be too much of a hassle we understand. But if we're here I figured we have to go to see that," Molly interjected after they all had stopped laughing.

"Oh yeah of course. The plan was to wait here for some other people to join us, and then head on around. But stop number one was going to be the park," Tomasz replied.

"Oh good! I noticed how close the park is to this place. I can't believe we were talking with you just a short time before that explosion. I was glad to hear that nobody was hurt. Aside from the one guy who was found unconscious there," Molly added.

"Yeah, it is crazy to think that happened only three blocks from here. Even though I've been to Crow District a lot lately I haven't gone there in a while. So I guess it will be nice to see how it looks now," Tomasz replied.

"Have they already decided on what they will do with what's left of the base of the statue?" Peter asked.

"Well, the only thing I know for sure is that talks about replacing the statue with another of Madam Sonali are dead. Enough people from Crow District spoke out against those plans and the city finally relented and decided not to go through with that idea. The citizens said they would show up en masse and pull it down themselves, no need for some crazy street gang to do the job. In the meantime, the base of the statue has been used as a stage of sorts. The locals love to come out and hold shows on top of it just to spite the City Hall members. I've heard they are pretty good. They might have one later when we go by." Tomasz added.

"I love it! That sounds like so much fun." Molly squealed.

The door of the restaurant opened and Tomasz turned to look. He could not help but smile when he saw who it was.

"Oh, there's our first addition for the day," Tomasz said as he got up. He went to the door to embrace Monique. She gave him a big kiss. She and Tomasz held hands and walked over to the table.

"Peter, Molly, this is my girlfriend Monique."

"Hi, I've heard so much about you guys," Monique said as she hugged both siblings

"Well, we've heard about you as well. We're so happy to finally put a face to the name." Molly said with enthusiasm.

"Tomasz is always raving about your musicals. He's also mentioned that on certain occasions you play live music at this bar we're going to later," Peter added.

"Oh, has he now? Well, we'll see, but if I am going to be on stage later tonight, it had better not be by myself," Monique mentioned as she eyed Tomasz.

"Oh of course I'll join you on stage. You know I can't pass up an opportunity to be upstaged by you. It makes me look that much better." Tomasz replied as they both sat down.

A large man in a chef's white uniform came out to the table with their food. The dark man carried their food on a platter resting on his metallic hands. Upon looking at the group he could not help but smile widely.

"So Tomasz this must be the group you've been talking about right? Molly and Peter!" Trevor said as he placed the food in front of them.

"Nice to meet you, Trevor. We've only heard great things about your skills in the kitchen." Peter said.

"Well I am sure Tomasz likes to oversell things, but yes my cooking is the best around here," Trevor replied with a slight grin.

"And how is the talented Monique doing today?" Trevor asked as he turned to her.

"Oh you know, getting ready for three shows this weekend. But can't complain. I assume you will be there for the Saturday one?" Monique said.

"You know we will. Rina made sure I did not try to sneak in any work this Saturday just so that we wouldn't miss the show. We also expect an encore afterward." Trevor added while looking sideways to Tomasz.

"There will be one," Monique replied while looking at Tomasz.

"I'll let you all get to it. I gotta get back to the kitchen. I hope you all enjoy." Trevor added and walked back.

The four of them dug into their meals.

"So what is on the agenda for today?" Monique asked Tomasz after they finished eating.

"Well, they wanted to see Yurok Park, since it has become quite the national sensation so I was going to take them there after here. Then we were going to take them on one of those riverboats."

"Oh, those are fun," Monique said.

"And then I was thinking we could go take them to Qabila."

"Qabila?" Peter asked.

"Oh yeah, that's the name of the bar we're going to later. One of our friends, her name is Mel, she runs it. The place is pretty new, only been around about three months. She used to have a different place, but she felt as if the time had come to move on. You'll love it," Monique said.

"Oh sounds great! I hope they have Cahuilla Sours, I hear they are really good." Replied Molly.

"Oh, they do indeed," Tomasz replied.

"So Monique, have you been to Yurok Park since the incident?" Peter asked in between bites of his food.

Tomasz and Monique shot glances at each other very fast. Nothing was said between the two.

"No, it's been years since I've been there. But I hear that you can barely tell that the statue was demolished. I mean aside from the base still being there, the place looks as good as new!" Monique said.

"I do hear it gets a lot more visitors than it used to beforehand though, so it might be a bit crowded," Tomasz added.

"So are we expecting anyone else?" Molly asked them.

Tomasz looked to the door again after the question. But no one else was coming in. Monique could see that Tomasz did not feel comfortable talking about it. She was about to speak up but Tomasz decided to chime in.

"Well, yes. I invited another friend that I had not seen for a while. I have been meaning to meet him for a while now in person, but we just haven't been able to. I told him about our plans today, and I hoped he would join us. But I don't know if he'll show."

Monique put her hand on his back. Tomasz smiled at her.

"I wanted him to meet the rest of the people we were going to be seeing tonight. I mentioned Mel, but there are other people I wanted all of you to meet. They're all great and friendly. I hoped I could introduce them to him," Tomasz said as he trailed off.

He had been so hopeful to make a change for the better, to capitalize on the chance he had been given. But it seemed that was not going to happen. He wanted Jacob to meet all of the people that Tomasz had grown so close to in the previous months. To give him the same sense of community Tomasz himself had grown to love. The sense of community he knew Jacob was missing.

"Wow, these people must mean a lot to you. It's a shame your friend can't come," Molly mentioned.

Tomasz snapped back out of his world. "Oh, huh?"

He looked around and saw Monique's concerned face.

"Oh that's right, yeah no, you guys are going to love them." He smiled back at them.

He was still not moving from his spot. They had finished eating quite a while ago. He knew there was no point in staying there any longer.

"Well, what do you say we take these guys on their tour? We don't want to miss the riverboats," Monique said.

As they all got up to leave the door opened. A tall young man entered. He seemed to be out of breath as he burst into the restaurant. His face was scrunched up in a look of concern. He scanned the place and locked eyes with Tomasz. As soon as he recognized him the concern in his face melted away.

"Tee! I'm so sorry, I went to the wrong restaurant and had to run all the way here. I'm glad I finally made it to the right one!" Jacob said as he went towards Tomasz.

Tomasz met him halfway and hugged the young man. The two took a step back.

"It's good seeing you again, Tee," Jacob said with an earnest smile.

Tomasz looked at his friend and could see shades of the young boy he once knew. He couldn't help but notice his smile. It was not the same as the one he remembered, but something in it brought back memories of a simpler time, a connection Tomasz hoped to rekindle.

"It's good seeing you as well, Jakey." Tomasz smiled at him.

"Again I'm so sorry for being late. I didn't want you to think that I was going to miss this!" Jacob said as he still tried to catch his breath.

"You have nothing to worry about. You're going to meet a lot of people today, but I'll start you small. This here is my girlfriend, Monique." Tomasz motioned towards her.

"Hi, Jacob! Tomasz has told me so much about you. It's nice to finally meet you!" Monique said back to him.

"Has he? Well, Tomasz has told me so much about you as well!" Jacob said with glee.

"And these are the sibling duo I've talked to you all about. Peter and Molly, this is Jacob!" Tomasz introduced the siblings and Jacob reciprocated without pause.

There Tomasz saw it again, Jacob's smile. The one he had not seen since before his brother passed away. There was never going to be anything that could replace the void left by Joshua in Jacob. Not even Tomasz could do that. But he could do his best to provide him with a community that would genuinely care for him.

As the group made their way to the door, Tomasz felt around in his back pocket and realized he had dropped something.

"Ah, sorry guys! I left something in the seat. I'll be right there."

Jacob, Peter, and Molly walked out. Tomasz went to where he was sitting and saw it. It was the detonator. He kept it as a sort of charm. It must have fallen out of his pocket.

Monique waited by the door, looking outside at Jacob, Molly, and Peter talking. It seemed as if the trio were already on their way to becoming friends.

Tomasz stood next to her and paused for a second. He took it all in. All that he had gone through since he first met the others in the Pink Tuxedos. Having found a group that would take him in. Having found a friend who needed guidance. Finding someone as amazing as Monique.

He understood how important all of that was to him, and how he was going to make sure to never let that go. Never again.

"Anything on your mind?" Monique asked him.

Tomasz came back to reality. He looked at Monique for a second and smiled.

"Nothing." He took her hand and led her out.